the
ever
end

Audrey Wilson

Bywater
BOOKS
2025

Bywater Books

Copyright © 2025 Audrey Wilson

Print ISBN: 978-1-61294-323-7

Bywater Books First Edition: August 2025

Printed in the United States of America on acid-free paper.

Cover design by TreeHouse Studio

Bywater Books
PO Box 3671
Ann Arbor MI 48106-3671

www.bywaterbooks.com

Advance Praise for *The Ever End*

"A chilling and unsettling story that will stay with you long after you finish."

—Jessica Huntley, *Don't Tell a Soul*

"So devilishly creepy it will make your skin crawl."

—Avanti Centrae, international bestselling thriller author

"This book is unsettling, cult-like and had me glued to the pages. I could not put it down . . . this is must-read."

—Chandra Claypool, *Where the Reader Grows*

"A fast-paced, addicting, binge-worthy book. I devoured it in one sitting."

—*Heidi Lynn's Book Reviews*

"From the prologue to the ending, this eerily unsettling blend of thriller and cult horror will consume you."

—Teresa Brock, *Best Thriller Books*

"A haunting thriller! There were so many twists and turns, Audrey has managed to create a masterpiece. I know I'd definitely read this again, and again."

—*LESBIreviewed*

"*The Ever End* is an unsettling psychological horror that lingers long after the final page. Fans of Shirley Jackson and *Hereditary* will find much to love in Wilson's atmospheric, nerve-twisting storytelling."

—*Shelf Unbound Magazine*

"Audrey Wilson delivers a chilling blend of horror and suspense in *The Ever End*, a novel that sinks its claws into you from the first page and refuses to let go. It's a book that lingers . . . long after you've turned the last page."

—S.C. Shannon, award-winning author

For my mother—with her, I never feel lonely.

Prologue

I COULDN'T HAVE been more than four years old the first time I remember feeling completely, utterly alone. We were living in the only house I'd ever lived in—a small ranch in the suburb of Skokie, just northwest of Chicago. A storm had rolled in in the middle of the night and I was afraid, so my mother let me sleep in her bed. With a particularly loud clash of thunder, I woke up to find her still asleep. When the sky lit up with electricity, my eyes darted to the window, and in the flash, I could see the shadow of a man standing in the street right in front of our house. He was tall, stiff, with long arms and broad shoulders. I wasn't sure if he was dressed in all black or if he was simply hidden in the blanket of night. If the thunder hadn't woken me, if the lightning hadn't struck, I never would have seen him. But I did.

Before I could scream, a voice that sounded like it was being whispered right into my ear silenced me. "Don't," the voice said. "Don't be afraid of what you don't know. Don't be like her." I looked down at my mother, sleeping beside me, and knew instantly that the voice was talking about her. "She'll lie to you. She's lying to you right now." I looked back at the man in the street. The voice was his. Even in the darkness, I could see his

1

mouth moving. Even from fifty feet away, I could hear him as clearly as if he were in my head. "Don't believe her."

I shook my mother to wake her up, knowing I had to be dreaming. Knowing that she would turn on the light and the man would be gone. But even after she was awake, even after the light was on, the man was still there. I didn't even need to point to him. She followed my eyes through the window. Without a word, she pulled on her robe and slippers, only turning to speak to me once before she left the room.

"Close your eyes and cover your ears," she said, and shut the door behind her.

I covered my ears as I was told, but I couldn't shut my eyes. I couldn't tear them away from the shadow outside our house. Because part of me knew, or at least hoped, that the moment my mother walked towards him he would disappear. That she would find him to be nothing but the shadow that he was—a trick of the light on a stormy night, a child's nightmare that was never real.

But he wasn't just a shadow. And he didn't disappear.

I waited for my mother to come into view outside the house, but for that moment it was just me and him. Like we were the only two beings in the world.

"You could have everything," the voice said. I pushed my fingers deeper into my ears, but it was no use. His voice wasn't in my ears; it was in my head. "Imagine it, Margo. Everything you ever wanted. It could be yours."

Before he could say any more, my mother approached him, confirming my worst fear—that he was real. If he was real, he could hurt us. He could hurt her. In my tiny little four-year-old world, I couldn't remember being truly afraid before. Not until then. I had never known fear like I did in that moment. I shut my eyes, certain that this could be the last time I ever saw my mother alive. I willed for the man to go away. I willed myself to wake up from the nightmare. And even though my mother never spoke of one, I prayed that there was a God and maybe He could save us.

When I opened my eyes, it was morning. There was no man outside the window and the space in the bed beside me was empty. My mother was nowhere in sight. I was alone. Completely alone in my little world. I lay beneath the covers, my heart racing, my hands shaking. "Mommy!" I cried. "Mommy!"

Seconds later, the bedroom door flew open, and my mother came rushing in to comfort her crying daughter. "Sweetie, what is it?"

Unable to speak, I sobbed uncontrollably. She held me and told me everything was okay, that she was there. I wailed to her about the man, about the voice. She consoled me, assuring me that there was no man. I'd had a bad dream. She had always been there to protect me from the monsters under my bed, and now from the man outside my window. And she reassured me that she always would. And I believed her. Not because she was right, but because I wanted to. It may have been the first time I saw that man, but it wouldn't be the last.

Chapter One

THURSDAY

THE DRIVE FROM Chicago to Fairbury, Iowa, is only about five hours, but somehow it feels much farther.

"When's the last time you were home?" I ask Sam, who's been uncharacteristically quiet for the majority of this trip.

"Uh . . ." He runs his hand through his disheveled mop of brown hair, which is the longest I've ever seen it. "Christmas, I think," he says.

My anxiety has been building ever since we crossed the Mississippi River. I wonder if agreeing to marry a man I've known only six months, before I've met his family, is the best decision. But it *was* my decision, and now is hardly the time to get cold feet. I just want his family to like me. I want them to be excited for me to join their family. Apart from my mother, I've never really had one of my own. And even though she's been gone for over eight months now, it's times like this, where I'm somewhere else entirely, that I can pretend she's still alive. I can pretend she's back at home, complaining to the neighbors about the increased traffic in the neighborhood, or watering flowers

5

that don't need more watering. Holding onto that thought is enough to keep my heart from breaking. I know one day it will. It will shatter into a million pieces because I'll finally let her death be real. But until then, I force myself to hold it together just one more day. And Sam is my glue.

I absentmindedly twirl the engagement ring around my finger, watching as the red ruby in the center glistens in the sunlight. "Does your family think us getting engaged after only six months is too fast?"

Sam raises an eyebrow at me. "Do *you* think it's too fast?"

"No," I say. "I love you."

"And I love you." He takes my hand and kisses it.

Six months may be a quick engagement, but coming at a time when I've felt more alone than ever, I don't want to wait too long to marry Sam. He's been the only good thing in my life since my mother died. He came into my world at a time when I was at my lowest. He gave me something to focus on besides the dark despair of my own grief. He made me laugh. He made me live. He made me forget. Agreeing to marry a man that I love will allow me to hold on to that good thing forever.

We continue driving and I continue staring out the window at the endless cornfields, trying to ignore the creeping sense of dread that comes with staring at their bony, broken stalks.

"You haven't told me much about them," I say after a few minutes of silence. "Your family." I don't mean for it to be an accusation, but more of a conversation starter.

"Sure I have," he says, an edge of defensiveness to his tone.

"Not really," I protest. "I mean, you've told me their names and what they do, but you didn't really tell me much else."

"There's not a whole lot to tell," Sam says indifferently.

"I'm sure that's not true," I probe. "Everyone's family is different." I pull my gaze away from the corn and toward Sam, sinking my eyes into his strong silhouette. "Tell me what they're like."

He lets out a long breath and glances over at me, his brown eyes grinning. "What's anyone's family like? A little crazy, a little kooky."

"Mysterious and spooky?"

"Hmm?"

"You know. *The Addams Family*." One of Sam's favorite childhood shows. We'd talked just the other day about going as Morticia and Gomez for Halloween.

"Oh, right."

Sam's quiet again, but I don't want him to be. I want him to tell me everything he possibly can about his family. I need to be prepared. Then Sam says, "There is one thing about them I should probably mention."

"Oh, no. Your family is in a cult, aren't they?"

Sam lets out a short laugh. "No. But I think I told you how they're pretty religious."

"You've mentioned it a few times," I say. "So what? We're going to be going to church with them Sunday morning?"

"No, they actually don't go to a regular church. They're kind of specific about their beliefs, and I don't think they ever really found a church that worked for them." Sam rubs his hands on the steering wheel. I'm starting to wonder if he isn't more nervous than I am. "But we can't sleep together."

"I know, we're waiting for the wedding—"

"No, I mean we're going to have to sleep separately. In separate rooms."

"Oh." I hear the disappointment in my own tone. Not because I had been expecting us to do anything—I'm fine waiting for our first time together to be our wedding night. Sam confessed to me early on in our relationship that he hadn't been with anyone else, so the idea of waiting to be together seemed sweet and romantic. Katerina and I had probably moved faster than we should have and look how that turned out. Fire burns out quickly when it's lit too soon. No, what bothers me is the idea of sleeping alone in someone else's house. It's more than a little unnerving. Especially when that house is old and creaky and in the middle of Nowhere, Iowa. "That's fine."

"I know it's not ideal." He takes my hand and kisses it again. "But just remember, in a few short months, we'll be married, sharing the same bed every night." He raises a suggestive eyebrow and I feel a little giddy. There is something very seductive about waiting to be fully intimate with your partner. It's made the chemistry between us feel even more real, more tangible.

Sam's face falls just slightly, and I brace myself for a shift in our flirtatious conversation. "I also didn't mention your . . . your dating history to my family."

"My dating history?" My tone probably sounds snarky, but I'm genuinely confused.

"Yeah. That you've . . . dated women."

Dated women? You mean that my only other serious relationship just happened to be with a woman?

"That's fine." My tone is intentionally short now.

"Come on, darling. You know I couldn't care less. But they're old-fashioned and stuck in their ways. It would be easier to not mention it."

I nod my head and try to soften my demeanor. It shouldn't matter that I have to hide part of who I am from Sam's family. The important thing is that I don't have to hide it from Sam, and I never had to hide it from my mother. I was a wreck the day I brought Katerina home to meet her. By that point, my mother and I were living in an apartment in Jefferson Park. I was in my senior year at Northeastern and had never mentioned to my mother that I liked both women and men. I'd never had a reason to. Not until I met Katerina in my English Lit class at the beginning of the fall semester. After dating for three months, as in love with Katerina as I was, and as certain I should have been that my mom would be totally fine with it, I was still beside myself the day I invited her to our house for dinner. But when

I introduced Katerina to my mother as my girlfriend and my mother didn't so much as bat an eye, any fears I had completely diminished. It was as normal as things ever were in our house. I had nothing to fear.

Sam and I had already gotten more intimate and more passionate the night I told him about Katerina. We were in my bed when he told me that he hadn't been with anyone else. Although he didn't consider himself to be particularly religious, his upbringing had been, and it was a promise he'd made to his family at a young age. He also said that, the guilt aside, he wanted to wait for the right person. I found it sweet; endearing really. And if I'm being honest, Sam and I had been doing everything but intercourse, which was enough for me. When I told him I'd only ever been with one other person, his face fell slightly, and when I mentioned her name, he seemed to perk up again. Sam didn't tell me why he was less bothered by my former partner being a woman, but I can assume the reasoning behind it. Maybe he felt less threatened by a woman. Maybe to him it didn't count. That possibility bothered me. To me, Sam and I had already had sex. I'd gone as far with him as I'd gone with Katerina. Besides, virginity is merely a heterosexual construct anyway.

Although Sam and I have yet to have intercourse, the intimacy I shared with Katerina went way deeper even than what I've experienced with Sam. And maybe that will change once we're married. Not because of the sex, but because there's a certainty that comes with marriage, a trust. I hope that's the case, at least. But whatever Sam's feelings were about it, it didn't change the way he felt about me. And that's what matters. Not what Sam's family thinks.

There's an itch on my leg, and when I reach down to scratch it, I see a black beetle over two inches long crawling up my jeans. "Oh, wow."

"What is it?"

"There's a huge beetle in here."

"Well, throw it out the window."

Adults who knew me as a child used to say I was fearless when it came to bugs, but I never understood what there was to be afraid of. My mother never killed a spider in her life. She never swatted a fly. "Every creature has a beating heart," she'd say as she picked up whatever insect had crawled into our kitchen. "They all deserve to be protected." Then she'd open the window and let the bug crawl onto the flowering pear tree. To not save an insect now feels like it would be a disservice to her memory. I cup my hands around the beetle and hold it carefully.

"It'll hit the car if I just throw it out the window. Can you pull over?"

"Seriously?"

I look over at him and try not to feel annoyed. "Seriously."

He rolls his eyes, slows the car to a stop on the side of the road, and turns on his blinkers. I get out of the car, the beetle still safe in my hands, and take it to one of the few remaining semi-green corn husks, but when I open my hands to set him on the stalk, there's nothing there. He's gone. I look around on the ground, on myself, through the air around me, but he's gone. I'd felt his tiny weight in my hands, his feelers grazing my skin, up until the very second that I'd separated my palms. That's when I catch a glimpse of black on the corn husk and lean forward to look. The beetle is crawling up it. He stops when he sees me, if he even sees me. But I think he does because he's facing me and holding completely still. I hear a faint noise that I can't quite make out and lean in closer. It sounds like a rustling, like a whisper. I can't tell if it's coming from the corn husk or the beetle, but I listen.

"*Is near . . . the end . . . is near . . . the end . . .*" the beetle says. But it can't be the beetle. Because beetles don't speak. And I'm not crazy. I'm hearing the wind blowing through the thousands of cornstalks. That's all. I pull away and the beetle disappears into the husk. My heart is beating fast and I just want to be back in the car.

I climb into the front seat and shut the door behind me, trying to shake my uneasy feeling.

"Did you save it?" Sam asks, but he sounds irritated.

"Yeah." Sam waits until I'm buckled in before he pulls back onto the road.

We drive without speaking for a few more minutes. Maybe Sam is irritated with me, or maybe he feels the same way about bugs most people do, that they're small and insignificant. I shouldn't have made Sam pull the car over. I should have just tossed the beetle out the window. He would have been fine. He probably would have just flown away. If he was even real. Maybe he wasn't. Sam never saw him. Only I did. I hadn't had anything like this happen since before my mother died. I'd gone almost an entire year without imagining something that wasn't real, a curse that I thought somehow died with her. After she passed, I thought my grief was the only mental burden I had to bear. I should have told myself the beetle wasn't real as soon as I saw him, before I heard him speaking to me. That way, I wouldn't be sitting here with a knot in the pit of my stomach because once again I'm hearing things that aren't real.

Chapter Two

"WELCOME TO THE WAILING homestead," Sam announces as we pull into a long dirt driveway half an hour later. My eyes fall on a white mailbox at the end of the driveway that has *Wailing* painted in red on the side in what looks like a child's handwriting.

Sam parks the car in the dirt patch beside the driveway. I gather my purse and phone, instinctively checking it before slipping it in my bag. I have no new messages or notifications and, upon a closer look, no signal either. I'm about to ask Sam if his family has Wi-Fi I can connect to, but he's already climbed out of the car and is shutting the door. I follow suit and climb out of the passenger's side, looking up at the house as I regain my bearings. Like the mailbox, the Wailing house is also covered in white paint that's beginning to chip. It's tall, three stories, with a large, wooden hatch on the side that I assume leads to a storm cellar. The shutters have all been removed, so the front of the house looks like the face of a ghost—white with gaping black holes—and the whole property is surrounded by acres of dying cornfields.

The cornfields.

They sway ever so slightly in the light fall breeze, a motion that should feel gentle and calming, but only makes me feel unsettled.

"What's wrong?" Sam asks.

It's only then that I realize I've been staring out at the cornfields for a few seconds too long. "I just didn't realize your family had a whole farm."

"They don't farm the land themselves. Too much work. But they fell in love with the property when they moved in back in '78." Sam walks over to me and puts his arm around my shoulder, admiring the home. I notice a beater 1970s Chevy parked near the barn and wonder if it's been there since they moved in. Nearby is a red 1990s Honda and a modern white SUV. There's also a black pickup truck parked by the field that looks like it might be the oldest of the cars, but it's hard to tell.

"They must have been young when they married."

Sam nods. "Young and stupid in love." He grins, assuring me that this trip will go by smoothly.

Before we can walk up to the front door, it swings open and a middle-aged woman with long chestnut-brown hair and over two inches of gray roots comes running down the front porch steps. "There they are!" She throws her arms around Sam.

"Hey, Mom."

"We thought you'd never get here!" She pinches his cheeks like he's five and I grin because I can tell he's embarrassed. Then she turns to me, her flushed, excited features softening into what appears to be admiration. Her smile widens. "Here she is."

Sam puts his hand on my back. "Mom, I'd like you to meet Margo, my fiancé. Margo, this is my mother, Mary."

I'm expecting a hug when she holds out a formal hand. "It is an honor to finally meet you, Margo."

I shake her hand. "It's great to meet you too. Sam has told me so much about his family." I say it because that's the kind of thing you're supposed to say when you meet your future in-laws, but it's hardly the truth. In reality, Sam has told me very little about his family, no matter how much I've asked. I was hoping to get more out of him on the drive here, but that didn't happen. In the past when he's talked about any one of them, he lumps them all together in an ominous "My family," with very little information about them as individuals. So now I feel like I know one or two facts about each of them, and nothing more. His mother is a recently retired teacher who loves to bake. His father is an electrician with a wry sense of humor. He has two sisters—Cheryl, who's older and married to Jimmy—and Alice, who's two years younger than Sam, aspires to be an actress while living with her parents, and who Sam is closer with than he is with Cheryl. Cheryl and Jimmy have a baby daughter named Selma, whose first birthday we will be celebrating with a party on Sunday (and who I still need to buy a present for, given that Sam mentioned this detail to me shortly after we were out of Chicago.) Then there's Ruth, Sam's grandmother, who isn't well. That's the extent of what he's told me, but in the end it's fine that I don't know much about them. For the better, actually. Because I'll get to know them all much better during our stay this week. And I have the rest of my life to get to know them even more.

"All lies, I'm sure." Mary play-hits Sam on the arm and laughs at her own joke. I laugh too, if only out of politeness. She throws up her arms in the direction of Sam's car. "Now, leave all your bags for now and we'll get Jimmy and Hank to help you unload after dinner. Come on in."

She gestures to the house as she bustles inside.

I turn to Sam. It can't be any later than one o'clock. "Dinner?"

"Lunch. Lunch is dinner, dinner is supper. I told you they're old-fashioned." Sam smiles and kisses me on the forehead without even having to bend down. I don't think I'll ever get tired of how tall Sam is. Six feet may not be abnormally tall by any means, but next to me, coming in at five-two, anyone over five-ten seems tall.

We make our way into the house and Sam lets the screen door slam shut behind us. There's a staircase right in the entranceway and a living room to the left. Sam guides me into the living room, and instantly the long, gold shag carpeting feels unstable beneath my low-heeled boots.

Like the outside of the house, the furniture and wallpaper of the living room also look like they haven't been updated since the 1970s, with muted olive green, dark gold, and burnt orange tones drowning the room. In fact, the most modern thing about the room are the playpen and assortment of baby toys that sit in the middle of it. The shag carpet leads into an adjoining dining room, so narrow that the cherrywood chairs surrounding the heavy, matching table look like they nick the walls on a daily basis. I wonder how we're all going to be able to fit.

I look back to the living room. There's a brown-and-tan-checked easy chair placed too close to the TV, and someone with white hair is sitting in it. Sam must notice me looking at them because he whispers to me, "That's Grandma Ruth." He goes over to the woman in the chair and leans down next to her. "Hi, Grandma."

She turns her head towards him and I catch a glimpse of her face for the first time, aged and pale. "Who?" she croaks.

Sam gives me a sad glance and turns back to her. "It's me, Grandma. It's Sam."

"Who?" she croaks again.

"It's me, Sam. Your grandson." Sam gestures me over and I come stand by him. "And this is Margo, my fiancé."

Ruth looks at him for a moment, then turns to me.

I bend down to meet her gaze. "It's so nice to meet you, Ruth."

Her eyes widen, and she raises a trembling, veiny hand to my face. Her fingernails catch in my hair and she carefully drags them through it, tugging at my roots. It hurts, but I don't tell her to stop. After a long moment, her fingers fall out of my hair, but

15

her eyes do not leave mine. When she finally opens her mouth, a throaty moan comes out, like a stammer of inaudible words during a nightmare.

"Shh," says Sam, lowering her hand the rest of the way to her lap. I notice the tips of her fingers are dark, almost black. "It's okay." She closes her mouth and turns her head back to the TV. Sam pats her hand gently and stands. I glimpse what she's watching on the vintage TV set. Some man with a thick head of auburn hair and a matching moustache and sideburns stands on a stage with a microphone attached to a long cord. The man looks familiar, and I wonder if I've seen him on TV before. The volume is down too low to hear what he's saying, but he's holding his free hand in the air the majority of the time, as though he's preaching. The stage behind him appears to be decorated like the front of a church, with three crosses hanging suspended from the ceiling and a red velvet curtain as the backdrop. The crosses are placed in a way that looks almost like modern art, with the two on the ends right-side up and the center one upside down. The program cuts to the audience, some of whom have one or both of their hands in the air, some smiling, some crying. I look above the television and see what appears to be a very old VCR sitting on it, with a solid red light glowing beside the Play button. The show isn't playing on TV. It's playing on the VCR. On the wall over the television and VCR hang three ornate, gold crucifixes, miming the same design of the crosses on the program.

I hear the faint sound of baby babble that I think is in my head until the floorboards creak and an athletically built man a little shorter than Sam enters the room carrying what I can only guess is Selma, upside down. She's laughing wildly and saying what sounds like, "Dada, no," but by the look on her face she doesn't seem to mean it.

"There she is!" Sam takes Selma from the man's arms, and she lets out a lighthearted yelp. "Sorry to steal her from you."

"Please, take her off my hands. I'm getting that carpal tunnel

I'm always diagnosing my patients with." The man looks at me and smiles. "You must be Margo."

"You must be Jimmy." I hold out my hand, as seems to be customary for this family, but he opens up his arms.

"Oh, come now. No need for formalities! You're joining the family, aren't you?" He pulls me into a brotherly hug. "Good to finally meet you, Margo. Now, if you'll excuse me, I'm going to see if the ladies could use any help with dinner. Don't run off with my baby girl, Sam."

"Can't make any promises, Jim."

After Jimmy makes his way through the dining room and into the kitchen, I lean into the adorable little girl in Sam's arms, trying not to imagine what a great dad he'd make. "And this little beauty must be Selma," I coo.

"The little princess." Sam bounces her in his arms. She's smiling at me with her hand in her mouth, and I feel like I've already won her approval. It's a small victory, but I'll take what I can get.

I hear a creak and a woman in her thirties with light brown hair and a strong jaw moves through the kitchen door and into the dining room, carrying a plate with a cloth over it. I'm pretty sure this is Cheryl. She sets the plate down and glances over at us. "Oh, hi there! I'm sorry, I didn't hear you two come in." She walks over and gives Sam a hug.

"Cheryl, this is Margo. Margo, my *much* older sister, Cheryl."

She rolls her eyes as she takes Selma from him. "You wait." She waves a finger at him. "Thirty will be here before you know it."

"Not if I can help it," says Sam.

Cheryl smiles at me and holds out her hand in what I've learned is true Wailing fashion. "It's great to meet you, Margo. I'm sorry you had to put up with my smartass brother for a five-hour road trip, but we're really happy to finally meet you."

I smile and laugh awkwardly. I wish I could come up with

some funny retort, but I fall short. "The drive wasn't too bad," I say lamely. "I'm happy to meet all of you too."

Cheryl squeezes my hand in hers and leans in a little closer to me. "You must be exhausted after your drive. Can we get you anything to drink? Water? Lemonade?"

"I'm fine, really," I say, although my mouth feels suddenly dry.

"Well, if you need anything at all, you let us know. Okay?"

I nod my head, feeling pleasantly disarmed by the warm welcome of Sam's older sister. But I remind myself that he's not as close with Cheryl. He always saw her as more of a mother or an aunt figure, he's told me. Alice is the one he's closest with. Alice is the one I already feel the desperate need to be liked by.

Cheryl takes Selma from Sam and heads toward the back of the house. In the brief moment of silence, the front screen door slams again. "If that doggone garage light breaks one more time, I swear—" Sam's father enters the room, tossing a tool belt onto the easy chair by the entrance. His gruff voice falls right in line with his appearance, a little old and a little hardened by life. He stops talking when he sees me, and a big smile comes over his face. "Well, pardon me, I didn't realize we had company."

He walks over to me, and I find myself posing as if I'm being judged in a beauty contest. He looks me over. Not in a creepy way, but like he's seen his daughter in a wedding dress for the first time. "Aren't you just a beauty." He shakes his head and looks at Sam. "Sam, you didn't tell us what a beauty she was! Fit to win Miss America!"

"Dad, don't be weird." Sam gives me a slightly exasperated look. "Margo, this is my dad, Hank."

I hold out my hand. "It's a pleasure to meet you, Mr. Wailing."

He points to my hand and looks at Sam. "What's this?" I feel my face grow hot as my outstretched hand begins to sweat. "So formal . . ." He laughs and takes my hand. "I can assure you the pleasure is all ours. And, please, call me Hank."

"Hank," I repeat, my smile stiff. "You have a beautiful home."

"Well, Sam here will have to give you the full tour later." He pats Sam on the back. With the two of them side by side, it's hard to imagine them as father and son. Hank is at least five inches shorter than Sam, although I'm sure he's gotten shorter and more hunched over the years. Even though their features may not be similar, their frames are, despite the height difference—both slender, teetering on bony. "It's not much, but we're awfully proud of it. Been our home for over forty years." He leans in closer to me, his wild salt-and-pepper eyebrows bobbing up and down. "Just don't be too spooked if you hear anything go bump in the night." The kitchen door swings open again, and in walks Mary, carrying a Crock-Pot-sized bowl full of what appears to be pea soup. Hank rushes over to her. "Honey, you shouldn't be doing that, let me help you . . ."

Sam touches my arm. "I'm going to give Alice a call and see if she's close—another audition," he says with a hint of exasperation in his voice. "Make yourself at home." And with that, he disappears into the other room, leaving me standing on display in the Wailing living room—a new mannequin in an old dress shop.

I shift my weight between my feet, looking around the room for something to focus on so I don't come across as too awkward, although the only person in the room to potentially judge me is Ruth. The others have bustled back into the kitchen, I assume to finish preparing dinner. Ruth hasn't taken her eyes off the screen since we met. I don't want to disturb her, but I also don't want to be rude. I've always hated seeing elderly folks be ignored, like people are afraid to talk to them, to treat them like another human being. Even though I know I'll never get to see my mother older, I did have the unfortunate privilege of seeing her mind deteriorate as if she were pushing a hundred, at least near the end. The very thought of it is enough to make me sick, and the only thing that might remedy it in this moment is showing kindness to a woman in a similar state. I take a few steps toward the TV, toward Ruth.

"Looks like an interesting program." I don't expect her to look at me, and she doesn't. "I don't watch too much TV at home. Mostly just in the evenings." Her eyes haven't moved, and although I feel as though her expression may have changed slightly since I started talking, it could be wishful thinking. "My mother and I used to watch TV together on Sunday and Tuesday evenings. Mainly reality shows, but sometimes a good British mystery." The silence fills the air between us again. "My mother also really liked old movies," I add. "Have you seen *The African Queen?*"

Ruth slowly turns her head to me. She doesn't say anything, but I seem to have caught her attention.

"She showed it to me when I was little. It was one of her favorites. She loved the costumes. I think in another life she would have liked to have been a costume designer." With that, I'm stuck on what to say next. "Well. I'll let you enjoy your show." I politely bow out of our one-sided conversation and glance into the dining room. Mary is now setting another dish on the table. I look behind me toward the hall and catch a glimpse of Sam in the other room, talking to Alice on an old, corded phone that could be forty years old. He's nodding and smiling and running his hand through his unkempt hair. The gentle reassurance of having Sam by my side, in my corner, has started to fade, and now I'm anxious again. Suddenly all I want is to be alone.

When my mother was still alive, I was never lonely, even when I was alone. But this year, I've found myself becoming so. Even though Sam came into my life when I needed him most, less than a month after she passed, I've still felt a loneliness since losing her that I've never felt before. That's the thing people don't always understand about loneliness; there's a big difference between being lonely and being alone.

"Hate to interrupt—" Hank's voice startles me, and I realize he's standing right behind Ruth, his hands on the back of her chair. "But I'm going to get Ruth settled at the table so we can eat."

Hank helps Ruth to her feet, and they shuffle through the living room and into the dining room. Her body moves so slowly, so cautiously, that merely watching her walk gives me anxiety. I find myself holding my breath until they reach one of the chairs in the dining room and Ruth is seated in it. Once my breath releases, I make my way into the dining room.

"Oh, there you are!" says Mary as I enter. "Take a seat, sweetheart, dinner's ready." I begin to take a seat in a chair next to Cheryl, but Mary stops me, "Margo, we have a seat for you right here." She pats the chair at the head of the table.

"Oh, are you sure? I thought you or Hank would sit there."

"Nonsense! You're our guest. Now, take a seat."

I don't argue and take a seat in the chair, which is plusher and more elegant than the one I was about to sit in. Hank finishes settling Ruth into the chair opposite me at the other end of the table. I try to smile at her, but her eyes remain unfocused. It's like she's somehow looking at me and right past me at the same time.

Sam takes a seat in the chair to my left. "Alice should be home in just a few minutes. It sounds like her audition did *not* go well."

"When is that girl going to realize she can't make a living acting?" says Hank, holding Mary's chair for her as she sits.

"Now, Hank, it's her passion." Mary scooches her chair forward. "We agreed to support her on this journey." She gives me a polite smile. "Do you have a passion, Margo?"

"Um—" I scramble for an answer, but I come up short. No one's passion is accounting. They'll think I'm the most boring person on the planet if I say that's my passion. That the only time I feel really, truly at peace is when I've just solved an equation or double-checked the sum of two hundred numbers and gotten the same exact answer. That math is the only thing in my life that's ever been certain, and that makes it my passion, even if it's true. "I guess . . . I enjoy reading. And math."

A wide smile spreads across Mary's face, her eyebrows raised. "Oh, how lovely," she says in a tone of feigned politeness.

With the window open I jump on one of my pocket conversation topics. "Your passion was teaching, right?"

Mary seems pleasantly taken aback by the question. "Why, yes, dear. It certainly was. Of course, I haven't taught in years."

"Oh, really? Sam mentioned you taught for thirty-five years, so I assumed your retirement was fairly recent."

"No, it was," she says quickly. "I just mean it feels like it's been years."

I nod my head, searching for a way to forward the conversation. "My mother was a teacher too."

Her eyes grow wide in surprise. "Was she really?"

My heart sinks slightly. I guess I'd assumed Sam had told them more about my mother, my only family. Even though he never met her, I talk about her often. "She was," I say. "She had to stop last year because she got sick, but . . ." I trail off, trying to find a way to turn the conversation back to something more pleasant. "She was always great at keeping up with the changing technology in education. She was an advocate for getting the school she worked at to change to a new LMS."

Mary stares at me blankly. "LMS?"

"Learning management software?" A term I heard my mother use many times since the late 1990s.

"I've never heard of that," she says, intrigued.

"Oh," I say, trying not to sound too confused. "Maybe that was after you retired."

She gives me a small smile, and with that I let the subject drop and look around the table. All the chairs are filled except for the one to Sam's left, which I assume is for Alice. Across the table is a full spread of sandwiches along with the Crock-Pot full of pea soup. Everyone is drinking water for their beverage. As I survey the food, I realize no one is saying anything. All I can hear is the faint sound of the man's voice on the television. "Praise our Almighty Father," he says. "Praise him with every fiber of your being!" The audience on the TV cheers.

I clear my throat, waiting for someone to speak, but no one does. When I look up, everyone suddenly shifts, and I realize they had all been staring at me. I feel my face grow hot and look back down at the table. The food no longer looks appetizing.

"The food looks delicious," I lie, to fill the uncomfortable silence. I feel a headache coming on, so I hope the food is at least enough to help subdue it.

Mary smiles at me and then averts her eyes. I want someone to speak. To say something. To say *anything*. But no one does. I look over at Sam, hoping he'll make eye contact with me and offer me some reassurance, but he doesn't. In fact, I feel like he's looking everywhere but at me. The man on TV continues to preach, his booming voice still carrying to my ears despite the low volume. I can't decide if his voice is making the silence better or worse.

We sit there for almost five minutes. I'm about to excuse myself to use the washroom if only to escape the painful silence for a moment, when the front door bursts open and a young blonde woman who must be Alice enters the room. Despite her youthful appearance, there's something jaded and sharp about her. Not just her features—a heart-shaped face that culminates in the pointed tip of her jaw, high, angled cheeks, and a thin nose—but her whole essence, like she's doing something she's very determined to do, and she must do it quickly. Her brief presence brings with it a feeling of unease rising in my stomach that I force down with a sip of water from my glass.

Alice drops her large cloth purse on the floor and walks quickly to the dining room table without saying a word. Once she takes her seat beside Sam, Mary smiles at her and holds out her hands, one to me and one to Hank on her right. Everyone else at the table follows suit, joining hands for what I assume is grace. I take Mary's hand and Sam's, feeling a vague sense of relief wash over me because this must mean that someone is going to be speaking soon.

Sure enough, Mary does. It's just not at all what I'm hoping to hear. "Margo, would you mind saying grace for us?"

The blood rushes back to my face and my mouth goes dry. "Um, I think I'd rather not—"

"Yeah, Mom, I doubt Margo would know what to say," Sam interjects.

"Oh, I'm sure she would." Mary smiles sweetly at me.

"I'd really rather not—"

"I'll do it," says Alice. Mary shoots her a warning glance, but Alice seems unfazed. She clears her throat loudly and closes her eyes. Everyone else closes theirs too. I keep mine slightly open. "Dear Almighty Father, we thank you for the food on our plates. Feed our souls with the bread of life you've given us. Nourish our bodies with the blood you've bestowed upon us. We give thanks for this meal, for our home, for our family, and for Margo." I glance at Alice. Her eyes are shut tight, but I could feel them looking at me a few seconds before. "Thank you for bringing her to us safely, and for allowing her to become part of our family."

I feel my heart rate speed up because I suddenly know exactly what they're going to say and do next. It beats even faster when I realize that I'm right.

"From now, till then, till the Ever End," they all chant, bringing their hands from right, to left, then out and in. My head swims with the confusion of what just happened. It swims with the words that came from their lips. The words that drifted through my mind before they were even spoken. How could I have possibly known the words they were going to say before they said them? And what's even more strange: why do those words sound so familiar? I feel myself suddenly grasping at a memory. A memory from my childhood, so far away and so intangible that it feels like a wisp of smoke. Before I can bottle the memory, it's gone, vanished into thin air.

It's just déjà vu, I tell myself, trying to shake my anxiety.

Everyone begins passing the food around and filling up their plates and bowls. "Eat up!" booms Hank.

"You go first, Margo," Mary says, positioning the handle of the ladle in my direction.

"Oh, thank you." I grab the handle and carefully ladle a spoonful of pea soup into my bowl, suddenly feeling everyone's eyes on me. When I'm done, I set the ladle back and slide the pot towards Sam.

"Plenty to go around!" Hank says, grabbing a sandwich from the tray in front of him. He takes a bite of it before it even touches his plate. "And you kids are going to need your strength for all that wedding planning you'll be doing this week," he says through his mouthful of food, gesturing toward Sam and me.

"Alright, Dad. One thing at a time," says Sam.

"What's the problem? We're all excited, and I'm sure Margo is the most excited of all of us. She's marrying the love of her life. Lightning doesn't strike twice." Hank leans in toward me. "Or does it?" He wiggles his eyebrows at me.

"Oh, Hank!" Mary pipes in. "Stop that."

"What? It's a fair question." He looks back over at me. "Any other past boyfriends we should know about?"

I blow on the soup in my spoon, wishing it would cool faster so I can eat instead of answer his question. "No, no other boyfriends," I answer truthfully, my eyes darting to Sam, but Sam isn't looking at me. He's filling his mouth with a sandwich.

"How sweet," says Mary in spite of herself. Soon there's some general murmur and chitchat. This is fine. This is good. A nice family meal.

"This soup is delicious, Mary." Jimmy is already reaching for another helping.

"You like it? It's a new recipe." She grins at me. "Vegetarian."

"That's very nice of you, to accommodate me," I say. Sam stops eating long enough to smile, no doubt proud of himself for remembering to tell his family of my dietary restriction.

"How was your audition?" Cheryl asks Alice, who stops chewing long enough to shoot her daggers.

"Why do you do that?"

"Do what? I'm making conversation."

Alice shakes her head and turns back to her plate. "I didn't get the part."

"Hey." Sam puts his hand on her arm. "You don't hear back from them until tomorrow."

"I know I didn't get it. I totally blew it. It was awful."

"We prayed for you last night," Hank chimes in between bites. Mary nods. Now that it's cool enough to eat, I take a bite of my soup. It's rather bland. I'd like some salt but there isn't any on the table, and I'm not going to ask. Asking for something not on the table at someone else's house feels like an insult to their cooking. Selma, who's sitting in a highchair next to Jimmy, waves her arms and chews on a soggy piece of bread. I look across the table at Ruth. Someone has loaded her bowl and plate with food, but she isn't eating. She's sitting there, staring ahead. Still not at me, just straight ahead into nothingness. I don't understand why no one's helping her eat, but it isn't my place to say.

"What play was your audition for, Alice?" Jimmy asks, blowing off a spoonful of soup and feeding it to Selma.

"I don't want to talk about it anymore," says Alice. "Let's hear from someone new for a change." She looks over at me and smiles, but I'd rather she didn't. It's not a warm smile. Everyone's head turns to me, and once again I'm under the spotlight.

"Mm—" Cheryl swallows a bite of food. "How was the drive?"

"Not bad at all," says Sam. "Left the city around eight, so just under five hours—"

Alice lets out a bark of laughter. "We don't care about the drive. We want to know about Margo. Your *fiancé*." She looks at me. "What is it you do, Margo?"

I swallow a bite of the bland cheese sandwich. "I'm an accountant."

There are a few polite nods, but I can tell they're hardly interested in my job.

"Sam, I don't think you ever told us how you proposed," says Cheryl.

Sam looks at me, flashing me that million-dollar smile of his. Whenever he smiles like that, I should feel butterflies. I should feel affection. But for whatever reason, I always feel slightly perplexed, like there's something I should remember that I can't. "Go on," he says. "You tell it much better than I do."

I swallow and pat my lips with my napkin. "Well, Sam took me out on a picnic for my birthday, actually. He took me to this really beautiful spot right on Lake Michigan. And he prepared this whole spread. Fruit salad, finger sandwiches, pastries . . . After dinner, he put on some music and we danced as the sun set—"

"What was the song?" Cheryl asks.

Sam jumps in. "'Shine On, Harvest Moon.'"

"Great song," says Hank.

I smile, feeling my body relax at the familiarity of the story. "Then, right when the song ended, he got down on one knee, and he said, 'I never thought I'd meet the person I wanted to grow old with until I met you.' And he showed me the ring and asked me to marry him and I said yes."

Mary waves her arms excitedly, quickly chewing and swallowing her food so she can speak. "Show us the ring! Show us the ring!"

I set down my napkin and show them the ring, grateful to have their eyes on my hand instead of my face. The beautiful red ruby in the center of it glistens in the light from the chandelier above. I'm not a girl who dresses particularly fancy or wears makeup, but something about the ring makes me feel glamorous. Special. Loved.

"Oh," she sighs. "How beautiful. Show Grandma Ruth." I hold my hand outstretched so Ruth can see it, although I doubt she can from so far away. "Doesn't it look beautiful on her? Looks like it was made for her, just like it was made for you."

I retract my hand slightly. "What do you mean?"

Mary looks at Sam. "Sam, you didn't tell her?"

Sam looks up from his plate. "Hmm? Oh, right. It was Grandma Ruth's ring."

My anxiety comes back with full force. I've heard of people giving their significant other their *deceased* grandmother's ring, but never while she's still alive. I have the sudden urge to take it off, but my fingers are sweaty and swollen. "Oh, I don't think I can accept this then."

"What? Nonsense!" says Mary.

"No, I mean—" I look at Ruth. "Ruth, I don't feel right taking your ring."

Ruth stares forward at a place right past my shoulder. Sam leans into me, his voice low. "Margo, it's fine. She's not . . . all there."

I'm not sure what to say to him. I want to cry. Just because she's not "all there" doesn't mean she's dead. I pull on the ring, trying to loosen it, but the harder I pull, the tighter it fits.

"Don't you take that thing off your pretty finger for one second," says Hank in a jarringly firm tone.

Mary puts her hand on my shoulder. "Really, dear, Ruth would want you to have it."

They don't know what Ruth would want. She's barely able to speak one word, let alone convey her thoughts and feelings on the issue. Her lack of autonomy in the situation sits in my stomach like a rock. This doesn't feel right. It feels like stealing. "I don't feel right—"

At that moment, Ruth opens her mouth and sings the first few lines of "Shine on Harvest Moon" shrilly at the top of her lungs.

Although everyone stops what they're doing and looks at her, the incident doesn't seem out of place to them. Cheryl reaches over and strokes Ruth's hair till she stops singing and goes back to staring blankly ahead. In the silence that follows her outburst, everyone has casually gone back to eating. I pick up my sandwich, trying not to look at the now-tainted ring on my finger. I'm not sure what has happened, but I'm certain that I'm no longer hungry.

As soon as everyone is finished eating, Mary, Alice, and Cheryl stand and begin clearing the dishes. Taking my cue, I start to stand as well, but Hank stops me. "Guests don't clean in this house, young lady," he says with a grin. I smile politely and shift in my chair. Jimmy is looking at an article in the newspaper, and Sam is picking at his teeth with a toothpick. I glance over at Hank to see his eyes haven't left me. When he meets my gaze, he says, "As soon as we're finished cleaning up this mess and kick these guys out—" he gestures at Jimmy, "we'll head on out ourselves."

"Where are we going?" I ask, taking a sip of water.

Hank looks at Sam expectantly. "You didn't tell your fiancé about today's plans?"

"Must have slipped my mind." Sam leans over to me. "My family wanted to take you to see a wedding venue."

"Ha!" Hank barks. "Not just any wedding venue—*the* wedding venue."

"The Evergreen Mansion." Sam looks over at me and with a hint of sarcasm in his voice says, "It's the most stunning property in all of Fairbury."

The wedding venue? I know Sam would like to get married close to his family. It's hard for his mother to travel in the health she's in, and even harder for his grandmother. Now that I've met Ruth, I can't fathom her traveling more than a short car ride to our wedding. Since I don't have any particular reason to get married in Chicago, I told him that Iowa would be fine with me, but I hadn't realized that his family had already picked out our venue. The way Sam made it seem when we were planning this trip was that it would be a chance for us to see what options Fairbury had to offer. That if his hometown didn't seem like the right fit, we wouldn't have to get married here. What if I don't want to get married at the Evergreen Mansion? What if I don't even want to get married in Fairbury?

"You know, Cheryl and Jimmy had their wedding at the Evergreen Mansion and it was just beautiful," says Hank.

Jimmy looks up from his paper, the fondness of the memory glazing across his eyes. "It really, really was."

I pull a smile onto my face, doing my best to mask my inner thoughts. "I'm sure it's beautiful."

Hank turns to me. As if reading the discomfort I'm hiding, he says, "Unless of course, you'd prefer to get married in a church. But Sam has made it very clear to us that that's not exactly your style."

I feel my face flush as I glance over at Sam. "It's not that I'm opposed to getting married in a church," I say, slightly defensively. "I wasn't raised with any particular religion."

Hank leans back in his chair and clasps his hands behind his head. His eyes are slightly narrowed as he looks at me, as if he's trying to figure me out. Just when I think he's about to speak, he doesn't. I look over at Sam, who's also looking at me.

"No religion," Hank says, as though pondering this new, unfamiliar thought. "You know, Margo. One of the reasons you may not consider yourself 'religious' is that you haven't found the right religion! There's hundreds out there. Thousands, even. And even more beliefs than that." In the distance, I hear the faint voice of the televangelist crackling through the TV, and I will the subject to change. I don't have anything against religion. It's people I have a problem with. People who have warped religions like Christianity over the years, turning them into something miles away from what they were. People who take the bare bones of a religion, borrow the pieces of it they like, and twist the rest into judgment and control.

I pull a smile onto my face. "Well, I can't wait to see the Evergreen Mansion."

After Jimmy and Cheryl leave with Selma, Alice excuses herself to her room, and Hank, Mary, Sam and I pile into Hank and Mary's old car. We've been driving for about twenty minutes and the whole time I've been feeling claustrophobic. I try to focus my attention on the small landmarks that Hank points out around town from behind the wheel, several of which he was responsible for wiring—the elementary school, a gas station, the community center—but nothing is exciting enough to keep me from thinking about the emissions oozing out of the exhaust pipe and into my lungs through the open window.

My phone buzzes a few times, catching up on missed emails and notifications as we go within range of a signal, but I don't check it. I'll probably start feeling nauseated if I look down while Hank is driving, but I also don't want to check it. I want to enjoy this time away from work for a while. Away from my life.

We turn a corner and drive down what feels like an alleyway—a wide alleyway between a strip of homes in great need of repair. A woman with white hair and a floral dress sits in a rickety rocker on her back porch. An old man pushes a mower across patches of grass and gravel. A young boy kicks a red ball around an overgrown yard. Every one of them stops and watches us as we pass, as if they recognize us. As if they're expecting us. The boy holds my gaze as his ball rolls into the street, slowing to a stop right in front of our car. Hank slows the car to a stop and stays silent as the boy walks in front of the car, picks up his ball, stares at us for a moment longer, then crosses the street. Even though my eyes stay focused ahead, I feel him watching us even as we drive away.

Finally, we arrive at the Evergreen Mansion, an elaborate estate with bright red siding, white trim, and cornfields surrounding it on all sides. Hank pulls up right in front of the steel gate. Mary gets out of the car first, as if she wants to be the first child in line for the roller coaster, running up to the gate faster than I knew she could walk. Hank is next, shutting the driver's side door behind him.

As I step out of the car and make my way over to the tall gate, I feel something thick and solid under my foot and nearly trip. Once I get my footing, I look down to see that what I've stepped on is a corncob encased in husk. Curious, I bend down and pick it up, feeling the roughness of the husk on my fingertips. I slowly peel back the husk, expecting to see a ripe ear of corn beneath it, but that's not what I find. Under the husk is something black, rotting, and rancid. I gag and immediately drop the cob. It lands with a light thud and rolls forward a few feet.

"What's wrong?" Sam's hand on my back causes me to jump.

I look at the corncob not far from my feet. "The corn, it was all rotted."

Sam gives a shrug. "Yeah, the harvest season has passed. Maybe that one got missed."

He leads me toward the gate, and I'm careful to step around the corncob, trying to get the wretched scent out of my mind.

We make our way over to a plaque on the gate that reads "Evergreen Mansion, 1959." Sam stands behind me, his hands on my shoulders. "What do you think?"

I look past the sign, through the gate, at the Evergreen

Mansion. To any passerby, it would be considered exquisite. A plantation-esque home with pillars framing the double-door entrance, over a dozen picture windows within view of the front gate, and manicured shrubs and flowerbeds surrounding it in strategic placement, despite their discoloration with the quickly impeding fall. The Evergreen Mansion looks more like a home that belongs in Louisiana than Iowa, standing brilliantly out against the dying cornfields behind it. But when I look at the Evergreen Mansion, I can't see it as anything but unsettling. With one glance, I feel the blood draining from my face, feel the life being completely sucked out of me until I'm nothing but a void—a shell of a person staring at the shell of a house.

"Cheryl and Jimmy used the grounds for the ceremony," Hank interjects. "That area back there by the cornfield is lit beautifully at sunset."

My eyes drift from the mansion to the cornfields, and the emptiness of my insides suddenly becomes filled with a creeping sense of dread. I wonder how many of the cornstalks are hosts to rotting corn like the one I'd picked up. I'd never known corn to rot like that, but maybe that's my naïve city upbringing talking. Even without the rotting corncob fresh in my mind, there's still something that feels strange about the cornfields surrounding us. There isn't more than a light breeze jostling the dying cornstalks, and yet their movement feels purposeful, menacing even.

I look over at Mary, who is holding onto two of the iron rods of the gate, her face pressed in the space between as if she's looking through a prison cell into the outside world, longing to be a part of it. "It gets more beautiful every time I see it," she whispers.

Sam leans in and hums "The Wedding March" in my ear before whispering into it, "I think I see wedding bells in your eyes."

The creeping sense of dread within me culminates in the form of a cramp in my stomach. Not that Sam has ever had a particular knack for reading my mind, but in this moment he's so far off, it's jarring. This doesn't feel right. None of it. I feel like I'm watching a movie of my own life, and it's nothing like I thought it was going to be. Not only had I imagined my mother being with me for occasions like this, but I imagined I would feel differently. Here I am with my fiancé's arms around me, looking at a wedding venue that probably costs more for one event than three months of my salary, and I feel sick with uneasiness at the mere sight of the building in front of me.

Just when I think I've gone someplace far, far away, Sam's voice pulls me back to earth. "You okay?" I blink at him, and for the first time, feel drops of water on my cheeks. Tears. With drying tracks in their wake. I quickly wipe my face and shake my head. "Yeah, a little emotional, I guess." Although I always try my best not to cry around him, Sam has been used to me breaking down at random since we started dating. He hasn't said anything about it. I'm not sure he knows what to say when I'm crying. What does anyone say to someone who's mourning? "I'm sorry," can only fall on deaf ears so many times. He puts his arm around me and pulls me into a hug, rubbing my back, but his touch is cold, and there's something robotic about his movement. "There, there . . . it's okay. Maybe this is all too much, too fast?"

He pulls back and looks into my eyes, as if searching for an answer in them. I shake my head. I can't bear to give anyone the satisfaction of knowing how I'm feeling right now. Not when I don't even know myself.

Before I can answer, Hank slaps Sam on the back as he surveys the property. "Pretty amazing, isn't it?" he says, nodding to the mansion.

Finally, Mary peels herself away from the gate and approaches me. Without saying a word, she takes my hand in hers. In her eyes are tears. They aren't the same tears as mine. They're happy, full of life and joy and promise. "Oh, Margo," she utters. "Do you love it?"

I pull my lips into the best smile I can muster and nod my head, but the lie hurts the muscles in my neck. Maybe it's the red color of the siding. Maybe it's the way the windows and doors and shutters seem to combine to make an eerily pleasant face on the front of the house. Maybe it's the unsettling movement of the cornfields around it. Maybe it's the fact that Mary is sobbing again, and I can't quite fathom how even the most beautiful wedding, even for your daughter-in-law, could stir up those kinds of emotions just by looking at the venue. Maybe it's the fact that my mother isn't here, and Sam doesn't seem to give a fuck that I'm standing here with my insides curdling, miles away from the life I thought I was going to have. But whatever it is, I don't like this feeling. I don't like this place.

Chapter Three

FROM THE TIME we leave the Evergreen Mansion to the time we arrive at the town square, Mary and Hank have circled the same argument about an electric bill six times and are gunning for a seventh by the time we pull into our parking spot in front of an empty storefront that looks like it's been vacant for thirty years. "With all the wires I've laid in this town, you'd think the electric company would have the decency not to overcharge us three months in a row!" complains Hank as I open my door. I'm the first to get out of the car and take the moment of peace to look around the square. In the center is a big, old courthouse and a red-and-blue playground that looks like it's seen better days. Around the square are a variety of shops and restaurants, about half of which are either closed or out of business. I can imagine the bustling hub of shoppers and families it probably was back in the day. But now it looks sad, another small Midwestern town forgotten with time.

I hear the faint sound of Hank and Mary's argument in the distance and feel Sam's hand on my shoulder. "I'm going to go help them sort out this issue with their bill. Do you want to come with, or do you want to stay here?"

"I'll be fine. I'll walk around the square."

Sam kisses my head and joins his parents, leading them across the street as they continue to bicker.

The sidewalks are empty enough for me—I don't pass a single person as I walk down the east side of the square. When I reach the south side, I pass a young couple and an older woman with a walker. Just as I'm about to make my turn onto the west side of the square, a small window sign that reads Home of Rebecca's Bridal catches my eye. I look up at the shop—in big, bold yellow letters above the awning are the words Dee's Flowers. I look over both my shoulders, scanning the square for Sam and his parents. With them nowhere in sight, I pull open the shop door and step inside. A little bell chimes as I cross the threshold, and instantly the perfume of flowers hits my nostrils, somehow easing my anxiety. Whichever flower it is that's slowing the palpitations behind my ribs, I'd do anything to bottle it.

I take my time walking past the abundance of flowers at the entrance, breathing as deeply as my lungs will allow, holding onto the scent. I turn on my heel to make my way over to the front desk, but something outside the shop window catches my eye, and I freeze. Across the street a man is staring at me. At least he would be if I could see his eyes. Despite the glaring sun, he's the only thing in view that's somehow shaded. I remember the figure outside my mother's window as a child, and the feeling of fear and loneliness that I had then wraps around me like a familiar coat. I don't know if this is the same man. If he is, he's as nondescript now as he was then. A dark figure is almost impossible to discern. Maybe he's the same man as that night— the same man who haunted me as a child. Maybe he's not. I may never know. A few people walk by along the sidewalk. Some cars pass. No one acknowledges him. I want to call someone over, to ask them if they can see him too. But I can't bring myself to move. And even if I could, if no one else can see him, I'll only appear crazy. I continue to watch the man as if there's nothing

37

around but him and me. Finally, I'm jolted by a voice in my ear.

"Can I help you, dear?" A woman in her sixties with short, gray hair and rectangular glasses is standing beside me with a tight smile on her face.

"Um, yes." I attempt to string together a few coherent words. "I saw your sign and, uh—Are you Rebecca?"

The woman laughs heartily. "Oh, dear, I'm not Rebecca! I'm Dee. Rebecca is in her office in back."

"Oh, sorry." I feel myself blushing.

"Don't be! I should be so lucky. Do you have an appointment?"

I suddenly feel deflated. "I don't."

"Not a problem, she might be free. Let's go give her a holler." I follow Dee through the maze of flowers, keeping my gaze forward, refusing to look back. Because I know he'll still be there if I do.

We come to a plain door that might as well have led to a janitor's closet. On the door is a sign identical to the one in the window, only this one is curling off the door from wear. Dee knocks on the door three times. "Rebecca? Are you free, dear?"

"Come in!" a voice calls from the other side of the door. Dee turns the handle and gestures for me to enter. I squeeze past several more flower stands as I make my way into Rebecca's tiny office. Her back is toward me, her body facing a computer screen. The office is cluttered with stacks of wedding books and magazines, folders, packets, ribbons, and samples of lace. "I'll leave you ladies to it!" Dee excuses herself, shutting the door behind her. Rebecca spins around in her chair. When she meets my eyes, a small smile spreads across her face.

"Hello." She stands, stretching out her hand in front of me. "I'm Rebecca."

"Margo," I manage. "I'm sorry, I know I don't have an appointment—"

"No problem at all. Please, have a seat." She gestures towards the empty dining room chair in front of me, and I take it.

Rebecca leans her elbows on her desk and looks at me, politely expectant. And that's when I realize it's my turn to speak, but I think I've forgotten how. In a word, Rebecca is beautiful. I'm not supposed to notice that. I'm fully aware that I'm not supposed to notice that. But anyone would notice it. I'm sure Sam would notice it. And if he did, I wouldn't even be jealous. Because she's beautiful—long, wavy brown hair falling over dainty shoulders, brown eyes with just enough flecks of green to trick you, high cheekbones tinted with rouge, and small, full lips that part into a crooked smile. Instantly, I'm reminded of Katerina. Rebecca doesn't share too many similarities with her—mainly the dark hair and dainty features—but what reminds me of Katerina is the feeling in the pit of my stomach I get when she looks at me. It's a dangerous feeling. One that I've tried very hard to feel with Sam and have yet to experience.

When I still haven't spoken, Rebecca offers a prompt. "So, you're getting married?"

I nod my head. "Yes. Um, actually I'm in town with my fiancé visiting his family. We're thinking of coming back here for our wedding in the spring."

"Fantastic." She opens up a large calendar notebook and lays it flat in front of her. The smile returns to her face, like she's switched into planning mode. "Tell me a bit more about where the two of you are at in the planning process."

"Um, sure—" I search for words, feeling a bit taken aback at getting right down to business. "Well, we really just started. We got engaged a few weeks ago." Before I can stop myself, I add with an awkward laugh, "We've only been together about six months, so it's all been rather quick."

I expect more of a reaction from her—an eyebrow raise or a small gasp—but if Rebecca is surprised by the short amount of time we've been dating, she doesn't show it. Of course, she's probably trained herself not to, in her position. She's probably learned to not show when she's fazed by the odd requests of couples or the drama of bridezillas. I hope I don't test her composure too much.

"Well, I'm happy to help in any way I can." I find her answer mildly disappointing. I don't know what I'd been hoping for. As much as I hate to admit it, I think I was hoping for validation. For her to say that plenty of couples get engaged after only being together for six months. Rebecca hesitates for a beat. "That is, if you're looking for a wedding planner. I don't mean to assume if you're just looking for a few local suggestions."

"No, we definitely are," I say quickly, although it's not quite the truth. Sam and I haven't discussed if we'll want a wedding planner. We're not even sure if we'll get married in Fairbury, but if we're even considering it, we might as well consider a wedding planner here too.

"Great," her smile returns, softer and more relaxed than before. "In that case, tell me a little bit about your story. How did you two meet?"

I should have our story down by now, but I don't. Probably because I haven't had many people to tell it to. Only a few colleagues at work, and some of Sam's friends when we went out to dinner to celebrate our engagement. "Well, we met on a train. Back in Chicago."

Her face lights up. "I love it. Very *While You Were Sleeping.*"

"Yes!" My heart skips a beat. "That's one of my favorite movies."

"Same here," she says, sounding genuine.

I think back to my childhood. To my mother putting in our worn-out VHS tape of the Sandra Bullock classic whenever I stayed home sick from school or during the holiday season. Even today, it's my go-to comfort movie. "I can't believe I never thought of that comparison," I say truthfully.

"Sometimes you need an outsider to help you see things clearly," she says. "Let's see . . ." She takes a quick breath and looks down at her notebook, and I wonder if she's consulting a standard list of questions. "Do you have a venue picked out yet?"

"Um, no. Well, sort of. Do you do wedding planning or venues or ..."

"Yes, yes, I do all of it. Essentially, I'm your one-stop shop for all things wedding."

"Great," I say. "That would be great. I think—" Before I can say another word, my phone vibrates in my purse, cutting off my train of thought completely. I pull it out. Sam is calling me. For some reason I feel instantly guilty even though I have no reason to. "I'm so sorry," I say to Rebecca as I answer the phone.

"Margo? Where are you?" says Sam's voice on the other end, muffled by the wind.

"I'm at Dee's Flower Shop."

"Dee's? Okay, I'll be right there."

He hangs up before I do, and I slip my phone back into my purse. "Sorry about that."

"Don't be. Was that your fiancé?"

"Yes, he's heading over here to pick me up if you'd like to meet him."

I squeeze my way back out of Rebecca's office and follow her lead out of the maze of flowers to the front of the shop. I look pointedly away from the window, going so far as to occupy myself with a bouquet of dying daffodils. Before I can think of something else to say to Rebecca, the small bell above the door chimes and in walks Sam, looking mildly annoyed. I tell myself he probably isn't annoyed at me, merely frustrated with his parents, but the way he looks over at me gives me my doubts.

"You must be Margo's fiancé." Rebecca holds her hand out to Sam, who shakes it briskly.

"Sam." His tone is a tad sharp. Sharper than normal. He turns to me. "You ready to go? Dad's got the car running. He and Mom are eager to hear what you think of their suggestions for the wedding."

"Um, yeah. I'm ready."

Rebecca hesitates. She turns to me. "Well, let me know if you want to schedule an appointment. The season is slowing down so I'm also open to walk-ins."

"Great, thank you." I smile, nod, and start to follow Sam out the door, when I feel a soft hand on my arm and freeze. I turn to face Rebecca, who is standing closer to me than I'd expected.

"All this—it can be overwhelming," she says quietly. "I've never been married, but I've planned enough weddings to know how stressful they can be, especially for the bride." She pulls out a business card and slips it into my hand. "Shoot me a text while you're in town. We can meet up over coffee and discuss what *you* want your wedding to be." Rebecca leans in, giving me a serious look, and I suddenly realize how short I feel standing next to her. "I'm not saying the opinions of your future in-laws don't matter, but in the end your voice is the one that's most important."

Sam, who left the shop without me, rings the bell as he pops his head back in. "Margo, you coming?"

I turn to Rebecca. "Thank you." I make my way out of the flower shop, determined not to notice the dark figure that's still standing outside the window.

Sam and I walk down the sidewalk towards the car, away from the man. I won't even look at him, even though I can feel him looking at me. I skip a few steps to keep up with Sam, but even once I'm by his side he doesn't say anything to me and I'm not sure why.

"Did you get the bill sorted out for your parents?"

"Yeah."

I nod and continue walking. When I spot the car up ahead, I stop and pull on Sam to stop too. "Did I do something wrong?"

"What? No."

"Do you not want to get a wedding planner?"

Sam runs his hand through his hair and glances from me to the car and back again. "It's not that, it's just . . . You know, my parents thought this was going to be something they planned

42

for us."

I feel my heart in my throat. "I don't remember us deciding that."

Sam hesitates. He doesn't have an argument because he knows I'm right. "You're right. You're right, we didn't." He looks back at the car again, antsy. "Look, can we talk about this more later?"

"That's fine."

We continue walking. Just before we get in the car, Sam lowers his voice and says, "Don't mention any of this to my parents yet, okay?"

He opens my door for me before I have a chance to respond, and I climb into the backseat. The arguing between Hank and Mary has stopped completely, and I can't decide if I prefer it to the deafening silence that's happening now. No one says a word as Sam walks around the car and gets in on the other side. In fact, no one says a word the whole ride back to the house. In my hands, I'm still holding Rebecca's business card low enough that it's out of view from everyone except for me, and maybe from Sam. Her name, Rebecca Colwell, an email, a phone number, and a sketch of two wedding bells surrounded by a ring of flowers are the only designs on the white card. Somehow, holding it, I feel a little bit at ease.

Chapter Four

MAYBE THE START of my relationship with Sam wasn't quite like *While You Were Sleeping*. There was no coma, no found family, no Bill Pullman, but there was a train, and we were in Chicago.

The first time I saw Sam, he was staring at me from across the car of the "L" train. His expression wasn't threatening but intrigued. Like he was trying to place me. I shifted uncomfortably in my seat. Of course, I'd been in uneasy situations on the train before, but typically they involved drunken men coming home from a late night out at the bar, or loners carrying on a conversation with themselves. Rarely did an attractive man attempt to make eye contact with me on my evening commute.

The train screeched to a halt at Irving Park, six stops away from mine. Only twenty-two more minutes until I would be home in my apartment, away from strange, attractive men with watchful eyes. I looked down at my phone and pretended not to notice him staring at me, which was at least better than trying not to cry, which I felt like I'd done every train ride home from work for the past three weeks, since my mother had passed away.

As the final few passengers boarded the car, Sam stood and

crossed over to me. He sat down a seat away and looked at me pointedly. I had no choice but to look up at him.

"Faye Dunaway," he said. "That's who you remind me of."

"Excuse me?"

"Faye Dunaway. The actress. You look like her."

"Oh. Okay, I guess." While the name sounded familiar, I couldn't picture her face.

"*Bonnie and Clyde? Chinatown?*" I shook my head. "I mean no offense." He waved his hand defensively. "She's very beautiful."

I didn't blush because I knew very well what this was. This was an attempt at flirtation that would, of course, never leave this train. I wasn't in the mood for a glimpse into a relationship that I knew was unattainable. I didn't need to tempt myself with the idea that there might be something out there that could distract me from the grief I'd been carrying, when in reality it would only be a few fleeting moments of excitement, followed by silence and pain.

I turned away from him and looked back at my phone. If the train hadn't been so crowded, I would have moved to another part of the car.

Out of the corner of my eye, I saw him lean back in his seat, defeated. "This is why I should never talk to pretty girls on the 'L,'" he said. "Please. Just look her up, and you'll see how gorgeous she is."

I glanced over at the man. Something about his casual attitude put me at ease. Not that I was flirted with very often, but the times I had been, the person doing the flirting had a pushy air to them, a one-track mind that I didn't care to get to know. But this man . . . there was something intriguing enough about him that it made me willing to chase the few fleeting moments of excitement. I turned my attention back to my phone, then angled it so I knew the man couldn't see the screen as I Googled Faye Dunaway. From her pictures, I could see she wasn't unattractive. Not unattractive at all. Especially in stills from *Bonnie and Clyde*. And the weird thing was I did kind of look like her. Just a homelier version with a bigger nose, and brown hair instead of blonde.

I looked back at the man, who was watching me with a confident smirk on his face. "These train windows are pretty reflective," he said. "I could probably read a text if you sent one too."

I put my phone away and let my body relax slightly. Maybe this man meant me no harm. Maybe he was sincere. With only eighteen minutes left of my commute and a train car full of strangers, I decided I was safe to not assume the worst. "She's very beautiful."

"Yes," he said. "You are."

And that time I actually did blush. "Sam Wailing," he said as he held out his hand.

I shook it. "Margo."

"Just Margo?"

"Until I know you better."

"Do you want to get to know me better?" he asked, his eyebrows raised. "Because I should warn you, I'm pretty boring."

"Oh?"

"Oh, yeah. I put myself to sleep sometimes, that's how boring I am."

I let out a short laugh and tucked my hair behind my ear. I could feel him watching me, but it didn't bother me as much as it did at first. Because it felt like he wanted to look at me. Because he thought I was beautiful. And even if this was just one of those weird interactions that I would think back on from time to time, there was no harm in sinking into it now.

I decided to play his game. I don't know how to flirt to save my life, but games I'm good at. "And what makes you so boring?"

"Well." He folded his arms. "For starters, I'm a sales representative in an office, which is pretty much the most boring type of job there is. I don't have much time for hobbies, so I won't be able to share any of my interests with you. I mostly read James Patterson novels—don't judge—and lately I've been on an *Ozark* kick. If that doesn't put you to sleep, I love classical music and will never turn down a game of chess. I've never had a broken bone and the only international travel I've done is on a business trip to Toronto. So, tell me." He leaned in, a half-grin spreading across his face. "Are you bored yet?"

I wasn't really sure how to respond, but I was far from bored. In fact, I was intrigued. Because this was the most conversation I'd had with another human being in weeks. Because I'd recently finished the latest James Patterson novel and had the next one already on hold at the library. Because there's a haunting beauty to classical music that I will never understand. And because I couldn't take my eyes off of Sam Wailing's smile. Not because I found it attractive, but because something about it looked strangely familiar to me. I'd seen that smile before. I didn't know where, but I had. His teeth were so white they looked like they belonged in a toothpaste commercial, and the only thing crooked about his whole mouth was his smile. I racked my brain trying to place him, maybe in the same way he had been trying to place me when I caught his eye from across the train car. But I couldn't. I couldn't remember where I'd seen that smile before. I just knew I had.

"Never trust a man with a million-dollar smile," my mother always said. There was a big part of me that believed her. Not because the memory of her voice and her wise words was all I had left of her, but because there was a good chance she was right.

"Sorry," Sam said when the silence grew two seconds too long. "I'm being too forward, aren't I?"

I averted my eyes from his mouth and shook my head. "Um, no. You're fine."

"No, I apologize. Here you are trying to relax on your commute, and you don't need some strange man flirting with you." So, it was confirmed. This was flirting. It had been so long since I'd flirted, I had trouble even recognizing it. "Are you coming or going?"

"How do you mean?"

He gestured toward my outfit: a brown skirt, black tights, a wrinkled white blouse, and my mother's oversized gray coat from the eighties, topped off with my embarrassing white sneakers, because no human can walk the streets of Chicago in heels. It certainly wasn't the most flattering outfit, but March has always proved to be a difficult month to dress for, when it's impossible to know if it's going to snow or reach seventy-five degrees. "You're dressed for work," he said. "But the question is, are you coming from work or going to work?"

"Ah." I tucked my sneakers beneath my seat. "Coming from."

I assumed his next question was going to be, where did I work? He was forward, but he wasn't that forward. He smiled and nodded and leaned back in his seat, waiting for me to bite. I couldn't help myself. I bit.

"I'm a CPA," I said.

He raised his eyebrows. "An accountant?"

"I guess that makes me just as boring as you."

"Hardly. All those numbers and calculations. It's exciting."

I almost laughed out loud. "I don't think anyone has ever called my job exciting."

"Do you enjoy it?"

It was a strange question; one I certainly hadn't been asked before. But I was kind of glad he did. "I do."

"What do you like about it?"

"Well, it's certain."

"Job security." He nodded like he got it, but he didn't.

"No, I mean the work itself is certain. You could take a million numbers, and no matter how many ways you add them up, you'll always get the same result. They're a guarantee." Then I added as an afterthought, "It's like the opposite of history."

48

"History?"

"You know how they say history repeats itself? Well, so do numbers. Only when history repeats itself, it does so in a sneaky, conniving way. You don't know when or how it's going to go about it. Some people may be able to learn from things that have happened in the past, but most of the time, the math is all willy-nilly." He smiled when I said "willy-nilly" and I felt myself blush again. "But numbers are different. Because if you calculated the same set of numbers that were calculated five hundred years ago today, you'd still get the same answer. They don't change with time. They're always the same. They're always certain. Sometimes it makes me feel like I can predict the future."

His grin widened as my words seemed to register. "And you say your job isn't exciting."

Chapter Five

I PULL MYSELF out of my memories and back to the dining room. I'd almost forgotten that I'm sitting here with Sam's family, in their home, eating dinner. Or supper, as they call it.

"Mary, this is delicious," I say, determined to let them know I'm present. Sam flashes me the very same grin as he did that day on the train, and for a moment it feels like I've finally gotten something right, complimenting his mother's casserole. I'm not quite hungry yet, still full from dinner, which feels like it was just a few short hours ago, but supper is served promptly at five-thirty so I'm not going to complain. "What do you call it?" I gesture to the casserole.

"Noodle bake," Mary says promptly and proudly as if she's been waiting all day to use the dish's formal name.

"It's normally made with bird meat," says Alice, "but Mom made it special just for you." Her odd use of the term "bird meat" nearly makes me cringe, but I manage to stifle it. Alice puts a big bite of the casserole in her mouth and gives me a smile, but I'm not sure if I like it. I think I prefer her resting bitch face.

"Are your parents vegetarians too, Margo?" asks Mary.

"My mother was. I don't know about my dad. I never knew him."

"Oh, what a shame," Mary says, her eyes big and sad.

"How about your grandparents?" asks Alice.

Taken aback, I find myself stammering. I don't want to tell them the truth, that my grandparents all but disowned my mother when she refused to have an abortion after getting pregnant with me. That she chose me over them. That if they could do something that cruel to their daughter, I was glad I never met them. "I never knew them either. It was pretty much just me and my mom my whole life." I feel everyone's eyes on me, and feel the need to add, "She passed away earlier this year."

Mary's expression is filled with remorse. "Oh, how tragic."

I'm not sure if Mary is putting on her response, or if she truly didn't know that my mother had passed away. It's another detail of my life the Sam hasn't shared with them. His lack of words about me makes me feel slightly insignificant even though I know it shouldn't.

"No siblings?" asks Alice. Maybe she's just being curious, but her question feels like a challenge.

I look her in the eye when I respond. "No. Just me."

Mary chimes in. "You must have been so lonely growing up."

I try not to sound defensive, but I can't help myself. "Not really. You can't miss what you never had, I guess."

There's a moment of silence filled only with the sound of silverware on dishes and the faint voice of the televangelist, whose video is still playing on the television set. I wonder if anyone even turned it off while we were out, or if Grandma Ruth just sat in her chair watching him all afternoon.

Just when I think I'm out of the woods, Mary pipes up again. "Now, did your father pass away when you were very young? Is that why you didn't know him?"

I've never had to explain to people before that my parents had never been married. That my mother was either intentionally vague about my father or really hadn't known much about him. Usually, people make their own assumptions. Now, I'm not quite sure how to respond without my answer receiving judgment. I never thought there was anything wrong with my situation. My mother never made it sound shameful. She never used her experience as a cautionary tale.

Apparently, I don't have to explain my situation to Sam's family because Sam answers for me.

"Her parents weren't married," he says casually. I want to kick him, but I'm pretty sure God may smite me if I so much as curse in this house.

Mary gapes at him and then at me. "No," she says. "Oh, you poor child."

The last thing I want from my future husband's family is pity. Especially not over something that I've never felt any shame for. If they want to pity me, pity me for no longer having my mother. Pity me for my tiny, moldy apartment. Don't pity me for a decision two people made a lifetime ago.

"Oh, it's okay," I say. "Really."

"Don't you worry," says Hank between bites. "He's very forgiving of our sins."

But it's not a sin, I want to argue. But I don't. I smile and nod and continue to not eat.

"Redemption," the distant voice of the televangelist says, "is our only key to a blessed life . . ."

I take the opportunity to deflect the focus from myself. "What television program is this?" I ask, nodding to the TV.

Mary and Hank look at me like they can't tell if I'm joking. Mary's brow furrows. "Don't tell me you've never heard of Redd Wright!"

"I can't say that I have."

"Mom, please give her the short version," says Alice.

"Where do I begin?" says Mary. "Redd Wright embodies all that is good and pure on this Earth. His spoken word is essentially scripture. We have every single one of his tapes and books. He believes in helping people. That if you are good, you will be rewarded."

"And he's a . . ." I hope my word choice isn't offensive. "Televangelist?"

Everyone in the room except for Ruth lets out some noise of disapproval. Hank chuckles. Alice snickers. Mary gives a perplexed laugh. Sam sighs. "He's much more than that," he says to me in a low warning voice.

"Now, Sam, it's true that he did begin his television program in 1972," Mary says. "But he had followers long before then. He was born and raised right here in Fairbury. Heavenly Father, rest his soul . . ."

"Oh." I nod, trying to appear interested. Clearly this man is important to them. "Did he, um, pass away?"

"He was taken," Hank says seriously. "Struck down by lightning with his wife while flying in his jet last Christmas."

Ruth lets out an audible noise, somewhere between a moan and a cry. When no one responds to her, I assume it's my turn to speak again.

"Oh gosh," I say. "I'm sorry to hear he died."

"He was *taken*," Alice emphasizes. "He was needed elsewhere."

I nod my head. The idea that God chooses who He needs or doesn't need has always been absurd to me. Accidents happen. People get sick. People die. My mother wasn't "needed elsewhere." She needed to be here, with me.

I glance over at Redd on TV. He must have been close to forty in the 1970s, which would make him at least in his eighties now. "How old was he when he died?" I ask, not sure what else to say.

"Wouldn't know," says Hank. "He kept his age to himself. Said it was just a number. Of course, no one had even seen much of him since his 1983 tour."

"He was very shy," says Cheryl, as though remembering him fondly.

I hear a sniffle to my right and look to Mary, who's staring at Redd Wright on the TV and crying silent tears. "He'll always be with us," she whispers. She turns her head to me and smiles widely through her tears. "He's with us right now."

"Mom," says Sam. "Don't scare her."

"Why would that scare her? I feel comforted knowing he's always with us." She turns to me again. "Life never really ends, you know."

I smile and nod and look over at the TV, trying to see what they all see in him. Had I known my question was going to open a floodgate, I never would have asked it. The whole drive here, I tried to prepare myself for meeting Sam's family. I tried to learn about their jobs, their habits, their quirks . . . but it was all pointless. The truth is, I know nothing.

Chapter Six

SAM OFFERS TO give me a tour of the house once everything is cleaned up from supper. I've felt terribly awkward for the past ten minutes, sitting as everyone else around me clears their plates, but Mary insists I don't lift a finger. I keep replaying the whole day in my mind, anxiety churning in my stomach. At some point this evening, I hope I get a chance to talk with Sam about our wedding plans. I want to make sure we're on the same page. I get the feeling that his family is going to have some very specific ideas for our wedding that I'm not sure I'm ready to relinquish to them, but being an outsider I'm in no position to balk. I only hope Sam is willing to stand up to them for me if it comes to that.

I'm about to stand and stretch my legs when there is a thud in the kitchen, followed by the sound of breaking glass and several yelps. I get up and run through the swinging door. Mary is being helped up from the floor by Hank and Sam, and there's a broken glass and a small puddle of water on the tile beside her.

"It's okay, we've got you—" says Sam to Mary.

"Stop making such a fuss, I'm fine," Mary says as they help her to her feet.

"Do you want me to call Jimmy?"

"No, she's alright—" Hank puts Mary's arm around his shoulder and leads her to the kitchen chair.

Sam looks over at me. "We can start the tour in the study. I'll be right there."

I nod my head and exit the room before Mary can see me. I'm sure she's embarrassed and I don't want to intrude, but my heart is racing, not just from the commotion, but from my own memories. I can hear the thud of my mother falling to the floor in our kitchen. The sound of her scream whenever it would happen. I'd rush to her side, help get her into bed. The treatment made her woozy, lightheaded. Sometimes it made her legs give out from underneath her. *It will get better*, I'd say to her. But it didn't.

I make my way into the study opposite the living room and scan the bookshelves for familiar titles. I don't recognize any of them, which is surprising for me. Sam and I often play a game of who can finish a book first. When a new one we've both been wanting to read comes out at the library, we always reserve two copies. I almost always finish mine before he does, but I wonder if he lets me win. He may be a fan of James Patterson, but he's proved to me since we started dating that he's not nearly as big a bibliophile as I am. When I try to have discussions about whatever book we just finished, I go into much more depth than he does. Part of me wonders if he even reads them cover to cover, or if he skims the main parts.

The books on these shelves appear to be mainly self-help, on subjects ranging from being the best version of yourself to keeping a youthful body and mind. The top shelf is entirely dedicated to books by Redd Wright. There must be a dozen of them, with titles like *Only You Can Heal Yourself*, *His Choice*, and *We Are Who We Are*.

I pick up *His Choice*. On the cover is a portrait of Redd Wright, smiling one of those million-dollar smiles my mother always warned me about. The logo on the spine of the book, on all of his books actually, is a small peacock, not like the NBC logo, but like a real photo of a peacock with its mouth open wide, like it's in mid-squawk. I open the book and thumb through it. The page I land on reads *Chapter Ten: His Choice, Your Fate*. I skim down to one of the passages:

> *Every choice leads us closer to our destiny. I've made many choices in my lifetime. Or at least, I think I have. But they aren't my choices. And they aren't yours either. They are His choices, His decisions. He decides your fate, your destiny. You can choose to pray for the path you desire. You can decide to follow in His footsteps. But, ultimately, the choice is His. Listen to His words, and they will guide you. But remember, His words are only as strong as you believe them to be. Which is why we must leave our choices up to Him. We must let those superior to us, like our Almighty Father or Amrita Diabolus, determine our fate. These are our superior beings, our saviors . . .*

I don't want to read anymore. I shut the book. I'm not sure who Amrita Diabolus is, but I can imagine she's some creation of their scripture, perhaps their version of Mother Mary. It doesn't matter either way, because almost everything he mentioned in that brief paragraph goes directly against what I believe. Free will is free will. There's no one being deciding our fate. We make our own decisions. I'm not about to get into this discussion with Mary and Hank, but I also am not about to be swayed by a popular televangelist that I hadn't even heard of until today.

I feel a hand on my shoulder and jump, but it's only Sam.

"Sorry about that," he says.

"Is your mother okay?"

"Yeah," he glances around and lowers his voice. "She's had some health issues lately."

"I'm sorry," I say.

"Don't be. Just the dark side of aging. Ready for the tour?"

He leads me down the front hall, where we pass a small table with an old dial phone on it—the kind I haven't seen since I was a young child. I look up to the wall above it and see a dozen photos. Sam's talking about the house—how Hank redid all the wiring himself, and how a tornado tore off a good chunk of their roof a few years back—but I'm transfixed by the photos.

Most of them are of Mary and Hank. There's one of them standing in front of the car I saw parked out front, and one of them in front of their house. There are also a few of them with the other family members: Cheryl and Jimmy on what appears to be their wedding day in front of the Evergreen Mansion—her in a vintage wedding dress with a lace veil and him in a dark blue tux. A younger Sam and Alice standing together by a lake. Cheryl and Jimmy sitting in the living room, holding Selma. Mary and Ruth standing in front of a store called Hansen's Dress Shop, both smiling and holding shopping bags. They only look about ten to fifteen years younger than they do now, but the photo itself looks old and worn. In fact, most of them look old and worn. Like they've been exposed to sunlight for too long, despite the lack of windows in the hall.

In the center of all the photos is one larger frame holding a picture of the whole family in front of their house: Ruth sitting in a lawn chair, while the others stand, Mary, Hank, Sam, Alice, Cheryl, Jimmy holding Selma . . . The trees and grass are all lush and green, the men wear shorts, and the women are in dresses. It must have been summertime. But Sam said the last time he visited his family was Christmas. And Selma looks just a few months younger than she is now. This wasn't taken last summer.

It was taken this summer. But it takes a while for my mind to make that connection because that would mean Sam had lied to me. And Sam wouldn't do that. Then again, maybe I'm too lonely to see the truth sometimes.

I feel a knot in my stomach. "Hey, Sam?"

"Hmm?" He stops and turns to me.

"I thought you said you hadn't been home since Christmas."

"I haven't."

I point to the photo of him and his family in front of their house. "But this was from this summer."

"I don't think so." He takes a closer look at the photo.

"It is. If it was last summer, Selma wouldn't have been born yet, and it's clearly not winter."

He studies the photo and sighs. "Oh, right." He steps a little closer to me and keeps his voice low. "Look, I'm sorry I didn't tell you, but that weekend I said I was going to Madison for business I actually came here. My mother wasn't doing well at the time and we were all really worried about her. You know how hard it is for me to open up sometimes. And I get protective of my family."

I nod my head, but the knot in my stomach doesn't go away. Is this the only lie Sam's told me? Have there been other things he's hidden from me? I think of the weekend he told me he was going to Madison. How he called me when he got there from what he said was his hotel room. How he told me the next night about the best fettucine alfredo he had at a restaurant called Highwood's, and how he wanted to bring me back to that restaurant so I could try it. How that weekend was my own mother's birthday, and it was a particularly difficult time for me to be alone, and I spent most of it in bed. How I saw Sam on Sunday as soon as he'd gotten back because I was desperate for something, anything, to pull me out of the hole I was spiraling into. And how everything he told me that weekend was a lie.

"Please, darling," he says, taking a step toward me, wrapping

59

his hands around my arms. "You know how it is when someone you love is sick."

I look at him, trying my best to understand his reasoning for keeping something like that from me. Trying my best to look at him the same way I had before knowing he'd lied to me. But as I look at him, the uneasiness in my stomach twists and turns from hurt to annoyance. Because now I'm thinking of my own mother and feeling irritated with Sam for making me do so. "It's okay," I say finally. I already feel out of place. Being on opposite sides with Sam will only isolate me further. He's my lifeline for the next five days. "I understand."

"Thank you. That means a lot." He leans in and kisses my forehead, then pulls his arm around me and leads me down the hall.

"Speaking of family photos," I say, trying to push through my slowly burning anxiety. "Will I get to see some embarrassing baby pictures of you?"

Sam lets out a laugh. "Not if I can help it."

He shows me the rest of the main floor, which pretty much consists of a bathroom and what used to be his dad's office but is now a bedroom for Ruth. The bed is neatly made, with a hand-crocheted blanket draping over it. On her dresser are over two dozen pill and vitamin bottles, with a few round green ones spilled out across the wood. On the wall at the foot of her bed is a painting of Redd Wright. He's looking straight ahead, and I can tell that he'll be looking directly at her when she sleeps. I brush off my chill as Sam takes me upstairs and shows me the bedrooms. Well, he shows me Alice's bedroom and his own. He doesn't show me his parents' or the guest room where I'll apparently be staying.

"It's not ready yet," he says when I ask if I can see my room. "Mom still wants to finish tidying it up for you before bed." He flips off the light to his room and starts to usher me out the door before I can even look around.

"Whoa whoa whoa, hang on." I grin. "This is the room I've been most anxious to see."

I turn the light back on and look around. I'd be lying if I said I wasn't disappointed. No photos, no embarrassing posters, no forgotten toys. It looks like an office that's been converted into an extra guest room, more so even than Ruth's.

I turn to Sam. "This was the room you grew up in?"

Sam shrugs, leaning against the doorway. "Yeah. What do you think?"

"Where are your toys? Your childhood things?"

"My parents aren't very sentimental. They donated most of my stuff after I moved out. I think they kept a few of my baby toys for Selma."

"Strange."

"Why is that strange?" I detect a defensive note in his tone.

"Well, they have every book and video recording ever made of that televangelist guy. It just seems strange that they wouldn't keep their only son's *Star Wars* action figures, or whatever you played with."

He laughs. "Actually, it was *Lord of the Rings*."

We go back downstairs and step outside through the back door. The house faces east so the backyard has a picturesque view of the sunset. The sky is a bit cloudy, but you can see the brilliant shades of orange and purple through the gray. I still don't feel quite right, but I want to. I want to feel happy standing here, looking at the sunset with Sam. I want to be present. I don't want to let my anxiety drag me into the past, but I can't get Sam's lie about his last trip here out of my head. It's one of those intrusive thoughts I despise so much. But I won't let it win. Not tonight. Tonight, I'll enjoy being here with my fiancé.

My gaze hovers over the cornfield, the stalks burning orange with the last bit of the sunset. I should say that it's beautiful. It should be beautiful. But if I'm being truly honest with myself, I don't think the cornfield is beautiful. I know I should, but I don't.

I find it sad. Strange. Ominous. Disquieting. "It's so beautiful," I say, hoping that if I say it aloud, I'll make it true.

Sam wraps his arms around me. "Yes, you are." He kisses my neck, then takes my hand and leads me around to the side of the house. Instantly, I feel a pull in my stomach, right behind my belly button, like a string is tugging me downward. I glance to the ground and catch a glimpse of the storm cellar, but before I can ask to see inside, he pushes me up against the house and kisses me deeply. I'm instantly reminded of our first kiss, outside of my apartment door. It was something we'd both wanted all night and I'd almost thought wasn't going to happen. That is, until he took me by surprise and pressed his lips to mine, the two of us leaning against the door frame for support as the passion overtook us.

For a moment, Sam's lie from earlier vanishes from my mind, and I'm lost in the soft pull of his lips. His hands run up the sides of my waist, simultaneously tickling me and turning me on, until they find my hair. He gently pulls my head back, holding it in his palm. My hands find his back, my fingertips pressed into the muscles beneath his shirt. I feel his tongue graze my lips, begging to be let in. I don't want him to stop, but I also don't want his family to catch us. We're not even allowed to sleep in the same room. I can imagine they wouldn't like us making out against their house. I pull away.

"Sam," I say. "What if someone sees us?"

He kisses my neck some more. "You look so beautiful I can't help it." He presses his body against mine, his hand slipping from my hair and moving quickly down to the small of my back.

"Dessert is ready," a sharp voice says from behind Sam. He pulls away and I see Alice standing there, her face expressionless, but her eyes fiercely pointed at me.

Sam runs his hand through his hair and doesn't make eye contact with either one of us. "Thanks, Alice."

Alice holds her gaze on me for several more painful seconds

before she turns and walks back to the house. Once she's out of sight, I straighten my sweater and smooth my hair. "I don't think your sister likes me very much."

"She's just moody," says Sam. He doesn't wait for me, starting to head back to the house. I glance over at the cellar and then run to catch up to him. "After dessert, maybe you can show me the cellar."

"Oh, you don't want to go down there."

"Sure I would. I've seen them in movies, but I've never actually been in one."

"Seriously, it's a mess. Mom would throw a fit if I showed it to you. Besides, there are bugs down there. You wouldn't like it." Bugs? Is Sam trying to use bugs to scare off the woman who insisted he pull over to save a beetle on the way here? I sometimes wonder if Sam knows me at all. Defeated, I start to follow him around the house, but somewhere behind me I hear a creak. I quickly turn, my eyes landing on the cellar. I hear the creak again, coming from the cellar doors, as if they're shifting just slightly on their hinges, like they're calling to me. Or rather, they're shielding something that's calling to me. It's like an itch I so desperately want to scratch but know it will scar if I do. I shut my eyes and force myself to keep walking toward the front of the house. Force myself not to scratch.

Chapter Seven

FOR DESSERT, MARY has fixed a pie. I'm not quite sure what kind of pie it is, but it seems to have a nutty base and a layer of whipped cream on top. It's fine, but like the soup and the casserole, there's something bland about it. We eat mostly in silence. No one has mentioned Mary's fall so I don't say anything, but I can tell by the tremble in her hand that she's shaken.

The sun has set and the only lights in the house are coming from the kitchen, the chandelier over the dining table, and the blue glow from the TV. With the curtain of darkness surrounding me, I'm feeling oddly claustrophobic. Winter is getting close, and with each day I'm filled with more dread than the last as I come closer and closer to closing the one-year circle since my mother fell ill. The short days and early nights do nothing but make me feel trapped inside my own head, itching for open space yet unable to find relief except during the hours of daylight.

"I might take a short walk," I say to the table once everyone has finished their pie. Everyone except for Ruth, whose pie slice is sitting untouched in front of her. "I feel like I could use a little air, if that's all right."

"You don't need to ask our permission, darlin'," says Hank,

cleaning up the crumbs on his plate with his forefinger. "Sam, take the little lady on a walk."

"I'm okay going by myself," I say. Sam doesn't argue. He knows how stubborn I can be.

Mary looks puzzled, at me, then at Sam. "She's a brave one, isn't she?"

I'm not sure what she means, but I let out a polite chuckle. "I'll be fine, really."

"I think she can take care of herself," says Alice.

I give Alice a smile that's unreturned and look back to Mary. "Can I help clear the table first?"

"Not at all. You take your walk," Mary says, almost briskly. She stands and takes my plate. "Just don't stray too far."

There isn't even a trace of sunlight left as I step outside. I take out my phone and use the flashlight to see the road. I don't go far, and make sure I can see the house from wherever I am. But part of me wants to go far. Part of me wants to get in the car and go back to the city, to my apartment. Because I never expected being around a family could make me feel so alone. I tell myself it's only nerves, that I'm still getting to know them like they're still getting to know me, but my reassurance doesn't do me much good. I feel off, and the outstretched road ahead of me that's now shielded with darkness somehow feels more appealing to me than the cozy Wailing farmhouse in the distance.

I suddenly have the urge to talk to someone. Not Sam, but a friend. I think of Rebecca. She's probably the closest thing I've had to one of those since we left Chicago, which is really pathetic considering I barely had one conversation with her. I'm already wondering when would be too soon to text or call her to meet for coffee to discuss other wedding options, like I'm some pathetic single woman wondering when it's okay to ask for a second date. I instantly want to slap myself out of it. I'm engaged. To Sam. And I'm in love. With Sam. I check my phone. I haven't had service since we pulled into the Wailings' driveway—and still nothing. How could I forget? Texting Rebecca isn't even an option as long as I'm in this house. But that doesn't matter. Because I don't need to text Rebecca. I need to focus on Sam, and why we're here.

The clock on my phone tells me I've been gone for nearly half an hour even though it feels like it's been five minutes. I take one last look at the dark road, and when I do, I see movement in the distance. I shine my flashlight up ahead and catch a shadow moving quickly across the road. Maybe a deer? Or a cat? Whatever it is, I think it's going to run into the cornfield, but it doesn't. I can still see the faint outline of it on the side of the road. I take a step closer, holding my phone outstretched. The animal seems to be some type of bird, maybe even a wild turkey. I can't make it out completely, but it has talons and even though it's turned away from me and I can't see its face, it appears to be ruffling its feathers.

"*The end . . .*" a voice whispers near my ear. I spin around, shining my light wildly, but I see no one. The phone light shakes with the tremble of my hand. I turn back to the bird. It's still there, still preening. "*Is near . . .*" the voice says. This time, I know better than to turn around to look. "*The end . . . is near . . . everything . . . can be yours . . .*"

I'm staring straight ahead, my eyes on the bird. Because as the voice keeps whispering, I realize that the bird isn't really a bird at all. That it's changing right in front of me, morphing from a crouched, feathered creature into the body of a man. Only he isn't fully a man. His neck is longer than it should be and his feet are still talons. The hairs on my arms stand on end as I find myself face to faceless face with him. He hasn't moved from his spot at the side of the road. It's so dark that I can't see his eyes (if he even has any), only the outline of him, but I know he's looking right at me. The same way he was this afternoon. The same way he did when I was a child.

"*The end . . . is near . . .*" His voice is getting closer to me even though the distance between us hasn't changed. *"Everything can be yours . . . Margo . . . You can have everything . . ."*

And with that his feathers fan out behind him like a peacock with an eight-foot wingspan. But he doesn't fly away. He just stands there.

"Margo," a voice that's not his says behind me. I turn, screaming before my brain registers that it's only Sam. I look back at the road. It's gone. He's gone. There's only a road. I turn back to Sam, trying to calm my breathing. "Are you okay?"

I nod my head and attempt to swallow. I can't tell him what I saw. He'll think I'm crazy. He'll think I'm just like my mother.

"I'm fine," I lie. "I saw an animal crossing the road and it startled me."

Sam takes my phone and shines the flashlight at the road. "What kind of animal?"

"I think it might have been a turkey." My mind flashes to the man's expansive fan of feathers. "Or maybe a peacock."

Sam gives me an odd look. "A peacock?"

"I don't know. That's what it looked like."

"Because there are so many wild peacocks in Iowa."

Even though what I'm telling him isn't exactly the truth, his dismissiveness still stings. I grab my phone from him. "It was probably just a turkey." I turn and head back to the house. After a few yards, I hear him follow me.

When we get back to the house, Alice is lying on the sofa reading, Hank is sitting with his feet up in an easy chair, and Ruth is back in her same spot, staring at the TV. It's still playing the Redd Wright program, only the picture looks slightly better, Redd's moustache is gone and his sideburns have been shortened. His suit looks a little different too, slightly more modern. I vaguely wonder if it's a later season of the show and try to let myself sink into the house. Having left and come back has made it feel slightly more familiar to me. I tell myself that by the time we leave on Wednesday, it will feel like a second home.

I just need to keep my negative thoughts at bay until then.

"Perfect timing," Hank says with a grunt as he gets to his feet. He walks over to me and pats me on the back. "Mary's got your room just about ready for you."

"Oh, shoot." I turn to Sam. "My bags are still in the car."

"Nope!" Hank says proudly. "We brought them in while you were on your walk. Everything is up in your room."

"Oh, thank you. You didn't need to go to all that trouble," I say.

"Nonsense. You're our guest. We won't settle for anything less than the best for you. Now, you two better get some sleep." Hank leans in just a little too close to me. "Don't worry, we'll put you hard at work on party-planning duty tomorrow."

I smile awkwardly. I'd almost forgotten about Selma's birthday party on Sunday. Before I'm forced to continue this conversation, Mary opens the door to the bedroom and calls down to me. "Margo, your room's ready!"

"I'll be right up," I call back, feeling uncomfortably formal. I look at Sam, thinking he's going to come with me, but he's now sitting on the couch talking to Alice. He makes some sarcastic comment to her and she laughs and kicks him. There's a comfortableness they seem to share that I have yet to unlock with Sam. I know I shouldn't be jealous. Of course he's more comfortable with his sister. He's known her his entire life. He's grown up with her. Maybe one day he and I will share a familiarity like the one he has with his family. Maybe once we're married, and I am part of his family, things will feel different. Until then I remind myself that I shouldn't be jealous of what Sam and Alice have. I shouldn't be. But I am.

I make my way up the wooden staircase by myself and knock on the door to the guest bedroom, even though it's ajar.

"Come in!" Mary singsongs. I enter the room and try not to audibly gasp when I see it. It looks like a princess's chambers in a castle. The bed is a four-poster canopy; the furniture is gold-painted and looks so heavy that I worry it may fall through the old floorboards at any moment. The bedspread, curtains, and canopy are all swirls of ornate blue and white designs. On the wall at the foot of the bed is a painting. It's different than the one in Ruth's bedroom, but it's about the same size and has a similar style to it. While Ruth's was a portrait of Redd Wright, this one appears to be of the Wailing farmhouse at night, surrounded by cornfields. Only the corn stalks seem longer than they should, more sparse, like naked tree branches growing up from the ground. Just like the real cornfields surrounding the Wailing farmhouse, these also give me a feeling of unease, and I pray they're not the last thing I look at before I fall asleep tonight.

The driveway is different too, stretching out in assorted directions and paths. In front of the house are eight beings, each one of them kneeling on the ground in prayer. They're various sizes, colors, shapes, and I realize that they're meant to represent each of the Wailing family members. There's even a tiny one for Selma. It's not that the painting is particularly strange, but something about it makes me uneasy. I can't help but feel I'd be much more comfortable on the living room couch.

Mary finishes tucking in the corners of the satin sheets and turns to me, beaming. "Well?" she says expectantly.

"I don't know what to say," I answer truthfully, feeling my face growing hot again. "It's beautiful. Thank you so much for such a warm welcome." I feel my words catch in my throat, though I'm not quite sure why. There's something deep inside of me that longs for Mary's affection. To show her that I'm the best soon-to-be-daughter-in-law she could ask for. "Um, Hank mentioned that you also brought up my bags?"

Mary smiles proudly and opens up one of the drawers on the dresser next to the bed. All my clothes and belongings lie neatly folded inside. I immediately wonder if she's opened my toiletries bag and found my antidepressants.

"Oh, thank you. That was . . . very thoughtful of you." I try to make my voice sound normal, but it comes out forced.

Mary looks at me nervously. "You're not upset with me, are you?"

"No, no," I say quickly. "Thank you again. I appreciate it."

"Oh, good." She takes a few steps toward me, and I swear there are tears in her eyes. "You know, we're very—" She stops mid-sentence, her eyes locked on mine, her face frozen into a perplexed smile. Ten seconds go by. Twenty. I'm not sure if I should speak or wait for her to.

"Mary?"

She seems to snap out of her trance. "Yes?"

"You said, 'we're very . . .'?"

"Oh, yes. We're very happy you're here, dear." She pats me on the shoulder and starts to leave the room. "If you'd like a glass of warm milk, just let me know, alright? We wouldn't want you having to go downstairs in the middle of the night," she says as she bustles out of the room. Before she shuts the door, she gives me one final smile. "Have a blessed sleep, dear."

"Thanks. You too."

She leaves the room, and I'm not sure if I'm happier alone or not. I open up the other drawer and find my bag of toiletries and pills. Everything seems untouched, but who knows. I start to change into my pajamas, hoping the sense of normalcy will give me some comfort. I'm only half-dressed when the door opens and Mary walks in, carrying what appears to be some blue satin sheets. I quickly pull my sweater back on.

"I almost forgot—" she says excitedly. "Here, I brought you this." She unfolds the satin sheets, which turn out to be a nightgown that looks like something I imagine my great-great-grandmother would wear if she were part of the royal family. It's long, pale blue satin, with lace sleeves and a high collar. "Isn't it beautiful?"

"Oh, wow." I gently touch the fabric, careful not to snag it on my unmanicured nails. "Yes, it's beautiful." I can tell by looking at the nightgown that I won't get an ounce of sleep in it. "Um, I think I might be more comfortable in my own pajamas."

Mary smiles. "Nonsense." She lays the nightgown on the bed. "I guarantee you will sleep like a baby in this nightie."

She smooths out the gown on the bed before giving me another smile and heading for the door. "Sweet dreams, dear!" she calls as she leaves.

I look down at the nightgown with distaste. If no one else comes in the room tonight, maybe I can get away with wearing my normal pajamas to bed, and then in the morning I can come downstairs in the nightgown. But part of me feels like they would somehow know if I did that. I take off my clothes and pull the nightgown over my head. It feels as uncomfortable as it looks, the lace scratchy against my bare skin, the satin unforgiving around my curves. There is a knock at the door. It's Sam, so I let him come in as I finish adjusting the nightgown.

He eyes me up and down as he shuts the door behind me. "Look at you," he says, baring his flirtatious grin. It doesn't work on me tonight. I'm too uncomfortable to be in a flirtatious mood.

"You may address me as *Your Highness*."

"Is that the nightgown my mother brought you?" He walks over to me. "You look beautiful in it."

"It's really uncomfortable," I say, already squirming.

"Really? It doesn't look too bad." He lifts my chin and loosely ties the ribbons on the collar. "And you look so beautiful. Do you think you can stand it, just for these few nights? It would really mean a lot to her."

Even though I'm not sure why wearing some old nightgown would mean that much to my fiancé's mother, I'll do my best to humor her. "It's fine. I'll wear it."

"Thank you, darling." Sam kisses me on the forehead. "You all settled in?"

"I guess so. Your mother kind of settled me in for me." I open the drawer. "She put away all my clothes."

He looks at the drawer. "That was sweet of her."

I don't agree, but I'm tired and already anticipating a restless night's sleep. "Yeah." I hesitate. "Do you think she saw my pills?"

"Hmm? Oh, I'm sure she didn't."

"But what if she did?" I press on. "I don't want her to think any less of me."

"For taking antidepressants? They know some people need medication."

I don't have shame in taking my pills. I've taken them off and on throughout my life since I was thirteen. When I don't need them, I don't take them. When I'm struggling to function, I go back on them again. I know I'll be off them again eventually. But right now, they help. "They don't seem like they would approve of anything like that."

"Hey." Sam takes my face in his hands. "They already love you. You have nothing to worry about."

He kisses me. He's gentle at first, but then I feel him pushing me against the bed, and I know he wants more. I don't know what's with him tonight, but in no way had I planned for our first time to be in the guest room of his parents' house. I pull away. "I should probably get some sleep."

Sam licks his lips and runs his hand through his hair, a sexually frustrated gesture I've grown to know well these past six months. "Yeah, you're right. You've had a long day." He kisses my head, but his demeanor feels cold. "Goodnight, my love."

"Goodnight." After I close the door behind him, I have to restrain myself from ripping off the nightgown. I climb into bed and turn off my light. But the moment I'm surrounded by darkness, the silhouette of the man on the dirt road appears in front of me—the same way he appeared earlier in the flower shop window, and the same way he appeared in the street outside my house twenty years ago—as if he had always been there.

Two years after the man stood outside our house in the middle of the night, I saw him again. I don't know what made him appear that day, or why I would then go on to live the next twenty years of my life without seeing him until today. I was in first grade, waiting for my mother to pick me up from school. Most of the other children had already been picked up by their parents, but my mother was late, as she often was. I was looking down at my shoes, kicking a stone back and forth between them, when I heard his voice.

"Margo."

I looked up and immediately saw him across the street. Even in the bright afternoon sun, he was still just a shadow. The only feature I could make out was his pale gray mouth. With every word he spoke, his mouth moved, even though his voice sounded like it was just inches from my ear.

"Do you want to be alone, Margo?" he asked.

I stop my mind from remembering any further. Any further, and I won't sleep tonight.

Chapter Eight

WHEN I TURN over for the ninth time, the clock reads 2:42 a.m. Last time it read 2:16 a.m. Despite my best efforts to not dwell on the demons of my past, I'm beginning to think I still won't be sleeping tonight. The bed feels like it's been stuffed with hay, there's a cold, damp draft coming from somewhere in the room, despite all the windows being closed, and as pretty as the sheets are, they scratch my skin even more than the nightgown does, but the nightgown is still the worst of it all. Every time I turn, the collar feels like it's choking me, even though I undid the ribbon hours ago. My nails snag the lace sleeves each time I move, and I wonder if I might have better luck sleeping naked. In my restlessness, my eyes fall on the painting at the foot of the bed. Against the backdrop of darkness, I can hardly make out the image. It looks like a jumble of lines and paint strokes. But even the lack of light doesn't help it appear any less unsettling.

I lie on my back and stare at the canopy, waiting for sleep to come. I let my eyes close, but the moment they do, I hear a rustling sound in the corner of the room and sit straight up. I scan the shadowy corners of the room, looking for the source of the noise. The only light I have to see by is coming from outside, but it's a cloudy night and there isn't much of a moon. I hear the creak of a floorboard in the same general direction as the rustling and stare at the corner of the room. All I see is a dark shadow, tall enough to be a person.

It's only a shadow, I tell myself. I lie down and turn over, away from the shadow, and tell myself I just need to sleep. That there is nothing in this room besides me and the furniture. But even with my eyes shut tight, my heart beats faster. I try not to think about that night long ago in my mother's bed. I try to block out the image of the man outside my window then, or that creature on the road tonight. But the rustling and creaking hasn't stopped. In fact, it's gotten louder, closer. I try to hold my breath so I can hear how close it is, but my heart is beating so fast my chest hurts. When I feel what my imagination tells me is breathing on my neck, I fling my arm through the air to my lamp and turn it on. The clock reads 3:42 a.m. It had been 2:42 a few minutes ago. My eyes dart wildly around the room. In the light I see that I am alone. And there is a good chance I am going crazy.

I slow my heart rate down as best as I can, but my chest still hurts. I want it to be morning. I want to sleep. Normally I don't have too much trouble sleeping. I'm a light sleeper, but not a troubled one. I usually drink a cup of tea, take my pills and—

That's when it hits me. I haven't taken my pills. I get out of bed and walk over to the dresser, where I take out my small bag and bottle of pills. Only I don't have any water and my throat's too tight to swallow them dry. I should have gotten a glass of water from Mary before bed. She told me to call her if I needed anything in the night, but the last thing I want to do is wake them at four in the morning.

I pull on my robe and tiptoe out into the hallway. I can hear the faint snores of who I assume is Hank in the room across from mine. The floorboards creak beneath my feet as I creep down the stairs. There's a faint blue light emitting from the living room, probably the TV, although I'm not sure who would be watching it at this hour.

I reach the main floor and begin to walk through the living room toward the kitchen. Sure enough, the TV is still on, and Redd Wright is still preaching to his audience. Even though the volume is all the way down, he still somehow leaves a bad taste in my mouth.

I go into the kitchen, where I find a glass and fill it half full with water before downing the pills in my hand. I set the glass next to the sink and go back into the living room. The TV is still on, but now the volume is up full. Redd Wright is going on about salvation, so loudly I worry it might wake the whole house. I look around for a remote and feel my heart stop when I realize Ruth is still sitting in the chair in front of the TV, the blue light turning her pale skin a ghostly white. Her eyes are burned into the screen, like it's the most amazing thing she's ever seen.

"And when this world has nothing left to offer you," Redd preaches to his followers, "take comfort in knowing He will be your ultimate salvation."

The remote is sitting on the table beside Ruth. I slowly walk over to it, careful not to startle her. But right before I can reach for it, Redd's words catch my ears, like he's speaking to me.

"Can you hear me?" he says. I look at the TV. He's looking right at me. Not at the camera. At me. "Can you hear me, Margo?" I look back at him, at his deep, brown eyes. Not because I want to. Because I can't look away. "Margo, when this world has nothing left to offer you, what will be your salvation?" The video rewinds and plays the same line again. And again. And again. "What will be your salvation? What will be your salvation? What will be your salvation?"

I look over at Ruth and see the remote in her slowly blackening fingers. Rewind. Play. Rewind. Play. Rewind. Play. *What will be your salvation? What will be your salvation? What will be your salvation? What will be your salvation? What will be your salvation? What will be your salvation?*

I take the remote from her hand and nearly drop it to the floor as I feel around for the power button. I press it hard, and the screen goes black. In the darkness, all I can hear is my own breathing. Then I hear sobs. Heavy, painful sobs. Ruth is crying like a wounded animal. Her voice is deep, guttural, mournful.

"Shh—" I lean down next to her, even though it's hard to even make out her profile in the darkness. "Please, it's okay. Shh . . ."

But she doesn't stop. She keeps howling, louder and louder. If she keeps going, it's only a matter of seconds before she wakes everyone in the house. I trace my shaking thumb over the remote and press the power button again. When there's enough blue light bouncing off the walls, I look over at Ruth. She's still staring straight ahead at the screen, her mouth open, the noise emitting from her throat like it's coming from deep inside her. It takes until the TV is fully powered on for her cries to stop.

The room slowly fills with the sound of Redd Wright's voice as he addresses his audience. He's no longer looking at me—if he ever was to begin with.

I set the remote back on the table next to Ruth and slowly back away. A wave of tiredness falls over me and I know I need to get back to my bed before I pass out. I grab the railing with both my hands and pull myself up the stairs. When I reach the top, my knees hit the floor before my feet, and I crawl on all fours down the hall to my bedroom. I can see it, but it seems so far away. I'm tired is all. I just need to get into bed. I crawl past Sam's bedroom on my right and notice the door's ajar. Had it been ajar before? I thought it was closed, but my brain has fogged over and I can't remember. I peer through the opening and my eyes adjust to the darkness, which is broken up only by beams of moonlight. I can see his bed from the doorway, and for a moment, it looks like he's sitting straight up in it. My eyes adjust further, and I see that it's not him. The person's hair is too long, and they're facing the opposite direction, toward where Sam is lying on the right side of the bed. The covers are pushed to the end of the bed, and Sam's legs are exposed. Even in the darkness, I can see the slight movement of the person who is sitting with Sam on the bed. Is it Alice? It looks like it could be Alice. She must be talking to him about something. Hopefully nothing is wrong with Hank or Mary . . .

I listen for a moment in my daze, trying to pick up on their words, but I don't hear any. Just the faint sound of Sam's breathing. It sounds shakier than his normal sleep breathing, but I can't tell if that's because I'm so tired I'm starting to shake myself.

My vision starts to darken even in the dark hall, and I feel it closing in around me. I manage to pull myself to my feet and stumble the rest of the way into my bedroom. Without even closing the door behind me, I tumble into bed. As soon as my head hits the mattress, everything around me goes dark. Maybe I'm dreaming. Maybe the man I've seen isn't even real. Maybe the voices are all in my head. Maybe I'm unwell. Maybe I'm crazy.

Maybe I am just like her.

Chapter Nine

FRIDAY

SOMEONE IS IN my room when I wake up in the morning. My eyes are still closed, so I don't see them yet, but I can hear the subtle creaking of the floorboards again. I open my eyes and attempt to orient myself as quickly as possible. I feel the presence of something next to me and whip my head to the left. Through the sleep clouding my eyes I see a figure towering over me. My heart races as I attempt to blink my eyes clear and see that Alice is standing right next to my bed, staring at me. It's such a jarring and unexpected sight that I have to question if I'm still asleep. If this isn't yet another apparition from my nightmares.

"Good morning, Margo," she says. Her deadpan voice orients me enough to recognize that I'm not dreaming.

I rub my eyes, and stare down at my bedspread, only just remembering where I am. The memory of Ruth and the television flashes into my mind and I flinch. Alice is staring at me. Though my eyes are still fuzzy from sleep, I can tell she's staring at my chest. I pull the covers up over my nightgown. Even though I'm not naked, I am braless, and feel very exposed through the clingy satin.

When I speak, my voice is hoarse. "What time is it?" I look around till my eyes land on the clock. It's 9:43, yet I feel like I've hardly slept.

Alice heads for the door. Before leaving, she turns back to me. "You slept through breakfast, but we saved you some eggs."

Before I can thank her, she leaves and shuts the door behind her. I lay my head back down on the pillow and try to find the strength to get out of bed. Sam was supposed to wake me whenever everyone else was getting up. And he didn't. And now I'm probably the last one to wake and I'm so embarrassed that I don't even want to go downstairs.

I unplug my phone and turn it on. Normally when I turn on my phone, I delight in the many notifications that pop up even if most of them are just from Facebook or emails from work. But not today. Still no service, no notifications. My phone is basically a clock and a flashlight at this point.

I pull my legs over the side of the bed and start to stand when all the blood instantly drains from my head, and I have to sit down. Once I've regained my balance, I stand again, successfully this time. I'm halfway undressed when I realize that Mary hasn't seen me in the nightgown yet. As much as I don't want to wear this thing for another minute, seeing me wearing it will make her happy. It will prove to her that I'll make a good daughter-in-law.

When I step back into the nightgown, I notice that my knees seem redder than usual, the skin burnt-looking and irritated. I pull the gown over my hips, then pause to grab my bra from the dresser. As I pull it on, I feel a dull ache in my left elbow. I turn it towards my reflection in the mirror and see a bruise just above the knob. That's when it starts to come back to me—the glass of water downstairs, the grogginess, the crawling. I'm trying to remember more about last night when I notice a small red dot on the inner bend of my left arm. I touch it. It doesn't feel sore, but it looks like a pinprick. That I don't remember. And unlike the bruise or the redness on my knees, this mark feels deliberate. How long has it been there? I can't remember ever seeing it before. Upon a closer look, I see that the prick is right over my pale blue vein, and that the skin around it is slightly yellowed, like a bruise starting to form. Suddenly, I'm reminded of getting a shot at the doctor. I think back to my grogginess, my body being so heavy with sleep last night that I had to crawl up the stairs. Was I drugged? Did someone inject me with something? It wouldn't be difficult to stick a needle through the lace fabric of the nightgown's sleeves. Vulnerable panic surges through my nerves as I try to justify the idea that I was possibly drugged. I rack my brain trying to think of who in this house would want to do something like that to me. The only person I can think of who seems to dislike me that much is Alice.

But a thought like that would be crazy. And I'm not crazy.

But Alice . . .

Did I have a dream about her last night? Something with her and Sam . . . It wasn't a dream. I saw her talking to him in his bedroom when I came back from taking my pills. I remind myself to ask Sam if everything is okay. Usually, people only wake each other up in the middle of the night to tell them that something *isn't* okay.

I take a few breaths, calming my nerves. I couldn't have been drugged. It's not possible. I'm reading too much into this. I need to stay calm. I need to stay sane. I pull on my nightgown and leave the room. Then I head for the bathroom, but someone is in it, so I wait in the hall. The bathroom door opens, and Sam emerges, all showered and dressed and smelling like shaving cream and cologne. He smiles when he sees me and leans in to give me a kiss.

"Good morning, beautiful!"

I let him kiss me, then pull away. "Why did you let me sleep so late?"

"I figured you were tired after the long drive."

"You should have gotten me up. I feel so rude. Alice said I missed breakfast."

"Don't even worry about it. I think they saved some for you. Trust me, my family just wants you to be as comfortable as possible while you're here."

Which is why they made me sleep in a Victorian-era satin and lace nightgown? I want to say. But I don't. Instead, I nod my head and start to go into the bathroom when I stop and turn back to Sam.

"Hey, Sam?" He turns to me. "Is everything okay?"

"Yes. Why wouldn't it be okay?"

"I saw Alice in your room last night. I wasn't sure if something was wrong."

Something seems to click in Sam's mind, and he nods. "Oh, that. Yeah, she had heard that some bad storms might be coming in and couldn't remember if she locked up the cellar."

I nod my head, but I remember the bedroom last night, the moonbeams that could only have shown so brightly in a clear sky. "It didn't seem like it was going to storm last night."

Sam laughs. "Welcome to Iowa. We've had storms hit and tornados touch down out of the blue here. One minute the sun is shining, not a cloud in the sky. . . the next, the world is turning green and the wind is blowing so hard you can't walk straight."

I let out a little laugh, but something about Sam's tone feels off. He's being unusually animated, and I get the feeling that he's hiding something. But I have no clue what he could possibly want to cover up. I don't want to let go of the conversation yet, but this one feels like it's over. I change the subject. "Do you have cell service? Mine hasn't been working."

He shakes his head. "This area is pretty much a dead zone."

"Does your family have Wi-Fi? It would be nice to at least check my emails from work."

"Oh, no. They don't have internet."

I feel my eyebrows raise. "Really?"

Sam shakes his head and lowers his voice. "They're a little behind the times. Sorry."

"No worries," I say, and head into the bathroom.

After washing up, I go downstairs. Ruth is still in front of the TV, only she's wearing a different outfit than she was yesterday. Of course, what's playing on the TV hasn't changed, and I feel my stomach turn at the sight of Redd Wright. I glance down at the remote, and Ruth's hand on the arm of the chair beside it. In the daylight I can see that it's no longer just the tips of her fingers that are discolored; all of the fingers on her left hand are now almost half black. I avert my eyes, feeling as though I've seen something I shouldn't.

Sam is sitting at the dining table, reading a newspaper, which he peers over to see me. "Coffee?" he offers.

"Yes, please."

Sam sets his paper down and goes into the kitchen. I glance in behind him. Alice is nowhere to be seen, and on the dining table is a single plate of eggs and toast in the same spot I sat at last night. I wonder how long it's been sitting there.

Before I can take a seat, Hank enters from the front door, throwing a dirty rag over his shoulder. "Well, well, look who's up!"

I try to stop my face from growing red. "I'm really sorry. I didn't mean to sleep so late."

"Pish posh, no need for apologies! We saved you some breakfast." He pulls my chair out for me and I take a seat. "Enjoy!"

"Thank you." I pick up the fork and take a bite of eggs. They're ice cold, but I don't want to be rude, so I quickly swallow. Sam returns a moment later with a cup of coffee that I can only hope is hotter than the eggs. I take a sip—it's lukewarm, but it will do.

Hank turns to Sam. "You think of anything we need at the

hardware store? I wanna get some rope for the birthday sign, and another can of lacquer for the—" He glances at me, then raises his eyebrows. "For the *gift*," he says cryptically.

"I can take a look up in the attic and see what other decorations we have," says Sam. "When are you heading over there?"

"Whenever! Thought we could all go together, if you want. Our little Margo didn't get much of a chance to explore our lovely town yesterday."

Sam looks at me. "You want to take another trip into town this afternoon?"

Either way I would have said yes, but the idea of having cell service for even a few brief minutes is reason enough for me. I also need to get a birthday gift for Selma. "Sure, that sounds good."

"And no need to beg, we'll gladly drive you by the Evergreen Mansion again," Hank teases. But it doesn't hit me like teasing. It hits me like a painful little reminder that our wedding plans feel like they're being slowly taken away from us. "Before I forget, I wanted to run a few things by you for the setup on Sunday." Hank walks past Sam, tapping him on the arm with the back of his newspaper. "Step outside with me for a sec, won't you?"

Sam flashes me a quick grin before finishing his coffee and following Hank out the front door. As the screen door slams shut, I'm left alone with Ruth, Redd Wright, and a plate of cold eggs. Once Sam and Hank are out of view, I pick up my plate and tiptoe into the kitchen. When I spot the garbage can, I carefully open it and scrape the remaining pile of cold eggs off my plate and into the trash. I set the plate on the counter as quietly as possible, then go back into the dining room. With Mary nowhere in sight, I go upstairs and change out of the nightgown that I've spent the last twelve hours squirming in.

† † †

After I get changed, Sam takes me up to the attic to help look for the decorations for Selma's birthday party.

"They should be around here somewhere," he says, shifting through some old boxes. Dust hangs in the stream of light coming through the attic window.

I look around at the dusty boxes and containers, but only half-heartedly. My mind is still back at the Evergreen Mansion. The thought of getting married there seems like the furthest thing from what I wanted. Not even because of the mansion itself, but because I feel like I'm getting no say in my own wedding. That people I've known for less than twenty-four hours are deciding what is done with "the most important day of my life," and to top it off Sam seems perfectly fine with it. If anything, he seems to think I'm the one throwing a wrench in his family's plans for us.

"*In the end, your voice is the one that's most important,*" Rebecca's words ring in my ears, her business card burning in my pocket. In a small way, it felt like she was standing up for me, validating me. I had been feeling overwhelmed, alone, and she saw that and extended her hand. Maybe what I felt for Rebecca yesterday wasn't anything but friendship from one woman to another—a commonality of feeling overwhelmed about wedding plans and lacking help from her male counterpart. That has to be it. That's all it is.

"If I don't want to get married at the Evergreen Mansion, we won't, right?" I say into a dusty box filled with some old cooking utensils. The question comes out of nowhere, and I surprise even myself.

Sam sets down a box he was holding and looks at me blankly. "Of course not."

The reassurance is blinding. "Really?"

"Margo, I would never make you get married anywhere."

85

He walks over to me and takes my hands in his. "This is *our* wedding. I just want you to be happy."

I smile and squeeze his hands. Of course we don't have to get married there. Of course he just wants me to be happy. There are many reasons I fell in love with Sam, and several of them come flooding back to me in that moment. The way he's been able to pull me out of my grief like nothing else has been able to do. The way he makes me laugh. The way he takes care of me. I know I worry too much. I know I'll always find the dark cloud in the silver lining. I know this about myself, and yet I continue to do it time and time again. I need to trust more. I need to trust Sam.

"We can get married here, in the backyard for example. I'm sure my family would be more than happy to host."

The good feeling starts to fade along with the trust. "I wouldn't mind meeting with Rebecca to discuss some other options."

Sam drops my hands, and even though it doesn't physically, the action hurts. "Margo, listen. There's honestly no sense in working with a wedding planner. She'll charge us a huge fee, show us nothing but the most expensive options. What's the point in that when my family is perfectly willing to do all that for nothing?"

Neutrality, I want to say. A wedding planner is a neutral party who is invested neither in the bride nor groom. They take both into account; they don't choose sides. I've been on the other side of Sam and his family since we got here, and in this game, I'm outnumbered eight to one.

"I think you're making a lot of assumptions about how your family will react to the idea," I say finally. "If anything, this would make a lot less work for them. And I wouldn't worry too much about the costs. I have some savings and, compared to weddings in Chicago, I'm sure anything here would be a fraction of those costs. I'll bring it up to them and see what they say."

Sam takes a breath, and I can't tell if it's because he's thinking or he's being impatient with me. "Fine." His tone is slightly defeated, slightly challenging. I'm waiting for him to follow up his simple word with, "But don't say I didn't warn you," but he doesn't. Instead, we resume our places in the dust bowl of an attic and continue our search for the party decorations.

I move a tall mirror out of the way to check one of the boxes behind it. Inside it is a stack of photo albums.

"So, here's where you've been keeping all your baby pictures." I lift the box out from behind the mirror and kneel on the floor in front of it.

Sam glances over but doesn't join me. "Oh, I doubt there would be any in there," he says.

"Why not?" I lift the top album off the stack and open it to the first page. The photos are old. 1930s old—most of the photos are of the same couple, taken in various places on what appears to be their wedding day. "Are these your relatives?"

Sam steps behind me and glances over my shoulder. "I guess so."

I let out a laugh. "You guess so?"

"Well, I hardly spent my childhood looking at old family photos." Neither did I, but it wasn't because I wouldn't have been interested in my family's history. It's because my mother didn't keep any family photos around. Given her history with her parents, she chose to forget about where she came from, and I couldn't blame her for that.

I take a closer look at the couple in the large wedding photo on the first page. The woman is wearing a long white lace gown, and the man is in a dark suit. They look like Mary and Hank. In fact, it's uncanny how much they look like Mary and Hank. "They look like your parents."

Sam kneels down next to me. He takes the photo out of the album and turns it over. Written on the back is *Wailing, Spring '33.* "They must be my great-grandparents," he says. I flip through the album. The further along I go, the newer the pictures get. On the last page, the photos look like they're from the 1970s. There are also a few more people in the photos, including an older woman with black hair and a young girl, maybe eleven or twelve. There's another photo of a couple standing in front of a big, old farmhouse with an old car. It takes me only a second to realize it's this farmhouse, and the old car is the same car as the one in their driveway. This couple also looks like his parents, even more so than the couple in the wedding photo from 1933.

"Are these your grandparents?"

"Yeah, those are my grandparents," he says certainly. "My dad's folks."

"And this is your house."

"It is. They must have visited when my parents bought this place."

"They look so similar to your parents."

"Strong family resemblance."

"But even your mom looks like your dad's mom. Don't you think that's kind of strange? It's not like Hank and Mary are brother and sister and these are their parents."

Sam laughs. "Don't be weird. Incest isn't our thing." He takes a closer look at the photo of the couple. "I don't think my mom really looks like her, do you?"

I look again. To me, Mary could be this woman's daughter. But I keep my mouth shut. "No, you're right. I guess she doesn't." I close the book and reach for the next album in the stack. "Now, where are those embarrassing baby photos of you . . ."

He takes the next album away and kisses me. "You are very curious, aren't you?"

I grin and try my best not to overthink. "Is it so wrong of me to want to see a glimpse of what our future children might look like?"

Sam grins back. "Oh really? Our future children, huh?" He leans in and kisses me deeper, so deeply that he lays me down on the attic floor. Although I wasn't in much of a mood last night, I suddenly am now, the secrecy of making out with my fiancé in his parents' attic exciting me. Sam runs his hand up my side until he finds my breast and cups it fervently, pressing his hips against mine.

I let out a soft moan and he buries his head in my chest. "Don't do that," he says.

"Do what?" I whisper, knowing very well that my moans are enough to send him over the top.

"You know damn well what." He kisses my chest, his hand running down to my backside. "God, I want you."

"Then take me," I say. And I mean it. "Just lock the attic door and take me now."

"We can't," he groans. "We have to wait for the wedding."

"We don't have to," I say, running my hands over his back.

He pulls away with a jerk. "No," he says firmly. "We need to wait."

I used to find Sam's dedication to his values admirable, but in this moment, I can't find it anything but frustrating. But I love him. And I want to marry him. And I will respect his wishes. I sit up and compose myself as Sam stands and goes back to the other side of the attic to look for the decorations. As though even being within feet of me is enough to make him lose his willpower.

I look over at the other photo album, tempted to have a peek. But before I can open it, the cover bumps open slightly as though there's something inside. I lift the cover up and gasp as a large black beetle crawls out from the pages.

Sam looks over. "What is it?"

I look around for the beetle, but it's gone. I've seen that beetle before. It was the same one that hitched a ride with us on the drive here. Or at least it looked like the same one.

"Nothing," I say. "Just a bug."

"Well, it is an attic," Sam says. He walks over to me, holding a box conveniently labeled *Decorations*. "Found them."

From downstairs, Hank calls, "Time for dinner!"

Dinner consists of ham sandwiches for the rest of the family, and a cheese sandwich for me. No pea soup today. I guess we ate it all yesterday. The sandwich is dry, but it's still better than the cold eggs I was left with for breakfast, so I eat it with no complaints. I haven't said much, but it's because I'm trying to think of a way to broach the subject of hiring Rebecca as a wedding planner. I'm almost certain Sam is underestimating his family. I'm sure they'll be fine with the idea.

As I search for the right introduction to the subject, Hank goes on in great detail about a big rat he saw out in the barn. When he's done and no one seems to have anything else to say, I think this may be my moment to bring it up, but Mary turns to me before I can open my mouth. "Margo, didn't you like your eggs this morning?"

I try not to look too taken aback. "Oh, yes. They were fine—"

"You don't have to pretend, dear. We found them in the trash," she says curtly, and takes a bite of her sandwich.

I glance at Sam, who's still eating as if nothing is wrong. As if I'm not sitting here on display in front of my future in-laws, being criticized for throwing away a plate of cold scrambled eggs.

"We don't like to waste food," says Alice without looking at me. "Even if you didn't like it, you shouldn't waste it."

I swallow the dry bite of sandwich in my mouth. "It wasn't that I didn't like them."

"It's okay, dear," Mary says indignantly. "If you didn't like the eggs, you could have just said so."

"No, it's not that. They were just . . ." I look for a way to lie my way out of this, but there's no reason for me to lie. "They were cold."

"Oh?" Mary raises her eyebrows judgmentally. "You mean to say you've never eaten cold food before? Is food always piping hot back in Chicago?" She lets out a laugh that I think is intended to be light but comes off sharp as a knife.

"Mom, come on. Let it go," Sam finally says. But he's two minutes too late.

Mary looks over at him. "It's wasteful. Especially when she could have gotten up earlier."

I'm about to chime in that Sam was supposed to wake me when Hank puts his hand on Mary's arm and smiles at her sadly. "That's enough, dear."

Mary looks at Hank and down at her plate. A wave washes over her, and I can practically see her guard come down. When she looks up from her plate, she's all smiles again. As if the whole cold eggs catastrophe had never happened. "How's the sandwich, Margo?"

I take a sip of water, caught somewhere between confusion and frustration. I try to lean on the side of confusion and move forward with her proposed shift in conversation. "It's good, thank you." I know it's not the best time. I know I should probably forget about the whole thing. But my wedding is important to me. It should be important. So I open my mouth. "Actually, I wanted to make a suggestion about the wedding." Almost in unison, they all turn to look at me. Everyone except for Sam, who's keeping his head down as he eats his sandwich. I feel a twinge of irritation at him for his lack of support. "I saw that Fairbury has a wedding planner and was wondering if it might alleviate some of the burden off of all of you if we hired her to help us plan the wedding."

I finish my statement more meekly than I intend to, my voice turning it into a question. For a moment, nobody speaks. They just stare at me. Mary's stare is the hardest to read. It's as if she's disappointed in me.

"Why would you need a wedding planner?" she asks blankly.

"Um, well I think that it could be helpful for all of us to—"

"Do you not want to be married at the Evergreen Mansion?"

she says in disbelief.

My hesitation is enough of a cue to put her over the edge. She covers her face with her hands and begins crying softly.

I try to backtrack even though it feels pointless to do so. "No, I'm not saying I wouldn't get married there. I just meant it might be nice to see some other options."

Mary keeps sobbing and I feel like the worst person in the world.

"You know, I don't think we've instilled enough confidence in our lovely Margo," Hank booms to everyone at the table like he's on the verge of a good laugh. He turns to me and his voice softens, but he still talks about me in the third person. "I think we ought to show her the photos of Jimmy and Cheryl's wedding. Give her a taste of what we can do."

"Oh, that's okay. I saw the one in the hall. It looked beautiful—"

But Mary is already on her way over to the buffet in the living room. At the very least, she's no longer crying, so I don't dare stop her. She rummages loudly through several cabinets before pulling out a gold-covered photo album.

"Trust me," says Hank with a wink. "We can make a better wedding than any wedding planner."

Mary sets the wedding album down beside my plate with a thud and pulls her chair up so she's sitting just inches from me. On the cover is a picture of Jimmy and Cheryl, beaming at each other, the sunset glowing behind them, peering out from behind the Evergreen Mansion. Beneath the photo in big cursive white letters are their names. Mary sniffles and opens up the book to the first page. "I do think that once you see what a beautiful wedding it was, you'll feel differently," she says in a very small voice that makes me suddenly feel sorry for her.

I smile and nod my head and allow her to show me every single photo in the book, each one with its own, equally important story. By the time she's done, all the dishes from dinner have been cleared and no one is left at the table except for me and Mary. I feel like I've been held hostage for over an hour. She closes the book and looks at me, the big smile from her last story still on her face. "I know it may not seem very important to you, but it is to us. And it is to Sam. Hopefully now you can see why there's no need for a wedding planner. We're going to take such good care of you, Margo."

I glance over at Ruth in the living room, who continues to stare at the TV. Then I glance at Redd Wright on the TV, who continues to preach to all of his followers. Even though the volume is turned nearly all the way down, I can hear his voice as clearly as if he's right in my ear.

Chapter Ten

AFTER DINNER, HANK, Mary, Alice, Sam, and I all pile into the family car, even though the backseat of the old Chevy doesn't feel like it's meant for three people. Through my window, I glimpse the top of Ruth's head in the Wailing living room. She hasn't moved from her spot in front of the TV.

"What time are Cheryl and Jimmy coming over?" I ask, suddenly thinking of Ruth being left alone while we go into town.

"Not until later this afternoon," says Mary. "We'll be back in plenty of time."

"I can always stay here with Ruth," I offer, nearing a panic attack at the thought of being crammed into this car for the next half hour.

"Oh, Ruth's a big girl. She'll be fine by herself," says Hank. Only she isn't a big girl. She's old and frail and sickly and can't even seem to walk without assistance.

Mary turns and looks at me from the front seat. "*He* keeps an eye on her." She winks and turns back around, but I don't feel any more assured.

Alice is being unusually chatty although the only person she seems to be chatting with is Sam. He laughs and jokes around with her while Hank and Mary are my primary company. Even though I don't think I did a very good job of getting through to Hank and Mary about my wedding concerns, I must have struck some nerve because we don't drive by the Evergreen Mansion. We go straight into town. During a short lull in conversation, Sam takes my hand in his, and although I'm slightly less uncomfortable I can feel Alice's eyes burning into our entwined fingers. She doesn't say another word until we pull into the town square. Almost instantly I feel my phone vibrate in my purse, over and over again as the notifications come in, most of which are probably from work. My heart skips a beat, because those buzzes mean only one thing: I can text Rebecca.

We drive past Dee's Flowers as we look for a parking spot, and my eyes follow the front door as if waiting for Rebecca to walk through it. She doesn't, of course, but I still look.

We park on the corner opposite the flower shop and one by one emerge from the car. "What a beautiful day," Mary says as she gets out of the car. To me, the weather is cold and cloudy, but who am I to say what's beautiful to someone else? "Let's see, Hank, do you have the list of things we need from Stan's Hardware . . ."

Among the open shops around the square, I spot a children's toy store. "I almost forgot—I need to get a birthday gift for Selma," I say to Sam.

"Sure," he says. "We can do that." Alice is already headed for a trendy clothing store on the corner called *Patricia's*. "Hey, Alice." Alice stops and turns to him, slightly annoyed. "Do you want to take Margo over to *J & J Toys*? Maybe show her around a bit?"

"Oh, that's okay," I say to Sam, probably too quickly. "Alice probably has her own shopping to do. You and I can just go."

"I have a couple errands to run myself," Sam says. "And Alice doesn't mind. Do you, Alice?"

Alice looks for a moment as though she's going to roll her eyes, but instead she smiles. I'm not sure which is worse. "Of course not." She looks at me. "Shall we?"

I nod my head and follow her down the street. I attempt to steal a glance from Sam, but he's already walking the other way.

J & J Toys isn't a huge shop, but I'm sure I'll be able to find something a one-year-old would like. Alice hasn't spoken to me since we entered the store, but maybe that's something I can change. Maybe I can bring her guard down too. "What kind of toy do you think Selma would like?"

Alice shrugs. "A doll, maybe?"

"That could be good," I say, although it was hardly what I was thinking of getting her. Sam described Selma as a very precocious child. I can't help but feel a doll would be an insult to her intelligence.

We mosey into the doll aisle. Alice grabs a soft baby doll off the shelf by the arm and hands it to me, dangling it in front of me like it's something vile. "How about this one?"

I quickly take the doll from her and hold it as properly as I can. Even though it's just a doll, it feels strange to hold it any other way. "It's alright," I say.

Alice furrows her brow as she watches me holding the doll. "Do you want kids?"

My words catch in my throat, and I feel oddly judged. "Um, yeah. I mean, eventually." That's as far as I'll go on the subject. Because as much as I want Alice to like me, it's no concern of hers that I feel my heart flutter every time I see a baby. That I have yet to have a serious conversation with Sam about reproducing. That, while I know he sees children in our future, I'm not sure how to tell him that I'd like that future to be sooner rather than later. That I'm aching to fill the mother-child relationship hole in my heart.

"I don't," she says simply.

"That's okay," I say. When I was younger, I hated when

someone would ask me if I wanted kids, and I would say "no" and they would respond by telling me I'm still young, that I'll change my mind eventually. Now I hate it even more because they were right. But just because they were right about me doesn't mean they'd be right about everyone. "It's not for everyone. And that's okay."

"I know," she says, and walks past me to the end of the aisle. "You need anything else?"

I look down at the baby doll in my arms. She looks kind of pathetic, even sad. Even though she's just a doll, I suddenly feel sorry for her. Like an animal in a shelter, I feel the need to adopt her and take her home. "No, I'm all set."

I pay for the doll and, as I put my wallet away, feel my phone buzz again in my purse. It's probably more work emails. Suddenly, I feel the thin piece of cardstock in the back pocket of my jeans. Rebecca. I could text Rebecca. I glance over at Alice, who's looking at a display of marionette puppets. "Is there a washroom here?" I ask the store clerk.

"Down the far aisle." She nods her head behind me.

"Thanks." I turn to Alice. "Do you mind if I use the washroom quick?"

"No," she says flatly, throwing me off my guard. After relishing the awkward silence, she grins. "Isn't it funny how when somebody asks you if you mind them doing something, and you don't mind, the correct answer is 'no'? Feels like it should be 'yes.'"

I muster a laugh. "Yeah, that always gets me too."

Once I'm in the bathroom, I lock the door behind me and pull out my phone. There are over a dozen notifications. Most of them are probably from work, which I couldn't care less about at the moment. I pull Rebecca's card out from my back pocket, juggling my phone in one hand and Rebecca's card in the other as I enter her number into a new text message.

Hi Rebecca, it's Margo.

I then proceed to type and delete a message four times until I finally settle on something that feels safe.

> *It was nice meeting you yesterday. What you said really meant a lot. It can be stressful planning all of this. If you're free in the next few days, I'd love to get together for coffee and to chat about the wedding.*

I hit "send" before I can change my mind yet again and leave the bathroom.

I find Alice standing outside the store, lighting up a cigarette. "Don't tell my parents," she says with a grin.

I smile back, pathetically proud that she let me in on her secret. "I won't."

She offers the pack to me. "You want one?"

I almost decline automatically, having only smoked a handful of times in my life and hating every one of them. But I can't pass up a chance for approval. And my heart hasn't slowed to a normal rate since texting Rebecca. Especially when I realize that if she doesn't text me back before we head home, I'll have to wait until the next time I'm in town, or at least close enough that I have service, to hear from her. "Sure." I take a cigarette from the pack and let Alice light it for me.

As we smoke, I keep a watchful eye out for Sam and his parents. The last thing I need is for them to take me for a smoker. I take another drag and try hard not to cough. My eyes wander around the square, to a building across the street that looks oddly familiar to me. It's not Dee's Flower shop. It's not a building I remember seeing yesterday. It's something totally new to me, and yet it looks familiar. But I've never been to Fairbury in my life. How could one of the buildings here look so familiar?

And then I remember where I've seen it before. It's the same building that Mary and Ruth were standing in front of in one of the photos hanging on the wall back at the house: Hansen's Dress Shop. Only the sign on the building no longer says "Hansen's Dress Shop. "It says "United Insurance."

I take another puff of the cigarette and turn to Alice. "Was that insurance building something else before?"

She looks around. "Which building?"

"That one." I point to it.

"Maybe. It's been United Insurance ever since I can remember."

We finish our cigarettes, stomp them out, and head back to the car. Sam, Mary, and Hank are already there, waiting for us.

"Find everything you need?" asks Sam.

"Yeah, I think so." I notice he's carrying a dark plastic bag with a "Hobbies & Things" logo on it. "What did you buy?"

"Oh, uh—" He hesitates and glances down at the bag. "Just a few things for Selma's party."

We get into the car and Hank starts the engine as Mary talks about how difficult it is to find the tools they need at the store these days. "And then the cashier tells me I should look online. Online! Like I'm a teenager or something. I just don't believe—" She stops abruptly and looks around the car. "What's that smell?"

I glance nervously over at Alice, who's looking casually out the window. "What smell?" I ask innocently.

"Cigarette smoke." She looks directly at me. "Do you smoke, Margo?"

I swallow and shake my head. "I don't."

Mary's eyes narrow slightly, but she turns back around in her seat. "I would certainly hope not. You're so young. You need to keep your health and youth as long as you can. Smoking will age you like nothing else."

I hold my breath as I roll down the window just a crack, even though it means the window crank is digging into my knee even more than on the drive here. We pull out of the parking spot and drive around the south side of the square, past the United Insurance building. "Mom, what did that insurance building used to be?" Alice smiles at me as though proud of herself for trying to be helpful. "Margo was asking about it."

"Hansen's Dress Shop," she says fondly. "Of course, they've been closed for, gosh, nearly forty years now."

Hansen's Dress Shop. That's the one that Mary and Ruth were standing in front of in the photo on the Wailings' wall. Even for someone who isn't a CPA that's easy math. I keep a close eye on the building as we pass as if the time difference between the dress shop closing and the photo of Mary and Ruth standing in front of it will suddenly make sense. Maybe it was a different shop they were in front of, and I'm mistaken. Maybe it wasn't even Mary and Ruth at all. Or maybe Mary's memory has failed her, and the shop didn't close forty years ago.

"Why do you ask about the shop, dear?" Mary says as we head out of town.

"No reason," I say. "It just looked like it was something else before."

The farther we drive from the town, the faster my heart beats. I glance at my phone—still no new messages. Of course, Rebecca's probably busy. It's not like she's just sitting around texting. She's probably working. Just when I think we're too far from town and too close to home to have reception, my phone buzzes. I check it, too quickly, and see her name.

> *That would be lovely. How's tomorrow at 2pm?*
> *Galileo's Coffee Shop on the square?*

I immediately swipe up on my phone to unlock it and type my response.

Perfect. See you then.

"Who you texting?" Sam asks, causing me to jump.

"Just sending an email to work." I quickly correct myself. "For work, I mean."

Sam looks at me skeptically. I hate lying to him. Honestly, I'm not sure if I ever have. Maybe I haven't been completely open about my mother, about her mental health throughout the years, but I've never lied to him. And Sam knows that. So he believes me, which makes me feel even worse. Then I remember that Sam hasn't been completely honest with me either. He lied about visiting his family when he told me he was going to Milwaukee. The thought of his lie churns my stomach. And the fact that I've lied to him twists it even more. The child inside of me wants to argue that he lied to me first, but that's irrelevant. In fact, I'm not even sure if that's exactly what's bothering me anymore. It's not just that I lied to Sam, or that he lied to me. It's not the single lie. It's that there might be more to come.

Chapter Eleven

CHERYL AND JIMMY come over with Selma to help decorate shortly after we get back to the house. They would do it tomorrow, so the décor only has to stay up for one day before the party, but Jimmy works Saturdays. I don't say another word to Sam about hiring Rebecca. Partly because the last thing I want is another walk down memory lane with Mary, and partly because I can already sense Sam's "I told you so," attitude seeping through.

I offer to get up on the ladder to hang the *Happy 1st Birthday, Selma!* banner Cheryl brought on the front porch, but Sam insists on doing it himself. It's soon clear that there isn't much for me to do in terms of decorating. Finally, after an hour of waiting around, Cheryl asks me to help her watch Selma while they decorate, and I'm happy to do so. Selma is the one person in the family I never feel judged by. So I sit on the living room floor with Selma as Ruth sits in her chair, staring at the TV like she always does. I try to tune out Redd Wright and his soothing Southern drawl, but with no one in the room to talk to besides a baby and an incoherent old woman, it's impossible to do so.

"Have you ever found yourself on the outside of life?" Redd

Wright asks. I look over at the TV as Selma occupies herself with placing different-shaped blocks into matching plastic holes. "Have you ever looked at the people in your life and thought, 'I don't belong here'?" There's a murmur of agreement from the crowd. "Well, I've got some good news for you. *He* has some news for you." Redd smiles his friendly half-grin. "You do belong. Where you are in this moment, with these people, in this life, is where you belong." He looks at the camera, but I know he's not looking at the camera. He's looking at me. "This is your destiny, Margo."

I grab the remote off the table beside Ruth and flip the channel up one, to some football game. Instantly I regret it because instantly Ruth opens her mouth and releases that same, ungodly sound she made last night. As much as hearing Redd Wright's wisdom pains me, hearing Ruth's screams is even worse, and I quickly change the channel back, but not quickly enough. Mary and Cheryl come running into the living room from the kitchen while Hank barges in through the front door.

"What in Sam Hill is going on in here?" barks Hank.

Mary runs over to Ruth. "Mama? Mama, are you alright?"

Hank walks over to the TV. He looks down at the remote, then at me. "You change the channel?"

"Yeah, I'm sorry. I didn't realize she'd react that way," I lie. "I am sorry."

Mary smiles sadly. "It's okay, Margo. You didn't know." She adjusts the pillow behind Ruth's back and gives her a kiss on the head before returning to the kitchen.

Hank looks at me. "Don't feel bad," he says. "Redd Wright is the only thing that keeps her going most days." He leans in a bit. "But I have a feeling she'll be turning a corner soon." He winks at me and heads back outside, leaving me feeling as confused as ever.

I expect Cheryl to follow her mother back into the kitchen, but she hangs back. "Don't worry," she says to me, like she can read my mind. She takes a few steps toward me, and half-sits on the arm of the sofa. "You're doing great."

"I feel like I keep doing or saying the wrong thing," I confess.

"Trust me, I get it." She glances out the window. I follow her eyeline to see Jimmy on a ladder, hanging something on the front porch. "They didn't take too well to Jimmy when I first brought him home."

"Really?" I say a little hopefully. Then I realize that their disapproval of Jimmy might have to do with race. I quickly try to correct my tone. "I mean, I'm sorry that was the case."

Cheryl shakes her head. "Don't be. They actually were the ones who originally set us up if you can believe it."

I can't hide my confusion. "Why did they set you two up if they didn't approve of you dating?"

Cheryl rolls her head back and forth like she's trying to find the right answer. "It's complicated," she finally lands on. "I think they liked Jimmy a lot as a person, but we've always been so close as a family that it was hard for them to let in a newcomer."

I nod my head, thinking of how close my mother and I were. How even when I was dating Katerina, I worried that bringing her into the picture would somehow throw off the balance of our small family.

"I think being the oldest also had something to do with it," Cheryl adds. "I was the first one to learn to drive, the first one to start dating, the first one to become independent." She lowers her voice and leans in a little closer to me. "If you haven't noticed, they're not big on change," she adds with a grin.

I glance around at the 1970s décor overflowing the Wailings' living room. "I've noticed."

Cheryl's gaze drifts to Selma. "I think the past is the best way to learn for the future."

I nod my head. Before I can say anything else, the kitchen door swings open, and Mary stands in the doorway. "Cheryl, I could really use your help. This Jell-O salad isn't going to make itself!"

Mary disappears back into the kitchen and Cheryl gives me a slightly exasperated look. "Duty calls."

Cheryl stands and follows her mother back into the kitchen, leaving me alone once again with Ruth and Selma.

I turn to Selma, who looks at me with her glassy, wide eyes. "Do *you* think they like me?" I ask so only Selma can hear. She smiles like she's just gotten the punch line of a joke and drops an octagonal block through its respective hole. I smile back at her, but I'm suddenly overcome with tiredness. I envy Selma, who will get to nap before too long. But even though I envy her, I still somehow feel more connected to her than I do anyone else in this house. Maybe even Sam. Because this little being is still pure, still naive, still unrattled by the world. She's what I wish I could be.

I'm reluctant to take a nap before supper, but Sam insists. I think he's worried I might doze off at the table. So I lie down for a short nap in my regular clothes, not that hellish nightgown, and am actually able to fall asleep for half an hour. I'm used to having very vivid dreams whenever I sleep, even if it's only briefly, but I don't during this nap. In fact, I didn't dream last night either. Like my cell phone, I feel like this house somehow impairs my reception.

Even though I don't dream, I find myself thinking back to memories I don't want to think about.

Suddenly, I'm fourteen again, in Lisa O'Neill's basement with five other girls, and I've realized that my antidepressants are in my purse, upstairs in Lisa's room. We're in the middle of playing *Never Have I Ever* and I have ten fingers outstretched while most of the other girls have three or four. Rather than being embarrassed at my lack of experience or confessing that I'm on antidepressants, I excuse myself by saying I completely forgot to take my allergy pill. Either the girls don't hear me or they don't care because they continue their game without any acknowledgment of my words. I silently make my way up the linoleum-covered staircase.

I reach the main floor and turn down the hall. The door to Lisa's parents' room is closed, and the faint blue flickering light from a TV escapes from the crack below the door. I walk past it toward Lisa's room in the back of the hall. I open the door, and naturally the room is dark. I feel around for a light switch but come up empty. There's hardly any light trickling in from the hall, so I'm forced to tiptoe into the room, feeling my way toward the bed. I think I left my purse beside it. As my eyes adjust to the darkness, I'm able to make out various pieces of furniture and the faint outlines of posters on the walls. Her bed is a tad messy, unmade—which is strange because I could have sworn it was made when I was in here earlier. I scan the floor surrounding the bed for my purse, and that's when my eyes fall back on her bed again. It's not just messy. The covers are raised. Someone is in it. I feel my heart punching my ribs as I take a few steps backward. I don't need my pills tonight. I'll be fine. I need to get back downstairs.

The someone moves and suddenly speaks—a throaty moan, like they're struggling to breathe. Caught between safety and morality, my hands are shaking at my sides. What if they're in pain? What if they truly can't breathe? I step forward and touch the shape beneath the covers. And as suddenly as I realized they were there, they're gone. The blankets fall to the mattress. As quickly as my legs can take me, I turn and bolt for the door, but something stops me. What feels like a hundred hands wrap their fingers around my body and pull me beneath the bed. I try to scream, but it's like my voice has been stolen from me. I try to move, but their grasp on me is too tight. Their fingers run up and down my body as quickly and erratically as spider legs, as if they won't rest until they've touched every inch of me. I'm drowning beneath their touch with nothing to protect me but the darkness surrounding me. It goes on for seconds, then minutes, until I'm convinced it will never stop. Then, in a single heartbeat, I'm sitting in the basement with Lisa and her friends, in the same spot I was in, with ten fingers outstretched in front of me as if I'd never left. I stare at my bony fingers, the strange way they attach to my hands, and I can still feel the hundreds that were crawling up and down my body just moments ago.

"Margo?" I look up from my fingers to see Jimmy standing in front of me. Only I'm no longer in Lisa's basement. And I'm no longer fourteen. I'm standing in the Wailing living room, my hands outstretched in front of me as if I'm still playing the game. "You okay?"

I slowly look down at my fingers, which are now trembling. I let them fall to my sides and try to act as calm and normal as possible. I nod my head. "Yeah, I'm fine." But my voice is shaking.

"Seems like that nap made you sleepier!" My head turns to Mary, who's sitting on the couch.

I muster a laugh and try to steady my voice. "I guess so." I hope that my tone comes off light, but inside I feel the darkness of the memory creeping in on me. At fourteen I was getting to the age where I knew my mother wouldn't always be able to protect me from the monsters under my bed. But, worse, I was also beginning to realize that maybe the monsters under my bed were never real to begin with. That my mother hadn't been protecting me from anything after all. That whatever I had experienced at Lisa's sleepover was an inheritance of my mother's own mind. And that no one, not even her, could protect me from that.

I glance around the room. "Is Sam here?"

"He's in the kitchen," says Jimmy. "You sure you're okay?"

"Oh, yeah. Like Mary said, I think I'm still a little groggy from that nap."

Jimmy hesitates, as if making certain I'm okay, then sits down on the couch next to Mary and continues what I assume was their conversation before I entered the room. If I even entered.

"So are you taking the full dosage?" Jimmy asks Mary.

"Oh, I try, but it makes me feel so unlike myself . . ."

I quickly walk past them and head into the kitchen in search of Sam. When I open the door, I'm hit with a strong smell of onions. Sam is mashing potatoes in a pan on the stove, and Hank is pulling something out of the oven. Whatever it is, it smells delicious.

"Hey," Sam says when he sees me. "Sleep well?"

I nod my head. There's no point in telling him about my memory or blacking out. I don't need to give him more evidence to believe I'm crazy. "What are we having?"

"Vegetable loaf," he says proudly.

"It smells great."

I help set the table and in ten minutes everyone is seated and ready to eat. Hank sets the vegetable loaf down in the middle of the table and takes a seat. I appreciate them accommodating me and hope they didn't go to too much trouble or that, if they did, they won't grow to resent me for it.

"Margo, would you like to say grace tonight?" Mary asks, her eyes bright and encouraging. For the briefest moment, her expression reminds me of my mother. But somehow that fleeting thought feels like a moment of betrayal.

I glance over at Alice. Part of me wants her to step in like she did last night, but another part of me wants to show my thanks for their hospitality by saying grace.

"Sure." I hold out my hands. Sam takes one, Mary takes the other, and everyone around the table does the same with the people beside them. Cheryl gently takes Ruth's, although with the discoloration of her fingertips, part of me wonders if holding her hand could do more harm than good. I close my eyes and clear my throat, searching for what to say. But my mind is blank. I try to recall what Alice said yesterday. Even if I could just think of a few words to string together, I could make it work. But I can't think of any. All I can hear is Redd Wright, talking through the television. Only he's not in the television. He's in my head. And he's not speaking to his followers. He's speaking to me. He's feeding me the words. And I'm speaking them.

Dear Almighty Father . . .
"Dear Almighty Father."

We thank you on this blessed day . . .
"We thank you on this blessed day."

For giving us one another, for giving us life . . .
"For giving us one another, for giving us life."

For watching out for us, when we cannot watch out for ourselves . . .
"For watching out for us, when we cannot watch out for ourselves."

We know that we are never alone, because you are always with us . . .
"We know that we are never alone, because you are always with us."

Your body is my body, your blood is my blood . . .
"Your body is my body, your blood is my blood."

From now, till then, till the Ever End . . .
"From now, till then, till the Ever End."

As if they all knew it was coming, they chant along with me the words that aren't even mine. I move my hands from right to left, then out and in, and feel the rest of the table do the same. Everyone opens their eyes, including me.

I look at Mary whose eyes are filled with tears. "I knew you could do it."

She smiles at me, then begins passing around the sides. For a moment, her praise warms my heart and I feel a surge of gratitude for Mary, but when my eyes land on the TV, the unsettling chill of reality coats my skin. Redd Wright's words entered my mind and found their way through my thoughts to my mouth. With nothing but a steady buzzing left in my ears I find my mouth has gone dry. Because as I stare at the TV, I see that he is interviewing a man in the audience. The volume is turned down so low I can't even make out their words. And yet when his words filled my head only moments ago, I could have sworn Redd Wright's voice was my own.

Chapter Twelve

I ASK SAM if he will lie with me in my bed tonight until I fall asleep, but he says he has to help Hank and Jimmy build something for Selma's birthday party tomorrow. A special bed of sorts, he says. So, instead I lie in my bed, wearing that awful nightgown, with the light on, hardly ready for sleep. Mary stands at the dresser across from me, folding white towels and putting them in drawers, and telling me stories of her girlhood as she does so. She's been doing this for over twenty minutes. I know I'm a guest in her house so I can't very well ask her to leave, but I really just want to be alone.

"Of course," she adds to a story about when she first learned to ride a bicycle, "that was a long time ago. I haven't ridden one in years."

I nod my head. Perhaps offering to help her fold will help move her along faster. I wait an appropriate amount of time after she finishes her story before I ask, "Can I help you with the folding?"

"Oh, certainly, dear."

I reluctantly climb out of bed and stand beside her at the dresser where I try to match her folding patterns. But when

111

I look over at her, I see she's no longer folding. Instead, she's looking at herself in the large mirror above the dresser. I try to busy myself with the towels and not stare, but after minutes of silence as she stares at her reflection, I feel the need to speak. "Everything okay, Mary?"

"I envy you your youth," she says. Looking at her, I feel she can't be older than sixty, maybe sixty-five tops. "They say aging is a beautiful thing, but it's not. It's cruel."

I understand what she means. Even though Mary may not be very old, she feels old. Just like my own mother, her body is betraying her. And that's the furthest thing from beautiful. In no way was my mother's battle with that horrible illness beautiful, if you could even call it a battle.

We found out about the cancer when it was stage four. She had no symptoms. No warning. No time. She had no history of breast cancer in her family that she knew of, but then again, she hadn't spoken to anyone in her family since before I was born. The survival rate was twenty-two percent. The treatments wouldn't have cured it. They would have only prolonged her life. I, of course, wanted her to do anything to keep going. To keep being my mom. But she didn't. She said it would be too painful, too uncomfortable, to go through the treatment for a few extra moments. The cancer took her forty-nine days after her diagnosis. I've never been angrier in my life. Not at her—I understood her decision—but at the illness. At how cruel life can be for no reason.

She told me eight days after her diagnosis that the voices wouldn't want her to fight it. The voices. She didn't talk about them often, but when she did, I knew better than to question her. She'd never sought mental health treatment. But I think it was because she never saw the voices as a problem. She said they'd only speak to her when she needed them to, that they protected her. As a teenager, I began to fear that the voices were a sign of her being mentally unwell. And the first time I heard my own voices I feared I was too. But neither she nor I ever exhibited any other signs of a mental illness. Aside from some anxiety and depression, I didn't feel like anything was particularly wrong with me or with her. On a good day, I told myself maybe this was just part of who we were. That maybe hearing voices wasn't always a bad thing. Maybe they were protecting us.

But after she died, the voices died too. That is, until the drive here. Until the beetle spoke to me.

"I lost my mother to cancer," I say finally. Maybe it's not the right thing to say, but it feels right to me. "It was the hardest thing I've ever had to go through. I'm not sure how you're feeling these days, but if it's any consolation, it looks like you're in really good hands with your family. Sam, Jimmy, Hank, your daughters . . . they all take really good care of you."

"That they do." She looks at me and smiles sadly. "Don't take one minute of that beautiful face of yours for granted."

Mary reaches out her hand and rests it gently on my cheek. With the touch, she lets out a long sigh and shuts her eyes. Finally, she removes her hand and opens her eyes as if awoken from a brief sleep.

Then she shakes her head and goes back to folding towels. "Oh, where does the time go?"

Despite how tired I am, I still can't sleep tonight. My nap this afternoon wasn't very restful, so I can't imagine it threw off my schedule that much. After over an hour of staring blankly up at the canopy I close my eyes, but that's as close to sleeping as I get.

At 3:20 a.m., I open my eyes. While I'm not sure if I've slept, I am sure that I have to pee. But I don't want to get out of bed. Because I feel like I'm being watched again. I see movement, and my eyes flash to the corner of the room by the door. The only thing I can see is darkness and a faint light coming from under my door. Only the darkness looks darker than it should, like something is there. And the strip of light spilling from the threshold of my door looks shorter, like something is in front of it. I tell myself I'm dreaming, that if I just shut my eyes for five seconds, everything in the room will be normal when I open them.

When I do open them, the darkness is lighter, the threshold is wider, and I no longer feel like I'm being watched. But that makes me feel more unsettled. Because if I'm certain that I am alone now, then I'm certain I wasn't before.

I'm afraid to close my eyes again. If I close them again, whatever was there before might return. Still, I don't think I'll be able to sleep without going to the bathroom. I climb out of bed, ignoring the wave of dizziness that washes over me as I stand, and shuffle to the door and out into the hall. When I get close enough to the bathroom, I see there's a dim light visible underneath the door. I take a step back and lean against the wall, waiting for whoever is in the bathroom to be done. I'm pretty certain there's a bathroom on the main floor, but I can't recall if it's in the front of the house or the back. Either way, after last night, the last thing I want to do is go back downstairs and risk Redd Wright speaking to me again. I need to keep my sanity as best as I can.

I wait. And I wait. And I wait. Finally, I tell myself I can hold it till morning and start to go back to my room when I hear a moan on the other side of the bathroom door. I stop and turn around. The moaning continues, louder this time. I should go back to my room. Whatever is going on in the bathroom doesn't concern me. The moan happens again. It doesn't sound pleasurable. It sounds pained. I take a few careful steps toward the bathroom.

"Hello? Is everything okay?" There's no break in the moans, even with my words, and I wonder if they even hear me over the mournful cries. The moans suddenly become garbled, and the thought hits me that whoever is in there could be drowning. I grab the handle of the door and swing it open.

Every surface in the bathroom is lined with flickering candles, and in the middle of it all sits Mary, naked, in a tub filled to the brim with crimson water that Hank slowly washes over her body. The moans are coming from her, and they don't stop even when she turns her head to see me. I almost scream, but I think I've forgotten how to.

I wonder if I must make some sort of noise because Hank turns his head abruptly toward me. Without a word he stands and rushes to the door, pushing me out and shutting it. I stand there in the hall, frozen and trembling from head to toe. I can't go back to my room. I can't go downstairs. I run down the hall and throw open the door to Sam's bedroom without even knocking.

Ever the light sleeper, he immediately grumbles, "Who's there?" in the darkness and flips on the light closest to his bed. "Margo?" He must see the look on my face, because his expression grows worried. "What's wrong?"

I run over to him and force his arms around me. My breathing is shaky, and I can't find the words to describe what I just saw.

Sam strokes my head and shushes me gently. "Did you have a bad dream?"

I shake my head and pull away from him, finding my strength as I look into his calming brown eyes. "Your mother—the bathtub—there was blood—"

"Blood?" He goes on alert. "Is she alright?"

There's a knock at the door. I start to shake my head, but Sam speaks without seeing me. "Come in."

The door opens and Hank enters the room, followed by Mary. Her hair is still wet but she's now wearing a dark robe. "You alright, honey?" Hank says to me softly.

I don't say anything. I'm too busy staring at the drips of red water rolling down Mary's calve. Sam looks at his parents.

"What happened? Is everything okay?"

"I'm afraid Margo accidentally walked in on me taking one of my special baths," Mary says lightly.

Sam exhales. "Is that all that happened?"

"You see, Margo," Hank explains, "Mary uses a special muscle relaxant medicine to help her sleep when her body aches."

"It looked like blood," I stutter.

The two of them laugh. "Just the unfortunate color of the medicine," says Mary. "Stains the tub worse than ink."

Sam looks at me, smiling slightly. "Feel better?"

I don't. Not just because of the blood-red water. Because I can still hear Mary's moans ringing in my ears. But with six eyes watching me, I nod my head.

"We're very sorry we frightened you," Mary adds.

Hank holds out his arm to me. "C'mon now, let's get you back to bed."

I clutch Sam like a child clinging to her parent. "I think I'll stay here for a while."

Hank and Mary exchange a glance. "I'm afraid we can't let you do that, dear," says Mary. "You know the rules."

I look at Sam, pleading for him to fight for me. He rubs my back and looks to Hank and Mary. "I'll make sure she gets to bed."

Hank and Mary hesitate, then Hank nods. "Alright, well don't stay up too late." They start to leave the room. "The water's been drained now if you need to use the bathroom, Margo."

"Sweet dreams," says Mary, and they shut the door behind them.

I'm still shaking as Sam reaches a hand up and pushes my hair out of my face. "You okay?"

"No. I feel . . . off."

"What do you mean?"

I'm not sure how to say what I want to say without offending him. How to explain that I've felt a knot in my stomach since before we even arrived at this house that I know has nothing to do with nerves. How to tell him that I practically jump every time someone enters my room. That there's something very off about this house, his house. His family. And definitely not how I've been hearing beetles and Redd Wright talking to me. Because that would completely discredit anything else I've said. Because that would make me crazy.

"I don't know," I finally settle on.

"Come on," he stands and pulls me to my feet. "I'll walk you back to your room. You probably need a good night's sleep."

I do need a good night's sleep. But I'm not going to get it here.

"No," I say, refusing to stand. "Something's not right."

"Not right? Like you feel sick?"

"No, I—" In a way, I do feel sick. Or at least I don't feel like myself. "Not sick. Strange."

"You're just tired," he says. "You've hardly slept. And it's stressful, meeting so many new people at once."

I nod my head. Not because I agree that stress is what's behind this strange feeling, but because I don't know how to describe what I feel, and the more I talk the less sense I know I'll make.

I ask him to wait for me in the hall outside the bathroom while I use it. When I'm done, I glance over at the tub. It's empty, but stained red, like Mary said it would be. Before tonight, the tub wasn't stained red at all. If it really is a dye from her medicine that she uses regularly, why hasn't it been stained red this whole time?

I take a closer look at the tub, at the drain. A small, watery red puddle has formed around the fixture. Suddenly the water is disturbed. A beetle crawls out from the drain, causing me to jump. It makes its way across the tub and up the side of the porcelain toward the window. Just as it reaches the window ledge, it stops and turns to me, looking at me.

"The end . . . is near . . . the end . . . is near . . . the end . . . is here . . ." the beetle whispers. Then it jumps through a small opening in the window.

Before leaving the bathroom, I unbutton the cuffs of my nightgown, roll up its lace sleeves, and splash my face with water. As I dry my hands, I glimpse the small red dot on the inside of my left forearm, the skin yellowing around it. Strange thoughts circle my mind, but I know that if I'm going to make it through the next few days in this house, I need to silence those thoughts before they consume me.

Sam is waiting for me in the hall as he said he'd be. "You okay?" he asks.

I nod my head and he walks me back to my room. Before he leaves, he kisses me on the forehead and reassures me that a good sleep is all I need. Then he shuts the door, leaving me alone in the darkness. Alone again in this house.

Chapter Thirteen

WHEN I WAS fifteen, I came home from school the day before Thanksgiving. My mother and I had planned on staying home for Thanksgiving, the way we did almost every year. The year before we didn't. We had been invited to my friend Teresa's house for dinner and my mother was sick at the last minute. She insisted I go without her, but I spent the evening feeling guilty and alone. This time, I was going to get it right. We'd even gotten all of our groceries at the store—white potatoes, sweet potatoes, cans of cranberry sauce, vegetable broth and breadcrumbs for stuffing, and this delicious vegetarian sage sausage you could only find at the Family Grocery three suburbs over. It was going to be a nice Thanksgiving. Was.

I walked through the front door to find several half-packed suitcases lining the front hall, clothes strewn around them—some of them mine, some my mother's. I closed the door behind me and let my backpack fall next to my beat-up, red Converse. It was all part of my punk phase—dark eyeliner, thick side bangs, and black or red attire whenever possible. On that day, it was black skinny jeans, an oversized black sweater, and of course, my black choker with the skull dangling from it. I looked like I felt, but not how I was. I wasn't tough. I was weak. And in that moment, I was also afraid.

"Mom?" I could hear her upstairs in her bedroom, the TV rattling on, but she didn't answer me. "Mom, are you there?"

She emerged from the bedroom, a pile of clothes in her arms and a bag dangling from her wrist. Her eyes were wide and fearful as she looked down at me from the top of the stairs.

"Is everything okay?" I asked, afraid of the answer.

"Shh!" She held a finger to her mouth, dropping several articles of clothing in the process. "You need to be quiet, Margo."

I lowered my voice to a whisper. "What's going on—"

"Shh!" she said even louder and made her way down the stairs until she was inches from my face. "He's here. He's outside the house. He's been here all day." Her eyes somehow widened even more. "He's been waiting for you."

Even though I was taller than her by that point, I felt like a small child standing there in front of my mother. "Mommy, stop it. You're scaring me."

She reached out her hands and took mine in hers "It's going to be okay." She touched a hand to my cheek, brushing my bangs out of my face. "Margo, I need you to listen to me. Pack up these suitcases and wait by the door. I got enough clothes for you for a few days. We're just going to stay a few nights in a motel until we lose him, okay?"

"No, Mom—" I tried to find the right string of words that would snap her out of this. I'd been able to do it before. I couldn't just deny what she believed. I had to play into it enough to keep her on my side. Enough to get her through that night. Tomorrow, things would be better. Tomorrow, we would have potatoes and cranberry sauce and vegetarian sage sausage and stuffing. "We could just stay here."

"We can't, it's not safe—"

"It is." I swallowed hard, trying my best to keep in character. To remember my motivation. "It is safe. He can't hurt us if we're in the house."

And that's when I saw a look on my mother's face I couldn't recall ever seeing before: pity. "Oh, Margo." Her eyes filled with tears. She leaned in even closer to me and in a deep whisper said, "Yes, he can."

We drove for over an hour until we reached a motel I'd only been past a handful of times before when we'd go up to Wisconsin for a day trip. It was a dark, dumpy place, with thick curtains in the windows and only two cars in the parking lot. We checked into a room that was, at my mother's request, "As far away from the road and as out of sight as possible."

Despite the strange looks from the motel attendant, he did give us the least conspicuous room there. It was located at the far east end, with a door that faced toward the dumpsters instead of the road. Once we were in the room, my mother locked both locks and had me help her pull the heavy wood dresser in front of it. Then we pulled the heavy curtains shut and covered them with the comforter to block out anything that might try to get through. The only light in the room was the glow from the old black-and-white TV. The light streamed across the white sheets strewn over us, making them glow too. My mother was lying on the left side of the bed, closer to the window so she could help protect me if *he* tried to get through, but now she was asleep, and I couldn't feel any less protected.

The TV was so low I couldn't make out what anyone was saying, but I didn't have the energy or the courage to climb out of bed and turn it up or off. I didn't know if even the slightest movement would wake her up or cause her to scream or spin around in her sleep like a waking nightmare. I was never afraid of my mother, but I was afraid of what scared her. Because something did. Something scared her to her core. From the moment I'd seen the figure outside my window when I was four years old, to this night in the dark, dank hotel room, I'd always known something terrified her. But the figure I had seen then wasn't real. I might have not known it as a small child, but I knew it by the time I was a teenager. But even though it wasn't real, I was afraid. I was afraid of what she was afraid of. Like her fear was contagious. I didn't think I could ever be scared of what scared someone else, but I was. I was so, so scared. And so, so alone.

The blue light from the TV hurt my eyes, and I closed them just enough to blear it out. I was so tired, but too afraid to sleep. I listened for my mother's familiar breathing, but suddenly I didn't hear it. How long had I not been able to hear it? Had she been breathing the whole time? I know she must've been. But now she wasn't. But when did she stop? I opened my eyes and refocused them around the room. In the corner, I saw shadows, but they must have been the same shadows that were there before. I looked over at my mother, who was now lying on her back, her eyes wide open. But that wasn't what scared me. Her mouth was moving rapidly, but no words were coming out. What was she saying? Who was she talking to? I slowly climbed out of bed and backed away. Something wasn't right. Maybe we weren't alone in this room. I ran over to the door. It was still locked. The dresser was still in front of it. The window was still covered. There was no way anyone could have gotten in. No one could have gotten in. No one could have gotten in.

At some point, my eyes must have closed because when I opened them next, it was morning. My mother was in a calm, pleasant mood. We talked about school, about movies, about anything and everything normal. We drove to the nearest Denny's and got pancakes for Thanksgiving dinner and ate them out of Styrofoam containers in the hotel bed. As if nothing had happened last night. As if there was nothing strange about spending Thanksgiving in a hotel with a comforter in the window. We stayed one more night, and then drove back home on Friday. She didn't mention anything about the figure. About a man. About *him*. When we got home, I helped clean up the house and we watched *Sister Wives* on TLC. Everything was fine. Everything was normal. Everything was over.

Chapter Fourteen

SATURDAY

SAM WAKES ME promptly at seven thirty the next morning, as if trying to make up for letting me sleep in the morning before. I eat every bit of eggs on my plate. They're only lukewarm, but I'm not about to leave a bite after the fuss that was made yesterday. They hurt my stomach as they land. I don't think it's the eggs. I think it's the fact that I have plans to meet Rebecca for coffee this afternoon and have no intention of telling Sam I'm going to do so after the whole ordeal yesterday. I shouldn't have to hide this from Sam. I shouldn't have to feel guilty about wanting to have some say in what I want for my wedding. But I am. I'm already thinking about what I can tell him to get him to take me into town so I can meet with Rebecca. I really am looking forward to meeting with Rebecca. Not because I feel anything for her besides friendship, but because I'm looking forward to discussing wedding plans for my wedding. Which is why I'm here to begin with.

The majority of my morning is spent with Mary teaching me how to crochet, and Ruth sitting next to us, staring at Redd

Wright on TV. I must not be very good at it because every time I manage to make a stitch, she says, "Oh, very nice, dear! Here, let me help you with that," takes my hook away, and redoes whatever I just did. I wish it was more of a distraction, but it's not enough to keep Redd Wright out of my ears and my mind off of lying to Sam. After the fifteenth undone stitch, I decide that I'm going to tell him there's a few hours' worth of work I completely forgot to do, and it needs to be done by Monday morning. I'll need internet to do my work, and since this house seems to be stuck in a time before modern technology, I'll need to go into town to connect to the internet. It's the perfect lie, really.

By the time Sam walks into the living room, Mary has practically crocheted an entire blanket, and I've watched her the whole time. "Oh, wow," Sam says, admiring the blanket. "That's looking great." He smiles at me.

"I can't take any of the credit," I say, a little too honestly. "Your mother is a crochet wiz." I turn to Mary. "How long have you been crocheting?"

Mary laughs. "Oh, more years than I can count."

"It definitely shows. I'll have to keep practicing."

"You'll get the hang of it eventually, dear. We can practice more after dinner." She pats my knee and gets to her feet, then shuffles into the kitchen.

I smile stiffly at Sam. "Oh, shoot," I say, like I've missed my cue by a half second.

Sam leans against the armchair. "What is it?"

"I completely forgot about the Edelson account."

"The what?"

"The Edelson account. One of our clients. I was supposed to finish their business audit before I left for vacation."

"Can't Jean or Harry take care of it?"

Considering Jean is my boss and Harry doesn't say more than two words to me unless he absolutely has to, I'm pretty certain that neither of them would be fit to take on my fictional audit. I shake my head. "I can't ask either of them."

I can hear Mary singing "Shine on Harvest Moon" in the kitchen as she prepares dinner. I stand and walk over to Sam, farther away from the kitchen, and far enough away from Ruth that she probably can't hear us. "I hate to do this, but would you mind dropping me off in town for a few hours this afternoon? I can connect to the Wi-Fi at a coffee shop or something there, get my work done, and be finished by supper."

Sam nods his head, thinking. For a moment, I think he's going to have some counter-solution or argument, but he doesn't. Instead, he says, "Of course, whatever you need." It's so easy the knot in my stomach tightens twofold. "Alice has an audition in town she asked me to drive her to later. We can drop you off on our way there. We'll head out right after dinner."

Half an hour later, we're all sitting down to yet another meal with a lot of chewing and very little conversation. Today, the cheese sandwiches are grilled, and I'm grateful for even this small improvement.

After dinner, I go upstairs to get my jacket, butterflies hammering the inside of my stomach at the prospect of seeing Rebecca. As I come down the stairs and pass the hallway, my eyes land on the photos hanging on the wall. I scan them as I pull on my jacket, searching for the photo of Mary and Ruth in front of Hansen's Dress Shop in a desperate need to validate what I saw in town yesterday. But it's gone. All of the other photos are still there, except for that one. And there isn't even a gap where it once was. Someone must have taken it down and rearranged them.

"You ready to go?" Sam's voice from behind me causes me to jump.

I look from him to the wall of photos. "Where did the photo of Mary and Ruth go?"

Sam looks at the wall. "Which photo?"

"It was a photo of Mary and Ruth in front of Hansen's Dress

Shop," I explain.

Sam's brow furrows. "I'm not sure I know which photo you mean."

Either Sam really doesn't remember the photo, or I'm being gaslit. "It was right here." I point to the place on the wall where the photo was. It's now a photo of what I assume is Sam and Alice as teenagers in front of a cornfield. She has her arm slung around his shoulder and is sticking her tongue out at the camera. Sam is in mid-laugh and looking at her, a grin on his face. It's a photo I don't remember seeing yesterday.

Sam is quiet for a moment as he surveys the wall, looking at each photo as if he's counting them. "There are fifteen photos," he says finally. "That's how many there have always been."

I want to prod the issue further. I want to understand what happened to the photo. But if we wait any longer to leave, I'll be late to meet Rebecca.

"Never mind," I say, making my way to the front door to put on my shoes. I know what I saw. I know the photo was there. Someone took it down. Maybe it was Alice. Or maybe I really am going crazy.

Sam, Alice, and I get into Sam's car and head into town. I sit in the backseat while Alice rides shotgun. It makes sense that I'd ride in the back since they'll be dropping me off first, but it still makes me the third wheel. I try to ask Alice about the show she's auditioning for, just to make chit-chat, but she hardly says a word. After several failed attempts at conversation, I give up and stare out the window at the depressed houses and dirty streets surrounding the square.

Sam pulls into a parking spot in front of the only other coffee shop on the square—a big chain one called Stan's that I saw several of on the way here. It's funny that Sam should choose this shop, not Galileo's, but I'm certainly not going to say anything. I'd rather he think I'm here, to lessen my chances of being spotted with Rebecca at Galileo's. I slide out of the backseat and get out of the car.

"Don't work too hard," he warns with a grin through the open window after I shut the door. I wave and watch as he pulls out and the two of them drive off, Alice not even looking in my direction. Once they're out of view, I cross the square to Galileo's Coffee Shop.

I spot Rebecca through the window before I go inside, and instantly the glass door feels like a force field. Suddenly, I feel like I've been lying to myself. I shouldn't be doing this. I was drawn to Rebecca when I first met her. Not just because she reminded me of Katerina. Maybe it was because I was feeling disconnected with Sam and on the outside of his family. Whatever the reason, something drew me to her, and if something draws you in that much, that probably means there's a good reason to stay away from it.

Just as I'm about to turn and find a way to kill the next two hours of my time, Rebecca catches my eye and waves. I give a small wave back and open the door.

I approach her table. She's sitting with a ceramic mug of coffee in front of her. "It's good to see you," she says brightly.

"It's good to see you too," I say, trying not to let her attractiveness distract me.

She gestures to the counter. "Please, order whatever you'd like. It's on my tab."

I try to protest, but Rebecca insists I order something, so I cave.

With my mug of pumpkin latte warm in my hands, I take a seat across from Rebecca.

"I'm sorry to see your fiancé couldn't make it," she says, her eyebrows slightly furrowed.

Defensiveness rises to my lips. I can't tell her that I'm here in secret, but I have to say something in Sam's absence. "Yeah, he's spending time with his family."

Rebecca opens her mouth to say something but seems

to catch herself. "Of course," she settles on, although I have a feeling that's not what she was going to say. "Well, don't worry. I often work more directly with the brides than I do the grooms." She gives a little eye roll that I find undeniably endearing. "Not to genderize, but you know how men are. You show them five different shades of pink and ask them to pick their favorite and they look at you like it's a trick question."

I can't help but laugh. Beautiful people aren't supposed to be funny too.

We spend the first twenty-five minutes going through several books of wedding décor—place settings, centerpieces, flowers—as casually as two girls browsing the latest bridal magazines. Every now and then, Rebecca will nod her head thoughtfully and jot something down in her notebook. Our conversation feels familiar, relaxed, and I'm able to sink into it. So much so that I almost forget I was ever drawn to Rebecca. Then she looks at me, that half-smile parted on her lips. "We also rent out a trellis, chairs, lights—everything you might need to make the ceremony special. And flowers by Dee, of course," she adds with a wink that makes my heart flutter shamelessly. And I'm not okay. Because all I want is for her to look at me like that again.

"What made you want to become a wedding planner?" I ask, shifting subjects from palette colors far too abruptly.

Rebecca raises her eyebrows. "Oh, um . . . I don't know, honestly." She takes a sip of her coffee.

Sensing her uncomfortable response, I try to back off. "I'm sorry, I didn't mean to pry."

"No, not at all," she says, waving her hand dismissively. "I guess I always was fond of weddings. And I'm fairly organized so I guess it makes for a fitting combination." She gives a small shrug. "Although it can get a bit monotonous, especially in a town like this."

"How so?" I ask, genuinely curious.

"Well—" She looks like she's searching for the right words, but I wish she wouldn't censor herself. After a day of masking around Sam's family, I'm craving authenticity. "I guess you could say that a lot of the brides I work with around here are rather traditional. No offense," she adds quickly.

I feel simultaneously taken aback and confused. "Traditional? Like, religious?"

She gives a reluctant shrug. "A bit."

"I'm not religious," I clarify.

Rebecca raises her eyebrows, not out of surprise, but as if she's worried she's offended me. "Oh, it's perfectly fine if you are," she says quickly. "I have nothing against religion. I just meant . . . Well, I grew up here, but for a while worked in Chicago. I got to work with a lot of different couples. It was more refreshing. More relatable, I guess."

My mind flashes to the Pride flag in Rebecca's window and my heart pounds. I assumed the flag meant she was an ally, but it hadn't even occurred to me that she might be more. I feel the sudden need to clarify that aspect of myself too. The urge to draw a fish in the sand.

"Well, I'm sorry it didn't work out for you to stay working in Chicago. But if it helps, you seem like a really good wedding planner."

"Really?" her face lights up, the flattered reaction at my genuine compliment a vulnerability I haven't seen on her yet.

"Definitely. You really seem to know how to work with couples," I say, trying to find my way to the words I really want to say to her. "I appreciated that you weren't surprised by how quickly Sam and I got engaged. Or, if you were surprised, that you didn't show it."

"I meant what I said. I work with a lot of different couples. Some who have been together for years and years and others who are on a tighter timeline, like you and Sam."

That's when I find it. My window. "Do you ever feel like all

130

relationships are on a timeline? Like, if you don't get engaged or married by a certain point, the moment passes?" Before she can answer, I keep going. "I feel like with my last relationship, she and I started out very madly in love—" I glance at Rebecca, searching for a change in her expression at the mention of my ex being a "she" and maybe it's wishful thinking, but I'm pretty sure I see it. "But after we passed the six-month mark, things started to fade. And after a year together, we broke up." I pause for a moment, wondering if I should say the next part aloud. "I think that's why I was so keen to marry Sam after such a short amount of time," I say, surprised at my own honesty. "I didn't want to lose the good thing we had."

Rebecca hesitates for a moment, either waiting to see if I'm finished talking, or searching for the right words. "I'm sorry it didn't work out between you and her."

Her. The word hangs between us, like an invisible thread connecting our bodies.

"But maybe that's part of what led you to Sam," she says optimistically, and I feel the thread between us snap. She looks away for a moment, then meets my gaze again. "I get the feeling you're pretty good at keeping secrets." Something catches in my throat, and I nod. "A few years ago, I was very much in love." She gives a sad smile. Not to me, but to a place just past her coffee mug. "But she came from a very religious background and no matter how hard I tried to convince her, she never believved that if we ran away, got out of this town, we could be together. But that would've meant choosing me over her family, and she didn't want to do that. She was actually fairly close with the Wailings as well. They didn't go to the same church or anything, but I think she felt a connection to them, to their faith. Anyway, she and I got into a bad fight one night. We were sitting in my car, right down the street from her house. I was frustrated and hurt and told her that if she wanted to really be with me, this was her last chance. We'd never even kissed, but we had this connection

131

that I thought was strong enough to outweigh anything else. But I guess I was wrong. Abby got out of the car and . . ."

She wraps her fingers around her coffee cup, holding it much tighter than she needs to. "And I never saw her again." She brings the cup to her lips and drinks. After she sets the cup down, she adds, "That's when I moved to Chicago. I thought I would have a better shot at meeting someone new there. Instead, I ended up throwing myself into work and running out of money a lot quicker than I'd expected. So, I came back here and started working for Dee and came to the sad realization that even if I can't have my own happily ever after, maybe I can at least continue to help other people have theirs." She briskly wipes her eyes and laughs. "Can you tell I don't have many people to talk to?"

It's probably not the right timing. It's probably inappropriate. But I reach out my left hand and place it on her wrist, wishing my engagement ring weren't on it. "Thank you for sharing that with me."

Rebecca looks at me as if she's going to ask a question, but she doesn't. She does pull her hand away to wipe her eyes again, even though they're mostly dry. "Thanks," she says. "Here I am, talking your ear off about my relationship drama. Tell me more about Sam. What drew you to him? What's he like?"

The shift in our conversation feels abrupt, but necessary. I don't know what I was thinking, putting my hand on hers like that. I hadn't even meant it as a come-on, just a moment of connection between two like people in a very restricted town. I shake off my embarrassment and mull the question over in my mind.

The few times someone has asked me to describe Sam, I always feel like I'm about to lie. Even if everything that comes out of my mouth ends up being true. Maybe it's because I'm only sharing the good things—enough to paint a picture of the man I've chosen to spend my life with and make people validate my decision. "Sam is . . . he's a good guy. He looks out for me. Cares about me. Takes an interest in what I like and what I do. My mother passed away recently, and Sam has been my rock through all of that." I let my thoughts wander to Sam, searching for the good moments we've shared. But all I can think about from these past few months are the times I wanted to cry over my mother. All the times I felt a need for comfort that only she could give me.

When something would remind me of her when Sam was around, I always tried my best to hold back my tears. Not because I didn't feel like I could cry in front of him, but because crying around Sam meant blurring the line between this great, happy thing we had and the sad reality that I would never see my mother again. The few times I did break down in front of him, he didn't comfort me and let me cry against his chest. Instead, he'd take me out to dinner or to a movie, or suggest we go out dancing. In those moments, I told myself that those were the best things I could do to help my grief, despite the fact that I had to push my way through the pain to act like I was enjoying any of them when in reality all I wanted was to cry against his chest.

This realization happening in real time in the coffee shop with Rebecca causes me to leave an uncomfortable pause in my story. "And I love him. I really do love him," I say finally. Before I can stop myself, I add, "But sometimes it doesn't feel like it's enough."

Rebecca nods. "I've heard a lot of good things about him from people in town," she says. "I know he hasn't lived here for a while now, but every time he comes back people's faces seem to light up when they see him."

I wish her words reassured me that I'm making the right choice in marrying Sam, but they don't. All they do is make me feel insignificant. I'd seen Sam's million-dollar smile right off the bat on the train. I knew he was charming. I knew he was someone people were inherently drawn to. But hearing it from

Rebecca only makes me feel like that charm isn't just for me. It's for everyone. Which means it's not special.

Rebecca shuts the wedding book in front of me and looks at me pointedly. "So," she says. "Do you have any venues in mind?" I find myself thrown off guard, not by the question but by the shift back to reality. To the distance that's grown between us. She seems to notice my hesitation and jumps in. "Not that you need to decide now, of course. I know you two are thinking about the spring. Is that right?"

"Probably May," I manage to get out. "I haven't seen too many options yet. Sam's family seems pretty set on the Evergreen Mansion, and I'm not saying it isn't a beautiful place, but I'm not as keen on it as they are."

Rebecca nods thoughtfully, but there's a stiffness in her expression. "It is a lovely house, if that's what *you* want." She emphasizes *you* in a way that makes my heart skip a beat. "I mean, I'm not particularly religious or anything, but it will be beautiful in the spring."

I take a moment to replay her words in my head. I think to the mansion and try to picture anything religious about it. No chapel. No cross. "What does religion have to do with the Evergreen Mansion?"

Rebecca looks at me blankly. "Oh, I thought Mary would have told you." I shake my head. "That's the former home of Redd Wright, the televangelist."

I feel a knot form in my stomach. Mary doesn't miss any opportunity to bring up Redd Wright. And yet she hasn't once brought up that the Evergreen Mansion was his home. I think back to Mary's sobs and cries when we went to see the Evergreen Mansion, like a piece of her was built into the walls. Knowing how she feels about Redd Wright, the dramatics all make sense now.

"She, um . . . she never said anything."

"Oh," Rebecca seems to be searching for the right words.

"Well, I'm sure she just forgot. I know she's had some health trouble in recent months."

An inexplicable, uneasy feeling washes over me, a coldness that comes from deep inside of me and seeps out through my pores. A vague, high-pitched noise sounds from somewhere within my ears and grows louder and louder until I'm finally able to recognize it as a voice. Not just any voice, but my mother's voice, as clear as if she were sitting here beside me. She's crying and screaming and yelling that we have to leave, he's coming for me. Pack up my things, he's coming for me. Stay away from the windows, he's coming for me. I feel tears streaming down my cheeks before I even realize that I'm crying.

"Margo?" I feel Rebecca's hand on my back and turn my head to face her.

It's only then that I feel my mouth moving. "I'm sorry."

"You have nothing to apologize for," she says, rubbing my back. "It can be a lot," she says softly. I nod my head. "I've never been married, but I've planned enough weddings to know how stressful they can be, especially for the bride. It's so hard to figure out what you want while also trying to appease the families. But in the end, it's your choice." She smiles.

My phone buzzes twice in my purse. I feel my heart begin to race, suddenly worried about what time it is and whether Sam is going to be picking me up soon. I told him I would be done catching up on work by four. I check my phone. It's 4:07 p.m. I quickly open my messages. There are three from Sam. The first one is him letting me know he'll be here in ten minutes, and the next two are him asking me where I am.

"Oh, God."

"What's wrong?"

"Sam's here. Not here, he thinks I'm at Stan's."

I toss my phone in my purse and get to my feet. As I grab my jacket, I realize Rebecca is looking at me with a furrowed brow and worried eyes. I must look like a woman under the control of her husband, the way I jumped at a few missed texts from him. I suddenly feel the need to explain myself.

"Sorry, I don't want to keep him waiting."

Rebecca gently rests her hand on my arm after I pull it through the sleeve of my jacket. "Margo, are you okay?" she asks seriously.

"I'm fine." I try to force a smile, but I have a feeling Rebbecca can see right through it. In my purse, my phone buzzes repeatedly. I let my smile fall and glance out the window. Sam is standing in front of Stan's, holding his phone to his ear. He's calling me. "Look, he doesn't actually know I'm here with you."

I wait for the judgment to come. For Rebecca to gasp at the fact that I've lied to my fiancé. But she doesn't. She continues to look at me with concern.

"I know that probably sounds bad. I'm sure he would be fine with it. It's his family. They don't think we need a wedding planner and—"

"Tell him you had issues with the Wi-Fi at Stan's and had to go to Galileo's instead," Rebecca says quickly, glancing past me out the window to Sam. "It's probably true. Stan's has notoriously bad Wi-Fi."

I look at her for a moment, feeling a rush of affection for her that I wish I didn't have. "Thank you." I glance over at Sam, who's now looking down at his phone, no doubt texting me again. He's probably worried. The wave of guilt I feel looking at him practically consumes me.

"Text me," Rebecca says, drawing my focus back to her. "If you need anything at all, I'm here."

I nod my head. She gives my arm a gentle squeeze and takes a step back, letting me walk out of the coffee shop and across the square.

Sam looks up from his phone as I approach him.

"There you are," he says, walking over to me. "I was starting to worry when I didn't see you in the coffee shop."

"Yeah," I say, slowly coming up with a response. "I was having some trouble with the Wi-Fi so I went over to that other coffee shop. Galileo's."

"Ah. I do recall Stan's having bad Wi-Fi, now that you mention it." He looks at me carefully, and I realize my eyes must still be swollen from crying. "Are you alright?"

I nod my head, but I'm suddenly fighting back tears again. I feel like I'm always fighting back tears around Sam. "I'll be fine."

He rubs my back and leads me towards the car, but doesn't press the issue, which somehow only hurts more.

"Did you get everything taken care of with work?"

"Yeah," I say, a little too quickly, hating how easily the lie comes. "Mostly."

As he opens the car door for me, my eyes catch Rebecca leaving Galileo's. With her sunglasses on, she walks down the sidewalk a few yards, then steps off the curb and climbs into a yellow Volkswagen beetle. I sit down in the front seat and let Sam close the door beside me. I watch as she pulls out and drives off the square, and my mind instantly drifts a million miles away.

Chapter Fifteen

SUNDAY

THE BIRTHDAY PARTY for Selma starts in less than two hours so I spend most of the early afternoon with Sam, helping him put up the final decorations. My conversation with Rebecca at the coffee shop looms in the forefront of my mind, as much as I wish it wouldn't. I can't wrap my head around the fact that Rebecca is more similar to me than I realized. Of course, she probably assumed I was straight. Not only because I'm marrying a man, but because of the family of the man I'm marrying into. They don't exactly come off as the most progressive.

But I'm not here for Rebecca. I'm here for Sam. And so, as I've learned to do so well with the grief over my mother this past year, I put any feelings toward Rebecca in the box deep in the darkest corner of my mind, shut it, and throw away the key.

"How many people are coming?" I ask Sam as I tie the string of a pink balloon to the front porch.

"Oh, it's just going to be the eight of us," he says from up on the ladder. "And Selma, of course."

I step back and take a look at the house. Since Friday

afternoon, it's been adorned with over two dozen pink balloons, streamers, a banner, and various jungle animal-themed decorations. "Seems like a lot of decorations for just the immediate family."

"You know how families are," he starts to say before catching himself. "I mean, you know how they can be. Always making a big hoopla of things." Sam finishes hanging up a cardboard cutout of an elephant and steps down from the ladder. "Come on, I want to show you what we made."

He leads me around the side of the house to where something about three feet tall and four feet long sits, covered in a white sheet. He pulls off the sheet to unveil a small, wooden bed with a fluffy, pink cushion for a mattress. On the headboard is an engraving of a large peacock, its feathers spreading across the wood. At the foot of the bed, *Selma* is engraved in cursive.

I kneel down next to the bed. "Sam, this is beautiful." I run my hand over the carved peacock, trying not to remember the creature I saw on my walk down the road our first night here. "Is this what you were working on with Hank and Jimmy the other night?"

"Indeed it was." He kneels down next to me. "It's kind of a tradition in my family that on the child's first birthday the family makes them a bed like this one."

"That's sweet," I say. I notice Sam is smiling at me. "What?"

"I was thinking how one day we'll be making a bed for our own kids."

I smile back, but I don't feel the giddiness I should. Instead, I feel a pang of guilt as my mind flashes to my secret rendezvous with Rebecca. How could I betray Sam when he's here planning out our future?

We gather in the living room for presents promptly at three o'clock. Ruth's chair has been turned so she can face the rest of us instead of the TV, which, for the first time since I've been here, is off. Hank and Mary sit near her, and Alice sits on the floor beside them. Jimmy sits next to Cheryl, who holds Selma on her lap. Selma's all smiles, clapping her hands at all the attention she's receiving. They've dressed her in a little pink headband and a ruffled pink dress. The fluff and lace suit her much better than my nightgown does me.

Sam and I take a seat on the couch. I set my present down on the table along with the others. I've wrapped the doll in a nice bag that Sam loaned me, and written a little note on a folded piece of card stock for a card. It's not ideal, but it will do.

"Alright, Selma, which one shall we open first . . .?" Cheryl reaches for the first gift, then the next, and the next. Cheryl and Jimmy open most of them for her, but Selma helps here and there, tearing at the wrapping paper and waving it around excitedly. Most of the gifts are puzzles of some kind, and all of them are in some way educational. Sam wasn't kidding when he said Cheryl and Jimmy take pride in Selma's intelligence. As I watch them open present after present, I take some comfort in the uniqueness of my gift. What little girl doesn't love a new baby doll?

Finally, Cheryl reaches for my gift. She reads the note first, "*For Selma, Happy 1st Birthday! Love, Margo.* Aww, thank you, Margo." She reaches into the bag and pulls out the doll. When she sees it, her face falls to a frown. I glance at the faces around me. Mary's is the worst; she's looking at the doll like it's something vile.

She turns to me and my stomach drops. "Why would you get her that?"

"What do you mean?" I lean over and take a closer look at the doll. Is there some inappropriate word written across its forehead that I somehow missed? Or did they actually take the gift as an insult to Selma's intelligence?

Cheryl's brow furrows. She starts to speak but seems at a loss for words. Finally, she manages, "Mom, don't worry about it." Cheryl puts the doll back in the bag and offers me a pained smile. "Thank you, Margo."

I glance over at Alice, who appears to be hiding a snicker. Mary shakes her head in disappointment as Hank pats her back. I see her whisper something to him, but I can't make out what it is. He shakes his head subtly and gestures toward the gifts. "Let's open the next one, shall we?"

Once the gifts are all opened, Mary announces that it's time to move outside for the big surprise, which I assume is the bed. As we make our way to the front door, I see Cheryl talking to Jimmy, pointing at the doll in the bag. Jimmy glances around, picks up the bag and goes into the kitchen, I imagine to dispose of it. Cheryl then makes her way over to Alice, who's sitting on the floor with Selma. Cheryl sits next to Alice, and I can see her face is still looking stern. Alice's smile to Selma fades as she turns her head to her sister.

"What?" Alice asks in an annoyed tone.

"You know very well what," Cheryl snaps.

"Come on," Sam says to me, opening the front door. Alice and Cheryl both look up, as if they hadn't realized we were still there. Cheryl turns back to Alice and lowers her voice to a whisper so I can't hear what she's saying. I avert my eyes and follow Sam through the front door, but I don't want to leave. I want to hear the rest of their conversation. Alice is clearly in trouble for helping me pick out the doll. And it's not that I want Alice to be in trouble, but I want to know why the doll is such an issue. And why Alice would think convincing me to buy it would be so funny.

After Sam and I are outside, I pull him away from the house.

"I don't understand," I say. "What was wrong with the doll?"

Sam lets out a long breath and half rolls his eyes. "It's not you. My family has this weird superstition that dolls are bad luck."

"What makes them bad luck?" I ask.

Sam searches for the right words. "They think they're

inhabited by child angels."

"Why would that be bad?" Hank and Mary emerge from the front door then, chatting among themselves. Although I don't think they'll be able to hear my conversation with Sam, I still lower my voice. "I thought your family believed in heaven and angels and all that."

He looks momentarily lost for words and ultimately shrugs. "You're right. It doesn't make sense. I told you, they're weird about things."

"Alice told me she'd like it. When we were at the store."

"Alice did?" Sam rubs his face. "Okay, I'll talk to her."

"No, don't do that. Besides, I think Cheryl already was talking to her about it."

I glance to the front door in time to see Alice walk through it. She doesn't look happy, and for the brief moment our eyes lock, she shoots me daggers before hopping off the front steps and kicking a rock off the dirt walkway.

"Well, I'll handle it, okay? She's probably jealous that she's not getting the attention she usually does."

We walk over to the sheet-covered baby bed where Mary, Hank, and Alice are now standing. I look through the front window of the house and see Ruth has been seated there so she can see outside. It's sweet, but a little unnerving.

We stand there in silence for a few minutes before I speak. "Are Cheryl and Jimmy going to bring Selma out?"

Mary gives me a knowing smile, but she doesn't respond. It feels like the same awkward quiet we've had at every meal since we've been here. I take the hint and don't say anything else. We wait for five more minutes, ten more minutes. I look across the cornfield at the sun low in the sky, peeking out from behind the gray clouds.

"Hello, hello!" says a voice from up above us. I look up to see Cheryl and Jimmy peering out of the attic window.

Mary, Hank, Alice, and Sam applaud. I'm not sure why, but

I join them. Mary turns to me. "Are you ready, Margo?"

Ready for what I'm not sure. "I am," I say, more than a little confused.

"Sam," Mary says, nodding to her son.

Sam reaches out and pulls the sheet off Selma's bed; then he goes to the foot of the bed and grasps it. He looks at me. "Margo, would you please take the head."

I stare at him for a moment, trying to figure out what head he's referring to. He picks up on my confusion and nods to the head of Selma's bed. "Do you mind?"

"Oh, sure," I say, stepping forward and holding onto the bed. "Where do you want it to go?" I assume he wants the bed moved somewhere else.

"Nowhere," Sam says. "Just lift it with me."

Still a little lost, I do as I'm told, and Sam and I both lift the bed in unison, so it hovers a few feet off the ground.

Hank and Mary are standing beside us, looking at the window. I lean forward to Sam. "Why are we doing this?"

"You'll see," he says. "It's okay," he adds reassuringly.

I'm not sure why he feels the need to reassure me, but the fact that he does makes me nervous. I look up at the window. Jimmy is no longer there, and Cheryl is looking out at something in the distance, something out in the cornfields, out of view. A moment later, Jimmy reappears, holding Selma.

"We're ready," Cheryl calls from the window.

Mary, Hank, and Alice clasp their hands together in prayer as Sam and I continue to hold the bed. My stomach suddenly feels like lead.

"Dear Almighty Father, at three-hundred-and-sixty-five days old, nineteen pounds, seven ounces, I present to you Selma Elizabeth Wailing-Cane." Cheryl holds Selma up to the open window and I feel my heart stop.

Before I can comprehend what's about to happen, Hank, Mary, Sam, and Alice all bow their heads and begin to recite a prayer in unison. I look to the front window and see that even Ruth is mouthing the words. "*Almighty Father, blessed are we that You bestow your good graces upon Selma Elizabeth Wailing-Cane, daughter of Cheryl and James, daughter of you. Watch over her on this journey from our arms to yours. Cradle her as if she were your own. Protect her as you protect us. From now, till then, till the Ever End.*" They finish their prayer with the same gesture they use after grace.

My hands have begun to sweat so much that the wooden bed feels slippery in my grasp. I should have kept my head down as they spoke. I should have shut my eyes and prayed. But I can't seem to take my eyes off the open window that Cheryl is now holding Selma out of at arm's length. Selma is looking around, wide-eyed. She isn't crying, but she looks like she could at any moment. I look down at the tiny bed in my hands, and back again at the window directly above it.

"What the fuck is going on?" I hiss at Sam.

"Shh—" He still has his eyes closed and his head is bowed to the ground.

"Don't shush me," I say, louder. I don't give a damn who hears me. "What is she doing?"

He doesn't respond, only keeps his head down with everyone else, his hands gripping the bed so tightly that his knuckles are white. Everyone, including Cheryl and Jimmy, are muttering something as they keep their eyes closed and their heads bowed. I can't make out what it is they're saying, but I don't care. It doesn't matter what gibberish they're praying because Selma is dangling out of a window thirty feet from the ground. Thirty feet from the bed.

"Sam, for God's sake, do something." My voice comes out guttural, desperate.

But Sam looks at me, stopping his prayer just long enough to say, "Hold on as tight as you can," before returning to muttering his religious incantation.

If Sam isn't going to do anything, I will. With my hands still firmly grasping the bed, I call up to Cheryl. "Cheryl, please don't do this!" She ignores me, her eyes still closed. Selma squirms slightly in her hands, beginning to fuss. With a little kick, one of her tiny shoes slides off her foot and falls through the air. My jaw hangs open as I watch it land three feet away from the bed. "Please, stop!" I scream at the top of my lungs.

A second after I yell, they all fall silent. For a moment, I think they're going to turn on me, begin yelling at me. But they don't even acknowledge my protests. In unison, they open their eyes and look up at Selma. As if in slow motion, Cheryl releases her grasp and I watch in horror as Selma's tiny body falls three stories.

"NO!" I fight every inclination I have to drop the bed and grab her, because right now the bed is her only chance of surviving this. Sam's eyes stay locked on Selma's tiny body, and he steps backward a few feet, accounting for her direction. I follow suit, only because my body is pulled as the bed moves. My brain isn't capable of even beginning to process what is happening. No matter how precise our aim, there's no way we'll catch her. There's no way she'll survive this.

That's when I think that the body falling through the air toward us can't possibly be Selma. It must be the doll I bought her. That's what it is. They're throwing the doll out of the window to get back at me for getting them a gift that they deem insensitive. This is one big joke. One big, sick, fucking joke. But as she nears the ground, I see her tiny arms flailing, grasping for the air around her. I see her head twist and her already large eyes looking enormous and terrified. I hear her little voice screaming through the abyss. It's not a doll. It's Selma.

As Selma lands in the bed with a thud, I'm brought to my knees with the pull of her weight. I'm sobbing because she must be dead. Her neck must have snapped. She couldn't possibly have survived.

I feel Sam's hand on my shoulder, then on my chin. He lifts my head until my bleary eyes meet his. I expect his expression to be grim, distraught, because he must not have known. He must not have realized what they were going to do. But his expression isn't grim or distraught. He's smiling as he helps me to my feet. "It's okay," he says, holding me up. "Look."

He nods towards the bed. I stop crying and stare in disbelief as Mary leans down and picks up Selma from the bed, holding her over her shoulder. "There's a good girl," she coos, rubbing Selma's back. She turns and Selma looks over at me, hiccupping between sobs. She looks rattled, but safe. She's alive. Somehow, she's alive.

Sam, Alice, and Hank surround Mary and Selma, each vying for Selma's attention. I look up at the window. Jimmy has his arms wrapped around Cheryl as the two of them look down at the scene on the ground, beaming like proud parents. I want to run. Run down the dirt road. Run as far away from this family as humanly possible. But I can't move. My feet feel like they're nailed to the ground. Even if they weren't, I'm certain I'd faint if I attempted to walk. I can see everyone talking, but all I hear is a ringing in my ears and the sound of my own heartbeat.

Once the excitement dies down, the family heads back inside the house with Selma, leaving me fuming at Sam in the far corner of the front yard, as far away from that house as possible.

"She dropped a fucking baby out a fucking window!"

Sam reaches for my arm, lowering his voice as if encouraging me to lower mine. "Margo, please calm down—"

"Don't tell me to calm down." I jerk my arm away. I don't care if his family can hear me. I can't help myself. This is no longer just about me. This is about Selma's safety. I know all too well what it means to take a child from their mother because they're deemed "unfit." I know how close my mother came to losing me on more than one occasion. I know what losing me would have done to her. But I was never in the kind of danger that they put

146

Selma in. I was never dropped from a fucking window. I need to get out of here. I need to call someone to come and help this child before the unimaginable happens. "We need to leave. I need to get out of here."

"Hang on, let's just talk—"

"What is there to talk about? Your sister dropped your niece from a third-story window. Who the fuck does that?"

"It's a ceremony," he says. "That's all it is."

"No." I get close to his face. He needs to feel what I'm feeling. He needs to understand. "A wedding is a ceremony. A baptism is a ceremony. That was a fucking sacrifice."

"Baby, it wasn't a sacrifice. They never intended to kill her—"

Sam never calls me baby. We always make fun of people who call each other that. I'm not sure where it came from now, and it only throws me even more. "She could have died."

"This is a tradition that has been passed down in my family for generations and not once has a baby died from it," he says.

"So your parents dropped you out of that same window when you were a baby?" I ask him, beyond horrified at the thought.

Sam opens his mouth like he's going to yell at me, but he lets out a breath instead. "Yes," he says finally. I want to question him, because the manner of his response doesn't feel honest, but I don't know why he'd lie about that. If anything, admitting to that being true is worse than any lie to cover it. "It's symbolic."

"How? How is it symbolic?" The air has grown brisk since the sun fully disappeared behind the clouds and I can no longer feel my legs, but I refuse to go back inside that house until Sam gives me an explanation for what I have witnessed.

"By dropping the baby, the parents put faith in their higher power to look out for them." I'm listening. My heart is still racing a mile a minute, but I'm listening. "It's basically them telling their God that they entrust their baby to Him, and by doing that, the baby will be protected forever."

I take a deep breath, but I'm still shaking. Sam rubs his hands up and down my arms to warm me up, but I'm not shaking because I'm cold.

"If you want to leave, we can leave," he says.

"Really?"

Sam nods, but I can't tell if he's bluffing. "I'm sorry this has made you uncomfortable." Uncomfortable may be the understatement of the century. "Trust me," he goes on. "I don't like it either."

"You don't?"

He shakes his head. "I think it's archaic, to be honest."

"Archaic?" The word practically catches in my throat on its way out. Archaic implies that what has happened is old, outdated, a thing of the past. Giving away the bride is archaic. Forcing a woman to take her husband's name is archaic. Corsets are archaic. What I witnessed wasn't archaic. It was dangerous. Absurd. Unthinkable.

I take another breath. Even though I can't justify any of what happened, Selma is alive. She's okay.

But the harder I try to convince myself that that's all that matters, the more lost I feel.

I look at Sam. My fiancé. The man I'm supposed to marry. I try to see the man I met on the "L" train. I search his face for the man who kissed me up against my apartment door. I look into his eyes, desperate to see the person who held me, night after night, who made me laugh until my stomach hurt, who told me he loved me, who gave me something happy to hold on to when nothing else in the world seemed to matter. I try to see that man in Sam now. I try with every fiber of my being, but the harder I search for him, the more it feels like he's slipping away.

Sam lifts my chin and looks into my eyes. "Listen, I know my family has their issues. And if you really want to leave, we can. But it would mean so much to me if we could just stick it out until Wednesday. I promise this is the craziest thing that will happen while we're here." I want to look away, but I can't pull myself from Sam's deep brown eyes. The eyes I've grown to trust so earnestly over the past half-year. "I know how you must feel. It's never easy joining a new family." He's touched a nerve, and I'm certain he knows it. I listen carefully to his next words, hoping that they'll be enough for me. "And as much as my family means to me, you mean more. Whatever bond I have with them . . ." He sighs, like he knows the next thing out of his mouth is going to pain him. "It's nothing compared to what we have."

While there isn't much more that I could ask for him to say, I don't know if it's enough. I can't think clearly with the image of Selma falling three stories running through my mind on replay. Right now, I need to push through. I have to make it through the next few days. Then we can leave, get married somewhere else, and go on with our lives. Maybe once Sam is away from his family again, things will go back to the way they were. Maybe he'll eventually see how toxic they are. And maybe, if he still chooses to visit them, at least I won't have to go with. I'll be sick. I'll have to work. Whatever excuse I have to make, I'm never coming back to Fairbury.

"What do you say?" Sam looks into my eyes, hanging onto the possibility of my response.

Finally, I nod my head. "Okay."

"You'll stay?"

"Yeah." He pulls me into a hug that should feel warm and comforting, but it doesn't. All I feel are Sam's bones and tight muscles against my body. I don't feel warm and I don't feel comforted. I don't feel like I know the man I agreed to marry. If this is who he is, and this is who his family is, then I'm certain now that my feelings of not belonging are real. That, despite aspects of my strained mental health, I am not entirely gone. There is truth to what I've been feeling, what I've been seeing. Something has felt wrong here since I crossed the threshold, and I now know something is.

After a moment, we pull away, and I follow Sam to the house, reminding myself that I only have to survive two more days before I can go home.

Chapter Sixteen

I SAY I need to lie down before supper, but actually I need to be alone. I need to process although I'm honestly not sure what I'm processing. Even though Sam said he wasn't keen on the tradition, he still stood by and let it happen. I'm the only one who seems to think there's anything wrong with this. Sure, I can grasp the concept of a ceremony for a one-year-old to show the family's faith in their higher power, but what kind of a higher power would want you to drop your child out of a window?

I think back to the conversations Sam and I have had about our possible future child. What we would name them. Whose eyes they would have. Whose hair. How we would tackle various parenting challenges together. We agreed we would discuss every major issue together before making a decision. We wouldn't spank them. We wouldn't swear. We wouldn't raise our voices. But I guess we never said we wouldn't drop them out of a three-story window. And if Sam ever so much as joked that we should follow in his family's "archaic" traditions, I would leave him faster than he had time to blink.

It's almost six, and Sam said to come down by six. I pull my hair back and leave the room, bracing myself for whatever insane event is planned next. Sam may have tried to reassure me that this afternoon's fiasco was the craziest thing that would happen while we're here, but somehow, I don't believe him. When I get to the top of the stairs, I hear whispered arguing downstairs and stop before my foot hits the first step. I hang back and lean my ear in the direction of the conversation.

"A doll? Really, Alice?" says Mary's voice.

"Come on, it was funny."

The doll? Their oldest daughter just dropped her baby out a window, and they're talking about *the doll?*

"You need to watch yourself, young lady," says Hank.

"Young lady?" Alice repeats in her deadpan voice. "Really?"

Mary lowers her voice even more. "Look, I don't know if you're jealous or angry or what, but it needs to stop. You're going to scare her off. Is that what you want?"

There's a pause. With no response from Alice, Hank chimes in. "You answer her, dammit. You know her health is getting worse by the day. Now answer the question. Do you want to scare Margo off?"

"No," Alice says reluctantly.

"Now, I'm going to go get Margo, and you're going to apologize to her."

That's my cue. I creep quickly back into the bedroom as Mary rounds the corner toward the stairs. "Margo?" she calls up the staircase.

With my door barely closed, I call back in a high-pitched voice, "Yeah?"

"Would you come on down when you're ready, dear?"

"Oh, sure," I try to say casually. "I'll be right down."

I give it a solid minute before I make my way downstairs. Cheryl and Jimmy are sitting with Selma at the dining table, feeding her, but none of the other places are set, which is odd this close to suppertime. I don't even smell anything cooking. The TV is still off in the living room, which means Ruth is sitting in her chair staring into the abyss. Hank is pacing around the living room, Sam is sitting on the couch, and Mary is standing next to Alice.

"Hi, dear," Mary says cheerfully. "Did you have a nice nap?"

I nod my head. "I did, thanks."

"Alice has something she'd like to say to you." Mary shoots Alice a sharp glance.

I expect Alice to mutter an apology and avoid eye contact with me, but instead she steps forward and takes my hand with both of hers. "Margo, I am *so sorry* I played that prank on you with the doll. It was very insensitive of me. As the baby of the family, you can imagine I'm used to getting all the attention around here, so when you arrived, I felt a little displaced." She gives a sad smile. "Can you ever forgive me?"

I find myself speechless, caught with my guard only half up. I know Alice is an actress, but without knowing how good she is, it's impossible to know if she's acting right now. It certainly feels like she is. But even if she is, it doesn't matter. Because I just need to pretend that everything is normal and make it through the next few days.

I offer her a smile in return. "Of course," I say. "It was kind of funny." Her smile widens. "I mean, suggesting I buy Selma the one gift I shouldn't buy her. What do I know?" I laugh, but it sounds slightly manic. At first, no one else cracks a smile. They stare at me, and I worry it's too much. Then they all break out into laughter at the same time.

"I guess it was a pretty good joke, Alice," says Hank, smoothing his moustache.

I bite my lip as the awkwardness of the laughter dies down. I wait for someone to say something about the baby-dropping, to acknowledge that they at least understand why it might upset me, but no one does. I'm beginning to think that no one in this room has even the slightest idea how truly disturbing it was. That the mild reassurance I got from Sam is the best I'm going to get. "So, what's for supper?" I ask the room.

"Margo," Mary steps a little closer to me. "You are in for a treat tonight."

Chapter Seventeen

INSTEAD OF SUPPER, Sam informs me that we're going to a church as part of Selma's purification ceremony.

"I thought your family didn't go to a regular church," I say to Sam as we make our way to the parked cars.

"They don't," he says. "Not in a traditional every Sunday sort of way. But this is a special occasion."

I'm reluctant to get in the car and drive twenty miles with this family in the dark, but Sam assures me that it will be fine, that nothing bad will happen as long as he's with me, and right now as much as I don't feel like trusting Sam, he's the closest thing to family that I have.

Before I climb into the cramped backseat, Cheryl approaches me, gently touching my arm. "Hey," she says softly. "I wanted to make sure you're okay after our tradition earlier."

"Oh, yeah—" As hard as it is for me to accept what happened earlier being deemed as a "tradition," I can tell Cheryl is trying to check in on me, and I'm in no position to pass up her concern. "I mean, I wasn't expecting anything like that," I say in my attempt to tiptoe around this topic as carefully as possible.

Cheryl lets out a light laugh. "I can imagine." She looks at me, her eyes warm. "Listen, I know how something like that might look to an outsider, but I wanted to assure you that I promise I would never, ever do anything to put my child's life in danger. This is something that has been passed down for years and years."

I nod my head. "Yeah, Sam mentioned that."

She looks like she's trying to read my mind, to get a gauge on how I'm really feeling about all of this. "Are you sure you're okay?"

I force my head to nod again. "Yes," I say definitively. "I'll be fine. Thank you for checking."

Cheryl smiles and pats my arm before walking over to her and Jimmy's car. I let out a long breath and brace myself as I squeeze into the backseat of the Chevy with Sam and Alice. We pull out of the driveway and onto the road, with Cheryl, Jimmy, and Selma following close behind us. Although I don't think I'll ever get over what I witnessed today, I am reassured by Cheryl's comfort, even if only slightly. But as we make our way farther and farther from the house, from any sort of civilization, the less comforted I feel. I'd considered offering to stay home with Ruth although I'm honestly not sure if tonight's activity would be any less concerning than being alone in the house with Ruth and Redd Wright. And while the idea of enduring any other form of ceremony for Selma's birthday fills me with unease, the idea that other people will be at the church for the ceremony calms me down. Other people are good. Other people are safe.

After about forty minutes, we pull up in front of an old, dark brown church with no cars in the parking lot and only a single yellow light illuminating the front steps.

"This is the church where Redd Wright gave his first sermon," Hank says as he parks the car.

"It doesn't look open," I say.

Mary gets out of the car. "It is."

I glance over at Sam, fear creeping into me again. Before I

can speak, he says, "Don't worry," which, of course, only makes me worry.

Much like the Wailings' house or the Evergreen Mansion, the church is also surrounded by a cornfield. And like the many other cornfields I've seen since arriving in Iowa, this one also gives me an impending sense of discomfort. The darkness of the sky exacerbates that discomfort. Against it, the cornstalks practically look like they're glowing, their yellow leaves broken and luminescent, like shards of glass. I rub my arms beneath my sweater, wishing my goosebumps would go away, but they don't.

We walk up to the front of the church. Hank takes out a key, opens the door, and we all file inside.

The inside of the church is nearly pitch black. The only windows are stained glass so not much moonlight is shining through. Upon a closer look at them, I realize the stained-glass windows are cutouts of different types of animals. I can't make out what most of them are. The only one I recognize is a rooster.

Jimmy leans over to me, and I glean the hint of a smile on his face. "Spooky, huh?"

Out of politeness, I smile back. It's not the darkness that's spooky. It's the people I'm sharing the darkness with.

Hank and Mary walk down the main aisle together as Alice and Cheryl begin lighting candles around the room. Jimmy takes a stack of chairs and begins placing them in a circle at the front of the church. Sam takes my hand and leads me down the aisle, past all the pews. I can see the faint outline of three large crosses up ahead of us—two right-side up and the center one upside down, the same position of the crosses in the Wailings' living room, and on Redd Wright's TV program. By the time we reach the end of the aisle, Jimmy has seven chairs set up in a perfect circle in the front of the room, right beside the podium, right beneath the crosses. Cheryl lifts Selma out of the papoose across her chest and sets her on her lap. I take a seat next to Cheryl, and Sam sits next to me.

Suddenly, I hear the screech of nails on a blackboard and swing my head around. Hank is hunched over, moving around the outside of the circle, marking the wood floor with a piece of chalk. I consider asking if we're allowed to do that, but I feel like we're not even allowed to be here at all, so there's no point in asking now. He completes the circle and hands the chalk to Alice, who walks over to me and kneels to the ground, drawing a circle around my chair. When she's done, she gives the chalk back to Hank, who returns it to his pocket.

"Why is there a circle around me?" I ask. "Isn't this Selma's purification?"

There's a short silence, and then Cheryl interjects. "It is. But we'd like it if you could hold her." She hands Selma to me. "She's not supposed to be held by anyone blood-related during the purification."

I don't question her explanation because there's really no point. Anything I ask they'll have an answer for, and it will likely leave me even more confused than before.

Mary reaches into her bag and pulls out an old thermos and a stack of paper cups. She passes the cups to Alice, who takes one and passes it around until each of us has our own. Mary then takes her thermos around the circle and pours a small amount of dark liquid into each of our cups. I look down at the substance. It smells like ginger and fresh tar. I'm already thinking of ways to get rid of it without having to drink it, but I'm coming up short. If it's spiked with something, it came out of the same thermos that everyone else is drinking from, so that means theirs would be spiked too.

"What is it?" I ask Sam, gesturing to my cup.

"Black koicha," he whispers back. "It's basically a thick tea."

I hold my cup with one hand and Selma with the other, bouncing her gently on my knee. She's the only thing keeping me calm in this moment. Not just because of her soothing disposition, but because, for whatever reason, she makes me feel strong, capable. I feel the need to protect her. The memory of her falling through the air from the attic window is still fresh in my mind and I don't feel she'd be safe here tonight without me. In some strange way, we need each other.

Mary pours the liquid into her own cup and takes a seat. Everyone is looking at Selma and smiling. Or maybe they're looking at me. Even with the candles, it's too dark to read their full expressions. Mary takes a breath and begins singing something in what sounds like Latin. Instantly, everyone else joins in. Everyone except for me and Selma. My eyes find Sam, who hasn't missed a beat in joining in with the song. A wave of dissonance watches over me as I marvel at how foreign Sam appears to me in this moment. He feels so distant, so far from the man I know, that I feel as if I don't know him at all. That the person I'm looking at is merely a stranger in a room full of strangers.

They continue singing the song, and every line, every word, causes my discomfort to grow more and more. The tone of the song is mournful, almost off-key, and gives me the chills. But that's not the worst part about it. The worst part is that the longer they sing, the more I hear of the melody, the more uneasy I feel. Because I don't feel like it's *my* ears that are hearing it. I don't even feel like I'm there. I feel distant, as though the music is transporting me someplace else. I'm not sure which is safer, the place I'm going or the place I am now.

When the song ends, everyone raises their cup straight into the air, over their heads. I do the same. Not because I want to, but because I look over and see that my arm is raised, and I have no idea how it got there.

"To the Ever End," Mary says, locking eyes with me.

We all repeat after her. "To the Ever End."

They all lower their cups to their lips and drink the substance. I pull mine up to my mouth, the puppeteer's grip tight around my strings. Before drinking, I tell myself this means nothing.

That it's some concoction they've made. *Black tea*, as Sam called it. I remind myself that this family doesn't even drink, so I can't imagine them doing drugs of any kind. I tilt my head back and let the warm liquid slide down my throat. Even though it smells like fresh tar, it doesn't taste like it. It tastes like slightly bitter oatmeal and goes down like it too.

I drain my cup and look around the group. They're all looking at me. Not at Selma. At me.

Hank begins slowly stomping his foot. Soon everyone else follows suit. Then they begin to chant. I don't know what they're saying. It's not English and doesn't even sound like Latin. As they stomp and chant, the distance between us grows further, like the circle is expanding the louder they get. And the farther we expand, the brighter the candles become. Before long, their flames have practically turned into a blazing ring of fire around us. For the first time, everyone's face is fully illuminated. I can see their eyes now; they're solid white. I look down at Selma to see if her eyes are white too, but they're not. They're her usual dark brown, although against the fire they look almost black. I hold on to her tighter. I need to protect her. She needs to protect me.

I look back up and, through the blur of darkness and flames and white eyes I see another pair of eyes. Only they're not white. They're red, burning like embers. As I look into them, I feel the rawest form of fear deep, deep in my core. I want to scream, but I'm completely frozen, completely at their mercy. I try to keep my focus on them, suddenly desperate to see who they belong to, but as quickly as they appear, they melt into the flames, disappearing right in front of me.

The chanting turns back into singing, and now everyone is up on their feet, dancing. I don't know when it happened, but now they're also naked. I want to look away, to shut my eyes at the intimacy of how I'm seeing my fiancé's family, but I can't. I can't look away and I can't shut my eyes. I'm only able to stare at them, mesmerized by the rhythmic movement of their bodies, the wrinkles and rolls and blemishes on their skin—details that only a lover or a mother would normally be allowed to see. I try to make sense of what's happening, try to wrap my head around the strangeness of what's going on around me, but I can't. In my confusion, I become suddenly aware of how cold I feel, despite the flames, and I realize that I'm naked too. I sit up straighter in alarm, and the scratchy fabric of the chair rubs against my back. I look around our distant circle. Hank stands behind Mary, holding her against him. Jimmy kneels in front of Cheryl, his hands running over her body. I look for Sam, but I don't see him. I just see Alice, moving her naked body against some other man, but I don't remember anyone else being here with us. That's when Alice moves her head and I get a better look at the man's face; it's Sam. I blink as my vision blurs and everything around me continues to move. It can't be Sam. Alice is his sister. His *sister*. I try to yell out, but the chants and singing have now turned into loud moans and my yells are lost in noise.

I look down at my lap. Selma is gone. I've lost her. She was my responsibility and I lost her. That's when I see Cheryl. She's now holding Selma against her naked body as Jimmy holds her against his. I look around for Sam again. I need to talk to him. We need to leave. I see Alice, but now she's dancing alone. I start to stand up when I feel large hands on my shoulders. They run down my chest and over my breasts. I look up and see Sam standing behind me. He makes his way around the chair and kneels in front of me, spreading my legs apart. I need to talk to him about Alice, what I saw him doing with her, but I'm suddenly consumed by the pleasure coursing throughout my body. I look down at him to protest, to remind him that his family is here, that they'll see us. To remind him that we agreed to wait until our wedding night to go any farther than what we've done so far. But when I look down, all I see is the top of his head, moving between my legs, and I'm overcome with another wave of pleasure coursing through me. He's not going further than we've already gone, so I tell myself that he should keep going. That he shouldn't stop. I want him to stop. I want to tell him not to do this to me, not here, not now. But I don't. Because I can't. I can't move, I can't breathe. With the flames engulfing us all, I'm completely lost inside myself, and I don't think I'll ever get out.

Chapter Eighteen

WHEN I WAKE, I'm sitting upright on the couch in the Wailing living room. The family is all around me, watching Redd Wright on TV.

"What do you think, Margo?" I turn to my left and see Sam, who has his arm around me.

The hair at my roots feels damp, and some of it is still sticking to my face, as though I've just run three miles. But I also feel cold and burned at the same time, like I was running through a blizzard. I had been wearing a sweater earlier, and now it's gone and my T-shirt is all I'm wearing on top, and it's soaked with sweat. I feel my lip quivering. When I speak, my voice is hoarse as though I've just woken from a deep sleep. "What?"

"Should I grow a mustache like Redd Wright?"

I look from Sam to the TV, and back to Sam, unable to orient myself or remember what has happened.

Before I can speak again, Hank does, smoothing his moustache, "He was certainly *my* inspiration."

Mary grins and touches Hank's moustache. "Yes, he was."

Alice is curled up in an armchair like a cat, asleep. Jimmy and Cheryl are leaning against one another on the love seat. Ruth is staring at the TV the same way she always does, blackness continuing to creep up her arms. I look around, but I don't see Selma. What if something bad happened to her? What if they dropped her out a window again? She was my responsibility. They gave her to me to look after. And I lost her. I spin my head around the room.

"Where is she?" I get to my feet, but as soon as I do the blood rushes to my head and I'm back on the couch again, seeing nothing but black.

I can hear Sam's voice asking me if I'm all right as he rubs my shoulder.

"Where's Selma?" I mumble, trying to see straight. "What did you do to her?"

"Shh, it's okay," Sam says. "Selma's fine. See for yourself." I follow his pointing finger until I see her sleeping in her new wooden bed on the other side of the room.

My breathing is labored, my heartbeat irregular. I don't know the last thing I remember. Selma being dropped? Alice's apology about the doll? Alice. Something happened with Alice. Not the doll conversation, but something else. But what was it? I feel like I've been gone for a while. We went somewhere. Where did we go?

Sam must notice the crazed look in my eyes because he leans in and asks, "Are you sure you're okay?"

I shake my head and get to my feet. "I need to lie down." I start to head upstairs, but my brain is still foggy, and I almost fall over again. Sam catches me and carries me up the stairs to my bedroom, the whole time whispering, "It's okay, you're okay . . ."

I want to ask him how he knows I'm okay. I can't even manage to walk. I feel very far from okay. But my jaw feels too heavy to speak.

As he lays me down on the bed, my eyes immediately dart to the painting on the wall at the foot of the bed. The figures are still kneeling in front of the house. The cornstalks are still willowy and ominous. But something about it feels different, even more menacing. I feel like I know something about it now that I didn't before. Like there is something hidden among the cornstalks. Something I can't see, but that I know is there. And whatever it is makes me feel very afraid.

"What's the matter?" he asks, holding my hands in his.

I look straight into his eyes, trying to find my strength. "What happened?"

"What happened when?"

"Tonight. Tell me what happened tonight."

"Um, well . . . We had the dropping ceremony for Selma. You freaked out. We talked. Then Alice apologized for the doll thing. Then we went to Redd Wright's church—"

I sit up straighter. "The church. What happened at the church?"

He seems confused. "We had Selma's purification. We sat around in a circle, had some black koicha that my mom made—"

"Black koicha?"

"Yeah, I told you when you asked me earlier. It's just thick tea."

"Then what did we do?"

"We said a few prayers for Selma, gave her our blessing, and then we left. You weren't saying too much, but you seemed fine at the time."

Even though I can't remember what happened, what Sam is telling me doesn't sound right. I suddenly see red, orange. Embers. Fire.

"There was fire."

He lets out a confused laugh. "Fire?" I nod my head. "You mean the candles? I think Cheryl and Jimmy lit a few."

I rack my brain for a shred of anything familiar about the night. Deep in my ears, I can hear music, singing. "Was there singing?"

"Singing? You mean the hymns? My mother sang some old

church hymns, and I think a few of us joined in."

I want to believe him, but nothing he's saying fits into my memories. Then the worst part comes back to me, only I can't remember quite what the worst part is. I just know Alice is part of it. "You and Alice."

"What about me and Alice?"

I search for the right words. Maybe I can't recall what happened tonight, but I can recall the uncomfortable feelings I've felt for the past few days. "The way she looks at you—something isn't right about it. And she was in your room late the one night. I . . . I know she's your sister, but I can't help feeling there's something more going on. Something is so strange with her, with everyone."

I expect him to get defensive. To pull away. To tell me I'm crazy. But Sam doesn't do any of those things. Instead, he lets out a long breath, gets to his feet and paces the room for a moment before he finally speaks. "It's probably because she's not my sister."

I stare at him. "What?"

"Alice isn't my sister. Neither is Cheryl. This isn't my biological family."

I can hear my heart beating in my ears. Not because it's so strange that Sam is adopted, but because it validates my suspicions. "You're adopted?"

Sam tilts his head back and forth. "In a way. Alice and I used to play together when we were young. My home life wasn't very good, so I spent a lot of time with her and her family. When my parents moved away, I stayed here. The Wailings took me in."

I blink, trying to process the information he's just given me. Thoughts swirl through my mind, but the first one I can grasp is the conversation Sam and I had after Selma was dropped out of the window. The conversation where he told me that, as a baby, he too had been dropped out of the same window in the same ceremony. I shouldn't be upset that my fiancé wasn't dropped out of a window as a baby, but somehow, I am. Not because I ever wanted him to be dropped out a window, but because that was just another lie that Sam told me.

I finally manage to formulate a coherent sentence. "Why wouldn't you tell me this?"

"It's not an easy thing to talk about. They think of me as their family, and I think of them as mine. I try not to look at it any other way."

"But Alice—does she have feelings for you?"

"It's complicated," he says. "We . . . had this . . . secret thing a few years ago. I ended it, but I don't think she's ever really gotten over me."

"Did you two ever . . . ?"

"God, no. Like I said, I'm saving myself for you."

I feel icky. I feel wrong. In my head I see more flashes of orange and yellow and red. "You need to tell her," I stutter. "You need to tell her it's over."

"Believe me, I have. She knows, but she still gets jealous."

I let out a long breath. The scariest thing about how I feel in this moment is that I don't feel very much. The usual ball of anxiety in my stomach has vanished. The headache that's been threatening to surface since we arrived here is gone. I feel vacant.

When I don't speak, Sam kneels at my bedside, taking my hands in his. "Margo, you're the only one that I want. You're the one I've been saving myself for. Just like I'm the one you've been saving yourself for, right?"

At first, I don't say anything. Sam never seems to put any weight in my relationship with Katerina, and it always hurts, but right now I feel indifferent. I'm not going to argue with him, especially not this close to our wedding. Sam seems to be hanging on my response, waiting for an answer with a note of desperation I rarely see in his eyes.

Finally, I nod my head. He lets out what appears to be a sigh of relief that he masks with kissing my hands. But his kisses go from gentle and reassuring to sensual, like he can't seem to get enough. His fingers tighten around mine. When he finally meets my eyes, his whole body seems to stiffen. "I need you, Margo. You have no idea how much I need you. And I promise I will do anything to make you feel safe."

He gives me a tight kiss on my forehead, then leaves me alone to get an early sleep. I change into my usual blue nightgown, which tonight doesn't feel as awful as it usually does. Then I open my dresser drawer and pour my two antidepressants out of their bottle. I pick up my glass of water, but right before I take the pills, I stop and look at them. I could have sworn they used to be white and oval. Now they're round and light green. Still, they look familiar. I've seen these round, green pills before. Probably because they're my pills. That's all it is. They can't have changed. I probably just didn't notice what they looked like. I down the pills with a sip of water and turn out the light.

For the first time since I got here, I fall asleep instantly. And for the first time I dream. If you can call it dreaming. The dreams I have are unlike anything I've experienced before. I feel like I'm on a carnival ride at night, and everything around me is a blur of people and lights and noise. In the center of it all is a man with a suit and a thick moustache. It's Redd Wright. He's waving his arms and speaking words I don't understand. With all the movement going on I should feel sick, but I don't. I feel calm, almost sleepy. Redd looks at me for a moment and falls silent. He holds out his hand and smiles. "Are you ready, Margo?"

I nod my head and take his hand. The moment I do his face changes. The moustache disappears, his hair grows long, his eyes shrink to the size of pinpricks. His whole body begins to shrivel in his suit until there's nothing there. He's gone. Suddenly I hear a baby crying. It must be Selma. I spin around, looking for the source of the crying, but I can't find it anywhere. Then I look down at my feet. The suit isn't empty. There's something in it, or under it. I sift through the fabric until I see a baby hand, then the rest of the baby. She's crying. I pick her up and try to comfort her. I look down at her face. It isn't Selma. It's me.

"Margo?" I utter.

She stops crying and looks at me. She knows her name. I know my name. Around us, the carnival lights have gotten brighter, and I realize now that they're flames, and they're moments away from engulfing us. I hold baby me close, knowing very well that if either one of us dies, we both die. This is when I should be afraid. This is when I should wake up screaming. But I don't. Instead, I take a long breath that feels cool and soothing despite the heat of the flames and let them swallow us whole.

Chapter Nineteen

MONDAY

I WAKE UP without my alarm going off, promptly at eight thirty, from the best sleep I've had in months, maybe longer. My heart feels strong, my eyes alert, and I actually feel comfortable in my own skin. I lift my left hand and look at the ruby engagement ring on my finger. It's not so odd that Sam gave me Ruth's ring. Maybe she wanted him to have it. It's a beautiful ring. I must mean a lot to Sam for him to want to give me something so important to the family. I love Sam. I want to spend my life with him. Maybe his family is a little strange, but whose isn't? I can live with strange. I lived with strange my whole life, even before I knew what strange meant. I spent Thanksgiving at a motel with my mother because she thought we were in danger. I've been ashamed to bring friends over because I was worried they'd judge my life without really knowing it. I've been haunted by a single, solemn figure who may or may not have existed for as long as I can remember. I'm in no place to judge someone else's family.

I walk downstairs in my blue nightgown that somehow feels

like the most comfortable gown I've ever worn. I'm not sure why I made such a fuss about it before. It feels like it was made for me. When I reach the last step, I turn and make my way toward the dining room, feeling oddly like I'm floating yet more strong and grounded than ever. Sam's family is all seated at the dining table. Their faces light up when they see me.

Almost in unison, they say, "Good morning, Margo!" Even Ruth has turned her head away from the TV to look at me, the hint of what appears to be a smile on her face.

Sam stands immediately and approaches me. He takes my hand and kisses it. "You look beautiful," he says, and I feel my whole body warm with his words and his touch.

I begin to make my way to the dining table for breakfast, but Sam gently stops me. Today I don't have to eat any cold eggs for breakfast because today Sam is taking me into town to buy me breakfast and a coffee and spend some time together—just us.

Once I'm showered and dressed, we get in his car and drive into town. Even though it's chilly today, I keep my window down, letting the brisk autumn air dry my hair and burn my face. As we drive into service range, I feel my phone vibrating in my purse, but I don't even care to look at it. Instead, I look over at Sam, admiring the beautiful profile of his face—his chiseled jawline, thin lips, high cheekbones... everything about him is beautiful and I love him for that.

We go to *Galileo's*, and I barely even think about Rebecca while I'm there. Our meeting feels so long ago, and even the idea of Rebecca feels so distant. I just hope the barista doesn't remark that it's my second time there in a few days. Her gaze on me holds for a second longer than it did last time, which makes me think she remembers me, but she doesn't say anything, and for that I'm grateful.

After we get our drinks—a black coffee for him and a pumpkin spice latte for me—Sam gives me that million-dollar smile of his and tilts his cup toward me in a gesture of cheers. But I don't "cheers" back. I stare at him. Even after he turns away from me, I stare at him. For a moment, I'm frozen, overcome with the most vivid *déjà vu*. I see Sam at *Carousal's*, a coffee shop I used to go to after work. It was out of my way, but their peppermint tea was my mother's favorite when she wasn't feeling well. I'd sit and enjoy a book and a coffee for a half hour or so after work on cold winter days, then take a peppermint tea home to her. I can picture him sitting at a table across the room, a paper cup in his hand, watching me. My eyes lock with his; he gives me the same smile and nods the same way he did just now. I stopped going to *Carousal's* after my mother passed away. After I met Sam. With no reason to buy their peppermint tea, there was no reason for me to go back. I never went there with Sam. At least not to my recollection.

"Did you ever go to a coffee shop called *Carousal's* back in Chicago? It was in Lincoln Park, I think."

He thinks for a moment. "Doesn't ring a bell."

"Are you sure? I feel like I may have seen you there before we started dating."

He shrugs and holds the door open for me as we leave the coffee shop. "Must have been some other devilishly handsome guy."

We walk down the sidewalk. It's a lot less busy than Saturday, not that it was swarming with people then, but now that it's Monday everyone is back to work. I'll be back in the office myself on Thursday, but until then I tell myself I should take this time to relax. To try not to overthink about Sam or *Carousal's* or any other thing that could jar me out of this comfortable feeling I just sank into. But as soon as the relaxation seems to fully engulf me, my phone buzzes again, and I instantly wonder if it could be Rebecca. I pull it out of my purse and glance at it, quickly enough so Sam can't see, and feel my heart sink when I see it's a text from Jean, asking me a question about the Smithe account. I shoot her a quick reply and slide my phone back into my purse.

It's for the best that Rebecca hasn't texted me since we got coffee. She shouldn't text me. I shouldn't want her to text me. I'm marrying Sam. Sam, who's been here for me since the day we met. Sam, whose family I'm spending the week with. Sam, who loves me unconditionally and who has brought me joy and happiness at my lowest point. Sam, who's been the light when my world was dark. Sam. I'm marrying Sam. And I'm okay with that. I'm okay with that.

For a moment, I think Sam is going to ask who texted me, but he doesn't. "You know what I love about you?" he asks, wrapping his arm around my waist.

I feel my lips spread into a grin. "What?"

"You're smart. Not sassy-smart. Really smart."

"You don't think I'm sassy?"

He laughs. "You're sassy. But you're more smart than sassy."

I smile and sip my coffee, letting it warm my whole body. "Well, you know what I love about you?"

"I'm going to guess it's not my family situation."

"I love your family," I say, but the words don't feel like my own. We stop walking and I look up at him. "But even more, I love your presence."

His eyebrows wrinkle. "My presents?"

I laugh. "No, your *presence*. You have a very calming presence. It makes me feel safe."

He wraps his arms around me and pulls me into a hug. "I'm glad I can make you feel safe."

We step inside an antique shop and spend a good hour browsing through old dishes and vintage toys. Sam gets caught up in the antique gun section, talking with one of the store clerks about antebellum rifles, so I mosey over to a booth filled with vintage clothes. A mint green coat catches my eye and I pull it out.

"Pretty, isn't it?"

I look over and see an older store clerk in a floral skirt

looking at me as she organizes a box of comic books. "It is," I agree. I take a look at the price tag: two-hundred-ninety-nine dollars is far out of my budget for a coat.

The woman must read my expression because she adds, "There's a reason for the hefty price tag."

"Oh?"

"Have you heard of Redd Wright? He's one of those televangelists. You know, gives sermons on TV and all that."

The lightness I had been feeling since I woke up fades slightly. I try to fight it, but the pull back down to earth I experienced when Sam grinned at me in the coffee shop is tugging at me again. "Yes, I've heard of him."

"When he died last year, they auctioned off a bunch of his things from his home here in Fairbury. That coat belonged to his wife."

I nod my head and gently tuck the coat back in the rack of clothes. "Well, I see why it would be worth so much then."

"We have a few other items of his, but not many. This one family swooped in and bought most of it." I feel my heart catch in my throat. "It was a little crazy if you ask me." The woman leans in and lowers her voice. "Apparently, they even took out a second mortgage on their house to afford all the things they bought. I mean, I get he's a big deal to some folks, but there's no celebrity I'm *that* obsessed with. I'm pretty sure they would have bought his home if they could have afforded it."

I give a light laugh, but I'm suddenly uncomfortable. I think of the pale blue nightgown I've worn these past three nights. The nightgown that Mary gave me. My mind wanders around the bedroom I've been staying in, and then around the rest of the house, wondering how many items in their home once belonged to Redd Wright.

I reach into my purse, take out my phone and open up Google. I hardly know anything about this man that Sam's family is so obsessed with. I only know what they tell me, which is undoubtedly biased. But there must be a reason for their obsession, something that makes him so revered. As I begin to search Redd Wright, I feel a hand on the small of my back. "You find anything?" Sam asks.

"No," I say quickly, sliding the phone back into my purse. "I'm ready whenever you are."

We leave without buying anything and head back to the house, stopping once at the grocery store to pick up some things for supper.

We get back to the house as a few dark clouds are rolling in across the once-clear sky. I help Sam carry the groceries to the front door, but before I go inside, I turn to him. "Hey, do you think they'd mind if I went for a short walk?"

"No, of course."

"Thanks." I give him a kiss on the cheek and start off down the road, trying not to think about what I encountered the last time I walked down this road.

Once I'm far enough away from the house, I reach into my purse and pull out my phone. No bars. No service. I keep walking, trying to race the sun. Still no bars. Finally, as the sun is beginning to dip behind a wall of dark clouds, one bar appears. I open up my Google search for Redd Wright and hit *refresh*.

Seconds pass, then a minute. Just when I'm about to give up, my search results appear. The first three are all ads for Redd Wright's audio books, self-help books, and DVD box sets. I scroll through the other search results, but there's nothing incriminating. I'm not sure why I was expecting to find something incriminating, but I'm still disappointed. I scroll back to the top of the page and click *News*.

The first few articles date back to December of last year, all headlining his death. As I scroll through, I come across one headline in particular that catches my eye: *Group of Redd Wright Followers Accused of 1ˢᵗ Degree Murder*. I click on the link, but the page is taking forever to load. After nearly five minutes, with the sun now completely eclipsed by the clouds, a blank screen with the words *Failure to load page* pops up. I refresh and refresh and refresh, but the same error appears every time. With my surroundings now much darker than they should be for only five o'clock, I close the window, turn on my phone's flashlight, and make my way back to the house.

Whatever the article said, it doesn't necessarily mean anything, I tell myself. It's like the "Helter Skelter" incident. Paul McCartney wrote the song "Helter Skelter" for The Beatles, but when Charles Manson heard it, in his twisted mind he took it as a sign that ultimately led to a killing spree. People are sick. People take things too far. Even though I'm hardly Redd Wright's number one fan, I haven't seen him preach anything dangerous. He just drones on about prosperity and salvation and praising their Almighty Father. He doesn't seem like the type to condone murder.

I can see the house up ahead and keep walking. But as much as I walk, I don't seem to be getting any closer. I walk faster, but the faster I walk, the farther away the house gets. As I slow to a stop to catch my breath, I feel something brush across my feet. I look down and catch the tail end of what looks like a black snake slither past me. I step back, shining my light around frantically, but he's gone. I keep walking, hoping that eventually the house will get closer.

"*The end isssssss near . . .*" a voice hisses. I stop walking again and look around. Nothing. No one. I am alone. I walk forward. "*The end issssssss near,*" the voice hisses louder. I look at the ground ahead of me and see the snake, six feet away. It raises its head off the ground, flicking its tongue as it hisses, "*Sssstay away. Sssstay away. The end issssssss near.*"

Before I can respond, the snake lowers its head and slithers past me, heading away from the house. For a second, I want to follow it. I want to run after it. Chase it back to Chicago, back to my home. But there's no point in running. I can get only so far on foot. Besides, I can't leave Sam. Sam is my home now. Sam is my family. I turn back to the house. It's the only thing I can see for miles. I walk toward it, expecting it to move away from me again, but it doesn't. Within minutes, I'm there.

Chapter Twenty

MARY FEELS LIGHTHEADED right after supper, so she goes upstairs to lie down while Jimmy and I take care of the dishes.

I hand him a plate to dry. "So how did you and Cheryl meet?"

"Oh boy." He blows out a breath of air. "That feels like ages ago. I was actually the Wailings' family doctor before I got together with Cheryl."

"Really?" I'd known from my conversation with Cheryl that the Wailings already knew Jimmy before the two of them started dating, but I didn't know it was because he was their doctor.

He nods. "I was always very fond of them. Hank had a strong appreciation for the care I gave to Mary. He used to tease me that I'd be a good match for his oldest daughter. So, to humor him I let him set me up. I took her out to dinner one night and we hit it off. The rest is history."

I let his words sink in, but they feel off. I think back to my conversation with Cheryl, about how she'd said they hadn't been keen on her dating Jimmy when they first got together. But maybe both stories are true. Or maybe Cheryl was trying to offer me some comfort. "Wow," I say finally. "That's a really neat story." I rinse another plate and hand it to him. "How long have you been together?"

He laughs. "Well, I can honestly say sometimes it feels like we've been married thirty years. The family likes to joke that we act like an old married couple. But in reality, it's been, uh, let's see … five years now."

I offer him a smile and continue washing.

After a moment of silence, he adds, "They're really good people, you know." I look over at him again. Out of everyone I've met in Sam's "family," Jimmy seems the most normal. Maybe it's because he's an outsider, like me. Maybe I can learn something from him. Even if it took some time, the Wailings welcomed him into their family, accepting him as one of their own. As rattled as I still am from the events of yesterday, there's a piece of me that very much wants to be accepted by them, to be loved by them. Maybe because I know that this is it. This is my only chance at becoming part of a family. "I know some of their …" He searches for the right word, "traditions might be a bit strange. To be honest, I didn't care much for that Redd Wright fellow when I first joined the family. But after seeing what he's done for them over the years, I've had a change of heart."

"What do you mean, 'done for them'?"

"Oh, I mean he's given them hope. More than hope even. In a way, he's brought life to this family like I've never seen before in all my years as a doctor." He gives a small laugh. "If I could harness their love of Redd Wright and prescribe it to my other patients … I would be one happy man."

We continue washing and drying until the sink is empty. After we're done, as Mary rests upstairs, the rest of us gather in the living room to watch more of Redd Wright. I used to watch *Dancing with the Stars* on Monday nights, but I don't dare ask them to change the channel. And maybe there is something to be said for Redd Wright. But the skeptical side of me can't stop thinking about what the rest of that news article might have said. And why my brain can't seem to fill the hours of missing time from Selma's purification with anything but fire and Alice. Then again, maybe those are one and the same.

I excuse myself to use the washroom after an hour of listening to Redd Wright and step into the small half bath on the main floor near Ruth's room. It's decorated in mint green floral wallpaper and matching mint-green tile. Even the dated ceramic sink is mint green. It's enough green to make me sick so I try to get out of there as quickly as possible. As I wash my hands, I look at myself in the mirror. The bags under my eyes that I've lived with for so long are starting to return even though they were gone this morning. I'm feeling much less fresh now than I was then, like the restful sleep I finally got is starting to wear off, and the doubts in my mind can no longer be put to rest. I catch a glimpse of silver in my hair and take a closer look in the mirror. I've never had gray hair before, at least none that I've noticed. Just as I'm debating whether or not to pull it out, another one appears, and another and another, growing from my scalp at rapid speed. Within seconds, my whole head is completely silver. Just as quickly deep-set wrinkles etch their way across my face, and my eye sockets grow wide and hollow until I look like an old woman on the brink of death. But the transformation doesn't end there. My now-white hair begins to shed, falling into the mint green sink until there's nothing left. My once peachy skin is now white, then gray, then brown and black as I descend into the form of a decaying corpse.

And then, with a single blink, I'm back to how I was. As if it had never happened. As if it's all in my head.

I turn off the light and leave the bathroom, trying to get a firm grasp on my sanity. Before I can return to the living room I hear a humming coming from Ruth's bedroom, which is odd because she's not in her bedroom. She's back in the living room, watching TV with the others. I glance around the corner to be certain—sure enough, there she is, the back of her white head all that's visible as she stares at the screen. I look over at her bedroom door. It's open barely an inch and the light is on. The humming grows louder, as though the voice is calling me into the room. That's when I recognize the song being hummed: "Shine On, Harvest Moon."

I take a step closer to her door and push it open, barely enough to step inside without the hinges creaking. I look around the room. No one is there, and now the humming has stopped. I should feel uneasy, baited, tricked. But instead, I feel curious, like someone wants me to find something in this room. I glance around, but nothing new strikes my eye. The painting above the foot of Ruth's bed looks the same. Everything else also looks the same. I look at her nightstand, at the plastic pill bottles reflecting under the light. I lean down to get a closer look at them, the orange bottles transparent. When I come across the bottle filled with small, round green pills, I pick it up and open it; they're identical to my antidepressants. I look at the label. They're not antidepressants. They're Ambien. Which means what I've been taking these past few nights aren't antidepressants either. They're also Ambien. Someone switched my pills. Someone wants me to sleep so soundly that I don't notice anything. So soundly that I'm completely unaware of another person coming into my room in the middle of the night. So soundly that I wouldn't even feel them making an injection into my arm. My mind races as I try to come to terms with this absurd notion. This absurd notion that is slowly becoming a reality as I stare at the label on the pill bottle. The wild thoughts swirling in my mind land on Alice. As jealous as she may be, I can't imagine her doing anything like this. But because I can't imagine something doesn't mean it's not real.

I push up my sleeve and look to the crook of my arm. To my surprise, the small red dot that appeared the other day is gone. I run my finger over the place it had been, as if touching the area will prove to me that it was real, that it had been there.

But not even that does anything to validate that it was ever there to begin with. My skin is perfectly clear. More than clear. It's practically glowing. Shiny and new, like I've spent hours in a steam room.

I shut my eyes and set the bottle back down where I found it. Then I quickly leave Ruth's room and barely stop in the living room on my way upstairs, only pausing to excuse myself for the rest of the evening. Sam is the only one who seems to hear me, but when he tries to ask me if everything's all right, I assure him that I'm fine and make my way up the rest of the stairs to my bedroom.

I shut the door behind me and immediately rush over to the dresser. I pull out my toiletries bag and fish around for my pills, nearly dropping the bag on the floor when I find them. I pop off the cap and pour them out in my hand. They're no longer round and green. They're oval and white, the same as they always were. And I'm that much closer to going crazy. I twist the cap back on the pill bottle and put it back in my bag.

Just as I finish closing the drawer, I hear Sam's voice, panicked, in the other room. "Mom? MOM!"

I leave my room quickly and follow his voice to Mary and Hank's bedroom. Sam, Hank, and Alice gather around Mary, who convulses on the bed. Her eyes have all but rolled back into her head, and there's a thick foam of saliva around her mouth.

"Oh, Almighty Father, please bestow upon Mary the miracle you have given us. Take away her pain and reverse the sickness inside her . . ." Hank prays as he attempts to hold her down.

Before I can react, Cheryl and Jimmy enter the room. Jimmy pushes past me on his way to Mary's bedside and begins examining her. Cheryl rushes to his side. After several fruitless attempts to subdue Mary, Cheryl glances over at me and whispers something to Jimmy that sounds a lot like, "What about Margo?"

"I'm sorry," I stutter. "I can leave—"

I turn to leave, but Jimmy rushes over to me. He grabs my wrist, his eyes pleading with mine. "No, come closer."

He guides me to the bed, to Mary. Her convulsions aren't ceasing. If anything, they're growing more violent. Jimmy takes my other wrist and places my hands on Mary's chest, just above her breasts. Instantly, I feel a transfer of energy from my body to hers. My hands and arms are warm and tingly, like metal conductors of power. After a moment, her body stops convulsing and goes completely still, but I don't let go. I don't think I could even if I wanted to.

After a few seconds, my whole body starts to shake until finally I go limp, falling into Sam. He holds me, smoothing my hair. I manage to open my eyes in time to see Mary open hers. Hank takes a damp cloth and lays it on her forehead. Her clothes are soaked through with sweat and she smells like urine. I'm afraid for her, but I'm also afraid for myself. Because I'm not fully aware of what just happened. I'm not aware of what I may be capable of.

Almost in unison, everyone in the room shifts their focus from Mary to me, looking at me with expressions I can't read. They look afraid, yet in awe. Alice's eyes are wide, like she truly can't believe what just happened. Jimmy's breathing is fast and irregular. Cheryl's hands are clasped over her mouth and tears are streaming down her face.

Sam helps me to my feet. "Come on. Jimmy and Hank will help get her cleaned up." His tone is mournful but casual, like this is an everyday occurrence.

The silence that's filled the room is deafening. As we make our way to the door, I feel everyone's eyes following me. Cheryl, who had been standing closest to the doorway, reaches out and gently places her hands on my arm. I turn my head slowly to look at her. Her eyes are red as the tears continue to come. "Thank you," she musters, her voice cracking.

I don't know what to say. I don't feel like I should be thanked.

I don't understand what happened. I don't even know if I liked it.

Sam walks me to my room and once we're inside he closes the door behind me. I sit down on the bed. "What happened?"

"She has congestive heart failure. It makes her blood pressure skyrocket, and sometimes when that happens, she has a seizure."

I don't mean to negate her heart condition. I can't imagine what she must be going through. But, in all honesty, I wasn't asking Sam about Mary. I was asking him about what I'd done to her.

"I mean, what happened with me?" I look down at my hands. They're pale, as if every ounce of blood that had been pulsing through them has been drained. "What did I do to her?"

Sam takes a seat next to me on the bed. He takes my hands in his, but I don't feel his touch. "You saved her life."

"I don't understand. How?"

Sam takes a long breath like he's going to say something prophetic, but ultimately, he shrugs his shoulders. "I don't know. Hank and Mary are loyal followers of Redd Wright. He believes in the powers of healing through gods and spirits. That sometimes certain people are able to channel powers within themselves to help others. If I had to guess, I'd say that's exactly what you did for her back there."

I shake my head. "But that's not something I believe in. I didn't even know what I was doing."

"You don't have to believe. My family has worshipped one God for most of their lives. Whether or not others believe in Him is irrelevant. Because He's real."

I look from my hands to Sam, thrown by his words. "So, you believe in Him too?"

"I do," he says with certainty. It's a side to him I'm not familiar with, and that realization makes my discomfort grow. My mind is suddenly wrestling with the Sam I used to know and the Sam sitting next to me, and I struggle to make sense of how they're the same person. While religion has never been a huge topic of conversation in our relationship, I always gathered that Sam felt indifferent about God. His decision to save himself for marriage always felt like a choice he made to appease his family, not because he believed what they believed. He'd even said that he didn't agree with a lot of the rituals they participated in. He always put his family's beliefs at a distance, so I'd grown to believe that his beliefs weren't aligned with theirs. But perhaps I've been wrong.

When I don't say anything, he speaks again. "He can protect us in ways I never knew were possible. I would never tell you what to believe, Margo. I hope you know that. But I do hope you'll keep an open mind. He's clearly blessed you with a gift of healing that I know my family has never seen before."

"Did you know I had this gift when we first met?"

"I'm not even sure if you had it when we first met." He pulls away from me slightly. "To be honest, I think it was awakened at Selma's purification last night. Some people are very susceptible to ceremonies of that nature. In trying to awaken Selma's spirit, maybe we awakened yours."

I nod my head, processing. The logical side of me doesn't believe this. Any of this. That side of me says there's no such thing as magical powers. That gods and spirits aren't real. That there never were any monsters under my bed that my mother needed to protect me from. That people are just people, and there's nothing special about them.

The other side of me, the hopeful side, can't stop thinking about what just happened in Mary's bedroom. How, if that had been my own mother, I would have bled myself dry to keep her well.

Maybe Sam's right. Maybe something in me was awakened at Selma's purification. But if it were such a significant night, why can't I remember it?

"Margo, I have a favor to ask of you." Sam leans forward again, looking so deeply into my eyes that I'm actually afraid to look away. "Marry me." I'm about to say that we're already getting married, but he continues before I can. "Marry me now. This week, before we leave. It doesn't have to be a big ceremony. Just something small."

"Sam, I don't know—"

"Mary has been sick for a long time. And to be honest, I don't know how much longer she has. I don't know if she'll make it to the wedding. I know . . ." His voice cracks and I see his eyes are brimming with tears. "I know they aren't my biological family. But they've been more of a family to me than my real family ever has. And I know it would mean the world to Mary to see us get married."

I don't say anything at first. I'm struggling to comprehend how the life I had only four days ago when we arrived here is the same life I have now. I don't even feel like the same person. I love Sam. I want to marry Sam. But to marry him right now, with everything that's happened, doesn't feel right. I wish it did, but it doesn't.

"Maybe we can move our wedding date up," I offer, trying to meet him in the middle. "Aim for next month." The next words out of my mouth are almost, I *can ask Rebecca about venues*—but somehow, I stop myself.

"I just thought that . . ." Sam lets out a long breath. "Since our wedding was going to be fairly small anyway, it wouldn't make much of a difference to you if we got married in two days or two months."

I feel my guard come up. "Because I don't have family?"

"No, no—" He tries to backtrack, but we both know what he meant. "I mean, we could always have a reception and renew our vows later on."

"I'm sorry, I—"

He shakes his head and wipes his eyes. "It's okay. I know it's probably difficult for you to understand. But think of your mother." His words sting my ears even though I don't want them to have enough power to do so. "If you could have given her anything in the world before she passed, wouldn't you have wanted to show her that you were happy? That your life would continue?"

My last moments with my mother are hardly something I try to think about. The pain is too great, the regret too overpowering. But whether I want to think about those moments or not, they're there now, at the forefront of my mind, as though Sam summoned them without my permission.

"I'm sorry," says Sam, reading the pain in my eyes. "I shouldn't even ask this of you. Please, forget I mentioned it." He stands and kisses me on the forehead before heading for the door to leave me alone. Alone. Although there may be a difference between being alone and being lonely, if it simmers long enough, alone eventually turns into lonely. I don't think I can bear to be lonely anymore.

"Sam, wait." He stops at the door and turns to me. "Okay."

"Really?"

"Yes," I say, unsure if it's the loneliness talking or my desire to marry Sam. "Let's get married."

Sam walks back over to me, takes my hand, and kisses it. "Thank you."

Before bed, Sam suggests we share the good news with his family. Hank has helped Mary bathe and cleaned her up, and there are now fresh, clean sheets on the bed she's sitting in. She has more color in her skin and energy in her voice than I remember her having before the seizure. Perhaps it's partly the fast recovery, partly the news we've shared with her. As soon as we tell her our plan, she claps her hands and immediately begins listing everything they need to do to prepare for the occasion. Jimmy and Cheryl seem surprised, but happy for us. Hank grins and says, "No time like the present," and Alice even hugs me. I feel, for a fleeting moment, like I've made the right decision. And, selfishly, this means that when we have our own wedding ceremony, with our close friends and obligatory business associates, Sam's family won't be there. As soon as I have the thought, I feel like the worst future daughter-in-law in the world. But I tell myself that's not true. That I'm doing a good thing for Sam's family by marrying him now. That even though it's hardly a gesture that will bring my mother back, it's something that I hope would have made her as happy as it's making Mary.

"That gives me two days to prepare everything. It's tight, but we'll make it work. An evening ceremony would be ideal, of course."

Two days would mean we'd get married Wednesday evening. We had been planning on leaving Wednesday, since I work Thursday. "Actually," I interject, "Sam, we were thinking of doing the ceremony tomorrow, right?"

"Tomorrow?" Mary jumps in before Sam can respond. "Oh, no. It has to be Wednesday. There's going to be a harvest moon! Can you imagine it?"

I'm about to protest that I have work on Thursday, but I have a strong feeling that this wedding will take total precedence over my lowly accounting job. The fact that I'm even thinking about work with my wedding happening in two days creates a hollowness inside of me. I feel numb, empty, raw. But I can't tell Mary any of this. I can't let her down. Besides, I haven't taken a sick day since my mother passed. I can afford to take one now.

"Anywho!" Mary concludes after a good half hour of wedding talk. "We should get a good night's rest. Lots to do tomorrow!"

Suddenly, Rebecca appears in my mind. I'll need to let her know we won't be needing her services anymore. That I won't be needing her anymore. I don't know when I'll have the chance. I could try to get far enough away from this house to text her the news. Or I could try to find a time to meet with her tomorrow and tell her in person. I'd prefer the latter. I want to tell Rebecca myself. I want to see her again. As if seeing her again will either confirm or deny that I made the right choice in moving my wedding up to two days from now.

Hank playfully shoos us out of their room. Sam walks me to my door.

"Thank you. This really means a lot to her."

I put on my bravest smile and lean into him as he kisses my forehead. We go our separate ways, him to his room and I to mine. As I get ready for bed, I can't help but feel a vague sense of relief. Perhaps it's because Sam's family is happy again. Perhaps it's because, with only two days left of this trip, I can see the light at the end of the tunnel.

I plug my phone into its charger and set it on the nightstand. Then I climb into bed in my restrictive nightgown and turn off the light. The moment I close my eyes I'm overcome with sleep. But no sooner do I fall asleep than I find myself fully awake and standing at the back of a long, dark church that feels more familiar to me than it should. The only light in the church is coming from the red stained-glass window with a rooster design on it. At the end of the center aisle, I can see the outline of four people, facing away from me. As I walk closer, I can see that the four of them are each a different size and height, and they are all kneeling on the floor.

The familiar voice in my head suddenly surrounds me, echoing off the walls of the church, but I don't understand the words it's saying. "*Statim finis . . . Statim finis . . . Quod umquam finis adest . . .*"

As I reach the front of the church, I have a clearer view of the four heads. The one farthest to the left is the smallest, hairless and black like coal. The one beside it is larger, with red burning through the black of the skin, like molten lava at the surface of a volcano. The third from the left is slightly smaller, charcoal gray in tone, with what appears to be straw for hair. The one on the far right is the most different. It's decorated with a lavish, colorful headdress made of what appear to be peacock feathers.

I stop in my tracks, suddenly terrified to move any farther. Something isn't right. I need to leave. I need to run away. But the moment I try I feel two invisible hands grab my wrists and drag me forward. I scream, but no sound comes out. Instead, the voice in my head gets louder. "*Semper in fine . . . Statim finis . . . Semper in fine . . . Statim finis . . . Est semper finis . . .*"

I fight harder, but there's no use. I feel the skin on my knees being scraped off as I'm dragged to the free space beside the body with the headdress. My wrists still clasped in front of me, bound by invisible ties, I kneel beside them, bowing to something I cannot see as the voice around me pains my ears.

"*Semper in fine . . . Statim finis . . . Semper in fine . . . Statim finis . . . Est semper finis . . .*"

I feel tears streaming down my face as my body remains forced in the bowed, contorted position that it's in. The voice around me turns to multiple voices, echoing in unison, right in my ear. I turn my head to my left and see that the person in the headdress is Sam. His face is bright white, his eyes are black, and he speaks the same words as the rest of the voices.

"*Semper in fine . . . Statim finis . . . Semper in fine . . . Statim finis . . .*" he chants, meeting my eyes with his black holes, willing me to chant with him.

I have the urge to scream again, but I know I won't be able to. So instead, I hang my head and let the only words that I can speak come out of my mouth. "*Semper in fine . . . Statim finis . . . Semper in fine . . . Statim finis . . . Est semper finis . . .*"

I'm freezing cold and wet. My knees burn, my wrists throb, and my body feels bruised all over. All I can see in front of me is a blinding pale blue strobe light that burns my eyes. I can still hear the voice chanting those words and I realize that the voice is mine. As my vision comes into focus, I see the outline of a figure through the blue light. It's the outline of Redd Wright. When

I finally grasp my surroundings, I realize that I'm kneeling in front of the TV in the dark of the Wailing living room, naked and drenched in sweat, with my hands clasped in front of me in prayer.

With a wave of consciousness spreading over me, I let my arms fall to the shag carpeting, my body going limp under its own weight. I gasp for air, shaking uncontrollably. When I try to stand, I find that my legs are too weak to hold my weight, and I stumble backward onto the couch. I can't pull my eyes from Redd Wright on the TV screen. Even when I feel a soft tugging on my hair on the right side of my head, I can't move. The tugging continues, and I realize it's a familiar feeling. Soft teeth like dull needles find their way through my hair in a repeated brushing motion. Finally, I manage to turn my neck and come face to face with Ruth. She isn't staring at the TV. She's staring at me, her feeble, blackened hand gripping the handle of an old hairbrush that she continues to run through my hair. Without breaking eye contact, I grab an afghan from the couch and wrap the scratchy blanket around me. We sit there for the longest moment, staring at each other. The only movement around us is her hand moving up and down. I feel as though I should be afraid, but something about the action feels soothing. A warmth washes over me as I fall back into my childhood, my mother's gentle hands brushing my wet hair after a bath. But this is not my mother. The memory fades away, and the fear that I thought I'd avoided takes its place and I begin to tremble. Ruth's hand freezes halfway through my hair. After a moment, she lowers her hand, holding the brush in her lap, and turns her head back to the TV.

I stand, keeping the blanket wrapped around me, and make my way over to the bottom of the stairs. I am going crazy. I feel it in my bones. Something is very wrong with me. There is a power pulsing through my veins. I can feel it. But it doesn't feel good. It feels dangerous.

I climb the stairs on tiptoe, praying for the floorboards not to creak. It isn't the first time I've sleepwalked. Which is what this was. Sleepwalking. My mother did it too, especially near the end.

Before she got sick, when I still lived with her, I once awoke in the middle of the night to find her standing in the entranceway of our house, completely naked, staring at the front door.

I approached her gingerly. "Mom? You okay?"

Her eyes stayed fixed on the door. "Let him in."

"Mom, no one's there."

"Let. Him. In."

"Mom, come on. Let's go back to—"

Before I could finish my sentence, something knocked three times on the other side of the door.

"Come in!" she called. The handle of the door started to turn, but I ran over and grabbed it. Without letting go, I put the chain on the latch and pulled a chair in front of it. When I turned back to my mother, she was already heading back to bed, still in her trance. She didn't remember any of it in the morning.

The same incident repeated itself for the next three nights. Then it stopped as suddenly as it had started. When I asked her if she was finally able to get a good night's sleep with no disturbances the morning after it stopped, she said yes. Then she told me about the visitor that had come to our house while I was at work the day before.

"A visitor?" I pressed.

"Mmhmm."

I felt my heart racing. "What kind of visitor?"

"Oh, you know," she said casually as she made her tea. "I invited him in."

"You invited him in?" I nearly knocked over my teacup. "Who? What did he look like?"

"Who?"

"The visitor."

"What visitor?"

I looked at her blankly. "The visitor you said came to our house yesterday."

She gave an amused laugh as she set her cup of tea down on the table and took a seat across from me. "We didn't have any visitors yesterday." She put the back of her hand to my forehead. "Are you feeling alright, dear?"

I didn't ask her about the visitor again. I just let the whole situation gnaw at my stomach all day and all night. The very next day she fell ill. A week later they diagnosed her.

I think about this as I shut the bedroom door quietly behind me, careful not to wake anyone in the house. My bed is perfectly made, and my nightgown lies primly across it without a crease. As if I'd never even slept in it, never even gone to bed. I don't want to put on the nightgown, but something tells me I have to. Something wills me to put it on, and I know that if I don't, something bad will happen. So I lift it up and step inside of it, letting the material scratch my damp skin as I pull it over my body.

Before I turn off the light, I catch a glimpse of my wrists. Around them are red marks, crevasses dug deep into my flesh. I turn the light off before I have to look at them anymore. But the pain isn't what prevents me from sleeping. It's the idea that maybe the voices are right, like they were right for my mother.

Maybe the end is near.

Chapter Twenty-One

TUESDAY

I DON'T SLEEP at all the rest of the night. Not only do I not want to sleep, but I'm pretty sure my body won't let me even if I wanted to. I lie on top of the covers, letting my sweat soak into the comforter, watching my room slowly lighten with the dawn. When the room is light enough, I examine my wrists, expecting the marks around them to fade and heal like the pinprick on my arm, but they don't. By daybreak the red lines in my flesh are as deep as they were when I awoke from that nightmare. I don't know how I did it to myself. Wire maybe? String? My hair ties sometimes leave indents in my wrists, but nothing like that. I only hope they disappear eventually.

I reach for my phone on the nightstand, but it's not there. I quickly sit up, feeling a sudden surge of anxiety. I look at the floor, behind the nightstand, in my bed, under my bed, but my phone is none of those places. I know I had it before I went to bed. I plugged it into the charger and placed it on the nightstand. And now it's gone.

I pull off the covers and get to my feet. If this is some sick

194

joke that Alice or someone is playing on me, it's the furthest thing from funny. As I head for the door, I pass my reflection in the dresser mirror. I've spent all night in this godforsaken nightgown and I'm not going to spend another minute in it. Whatever peace I felt yesterday feels like it's fully worn off now, and I could care less about Mary's stupid nightgown. I peel the lace and satin off me, rolling down the sleeves and tugging my wrists through the delicate cuffs. I pull on leggings and a sweatshirt and go downstairs.

Ruth is sitting in her chair, staring open-mouthed at Redd Wright on TV. The very sight of the living room sends a chill down my spine as whatever the hell happened last night comes flooding back to me. My wrists throb. My knees burn. And I can practically feel the teeth of Ruth's brush tugging through my hair. The thought of the action doesn't seem calming anymore, and I don't know how I ever thought it was. The idea of it now makes me shiver. I push down the urge to scream, to shut my eyes, to pinch myself, to make sure I'm no longer dreaming.

I swallow, my mouth dry. "Good morning, Ruth."

She slowly turns her head toward me. A noise comes out of her mouth, followed by silence, and then she turns her head back to the TV.

Sam is drinking coffee and talking with Hank at the dining table. Before I enter the room, I take a breath. One more day. I just need to survive one more day. Maybe no one took my phone. Maybe I misplaced it. Maybe Sam has it for some reason.

Hank spots me before Sam does. "Good morning, darlin'!"

I pull the smile onto my face. "Good morning."

Sam turns in his chair, a smile spreading across his face. "Well, if it isn't my blushing bride."

"Bride-to-be," I correct him. I rest my hand on Sam's shoulder. "I'm sorry to interrupt—"

"Not at all," says Hank, getting to his feet. "We're just talking shop—getting ready for the big day and all." Hank gives me what feels like a misplaced wink, then picks up his coffee mug and heads toward the kitchen.

Sam rests his hand on mine, rubbing it with his thumb, and for a moment my mind goes blank. Sam's always had that effect on me. I used to find it intoxicating, but right now, in this moment, I find it rather frustrating.

"You're not wearing the nightgown," he says, his million-dollar smile faltering as he looks over my outfit. "Look, I know it's uncomfortable, but my mother really—"

I wave my hand dismissively. The last thing I want to talk about right now is that nightgown. "I know, I just needed a break," I say quickly, needing to get to the point of why I interrupted him and Hank to begin with. "Have you seen my phone?"

Sam's brow furrows and his lips curl in like he's thinking. "Not since yesterday."

"Are you sure?" There is a clank in the kitchen, followed by the chatter and laughter of Mary and Hank. I lower my voice slightly. "I know I left it on my nightstand before bed, and when I woke up this morning it was gone."

Sam glances to the kitchen too and gets to his feet. "Do you think someone took it?"

"I don't know," I say, feeling suddenly foolish. "Maybe. I just—you know me. Have I ever once misplaced my phone since we started dating?"

Sam thinks for a moment. "No."

"Exactly. I never misplace it. I have the feeling that someone might have—"

I don't get to finish my sentence because before I have the chance, something catches my eye out the window behind Sam. On the road, parked down the street from the Wailings' mailbox, is a yellow Volkswagen beetle. I feel my heart rate begin to rise.

Sam seems to notice that my attention is elsewhere and starts to turn to see what I'm looking at, but I put my hand on his arm, trying to keep his attention with me. "Sam, I—" He looks back to me. "I can't find my phone," I finish lamely. "If you do see it, would you let me know?"

"Um, yeah, of course," says Sam, clearly confused.

"Do you mind if I go for a run this morning?"

He looks taken aback. I'm not sure if it's because I rarely go running, or if it's the timing of me wanting to go for a run now. "A run?"

Before I can answer Mary comes bustling through the swinging kitchen door, followed closely by Hank.

"There she is!" Mary coos upon seeing me, walking towards me with her hands outstretched. "There is the beautiful bride-to-be!"

I force the smile back on my face and try my best to slow my heartbeat. "Good morning, Mary."

Mary turns to Sam, and I take the opportunity to glance out the window again. The yellow beetle is still there, although I'm not sure for how long. "Sam, isn't she beautiful. Even if she's not wearing her nightgown!" she says to me, twisting her tone into a mock-scolding one that throws me off-kilter. "Are you all ready to get started? There's plenty to do before your big day!"

My mind reels as I try to think quickly. I can't let Rebecca drive away without seeing her. Especially now that I can't find my phone. That was the last thing I had that connected me to the outside world. "I can't wait," I say brightly, forcing my smile even wider. "But I was actually telling Sam that I'd like to go for a run first if that's okay."

Mary looks at me, a crease forming between her eyes. "A run?" she says, like the word is completely foreign to her.

"Yeah." I awkwardly bend down and rub my right knee. "My knees get so stiff when I'm not exercising."

Sam looks like he's seeing right through me. I will him not to open his mouth, but he does anyway. "You really want to go for a run? You hardly ever exercise—"

I force down the urge to roll my eyes. "But I walk a lot. And

I've hardly walked at all since we got here. I really need to go for a run. I won't be long."

With that, I quickly walk to the front door and step into my gym shoes, pulling them on as fast as I can. In my wake, I hear Mary murmur something to Sam. She sounds worried, concerned. I hear Sam's voice, consoling her, and then, "Margo—"

I turn the doorknob and am about to open the door when Sam comes rushing around the corner. "Hey—" he slows to a stop in front of me. "Do you have to go for a run this morning?"

"Why? What's wrong?"

Sam nods his head toward the dining room. "My mother, she—she was really looking forward to preparing for the wedding with you."

"And we will," I say quickly. "When I get back. Okay? I promise. I just need to do this."

He looks at me, his face unreadable. For a moment I think he's going to stop me. That he's not going to let me leave. But that's not how Sam is. That's not how he's ever been. So he nods his head and steps out of my way.

I offer him a genuine smile. "Thank you."

I close the door behind me, silently praying that he won't look out the window. That he won't be suspicious about where I'm going. When I'm halfway down their driveway, I glance back at the house. From what I can see, no one is watching me. At least no one that I can see.

The yellow beetle is still parked down the road. Through the slightly tinted windows, I see her, sitting in the driver's seat, sunglasses on, jaw tight. Suddenly her body shifts and she pulls off her sunglasses. She sees me. And I see her. She's here.

I get to the end of the driveway and go left at the mailbox, despite Rebecca being parked to my right. I can't go toward her car. If anyone is watching, I need to get out of their line of view. I start at a jog down the road, behind the tall grass, until I'm shielded from the view of the house. As I jog, I hear a motor start up, and the rev of an engine growing closer to me. I shut my eyes and let my legs slow to a stop. I turn to my right in time to see Rebecca pull up a few yards away from me. I bolt across the street, go around to the other side of the car, and climb into the passenger's side.

Without so much as a hello, Rebecca steps on the gas and drives down the road until we can no longer see the Wailing house in the distance. Finally, she slows the car to a stop and puts it in park. I haven't taken my eyes off her. My heart is pounding against my ribcage, and I know it's not only from the run. "Rebecca, what—what are you doing here?"

She looks at me for the first time since I got into the car. "I know, I shouldn't be here."

She's right. She shouldn't. But I don't care. I'm so relieved to see her I have to stop myself from smiling. "It's okay," I say quickly.

"I just—after our last conversation, I've been worried about you. I know the Wailings can be . . ." she seems to be searching for the right word. "Private," she settles on. "I tried texting you and calling you, but your phone went right to voicemail."

"The service is terrible out here," I say. "Plus, I can't find my phone."

She looks at me for a long moment. "Is everything okay?"

I open my mouth to say yes, that everything is fine, but that would be a lie. And I don't want to lie. "Sam and I are getting married tomorrow."

Her eyebrows rise, the mask of the wedding planner vanishing. "Tomorrow?"

I nod. "Yeah."

"Is that . . . is that what you want?"

I let out a laugh that comes out sharper than I mean for it to. "Honestly, I don't even know what I want anymore," I say truthfully. "I love Sam. I do. And he loves his family. He doesn't know how long his mother's health is going to hold up. This is what she wants and he's trying to make her happy. And I know I shouldn't do something like this just because it will make someone else happy, but if my mother were here, I know I'd want to do whatever I could to make her happy."

Rebecca nods her head, sitting back in her seat. She's going to say something, I can practically hear her sorting through her thoughts. I want to speak, but I know I need to give her the silence to think.

"How long do you have?" she asks.

I glance at the clock on the dashboard. "Forty-five minutes? An hour, tops."

"Come on." She puts the car into drive. "I want to show you something."

We're silent as she drives in a direction through town I've never been before. There are very few homes and businesses, and I soon realize that she's turning onto the highway. Rebecca must sense my concern, because it's then that she says, "Don't worry, it's not very far."

We drive along the highway for about ten minutes. Up ahead, I see the first sign of civilization since we left downtown Fairbury—a roadside sign that reads *ROBERT MILLER'S MUSEUM OF DEATH NEXT EXIT*. I don't give it much thought until Rebecca takes the next exit. Surely the Museum of Death can't be our destination. But I'm proven wrong when she turns into the nearly empty parking lot and pulls into a spot right by the entrance. I look at Rebecca, my brow furrowed. She turns to me, her small half-smile hanging on her lips.

"Do you trust me?" she asks.

I nod my head and we get out of the car.

The entrance of the museum is hardly interesting. It feels more like a waiting room at a dentist's office than a museum, with wall-to-wall beige Berber carpet, a half-dozen black chairs that look like they belong in a conference room, and a ticket booth at the center of the room on the farthest wall that reminds me of the ones at the DMV—covered in fake wood paneling, with a metal speaker centered on a panel of smudged and scratched plexiglass. Behind the glass is a young woman with jet black hair and a nose ring. "How many?" she asks without looking up from her computer screen.

"Two, please," Rebecca answers.

The young woman types a few things into the computer, then prints out two tickets for us. She hands them to Rebecca through a small rectangular gap at the bottom of the glass and recites what sounds like words she's said a hundred times. "Welcome to Robert Miller's Museum of Death. Absolutely no photographs or video recording is allowed inside the museum. There is no time limit on how long you can spend inside the museum, but please keep in mind that we will close promptly at 5 p.m., and if for any reason you exit through the curtain behind me on your left, you will not be able to go back in. Some of the images and videos you may see in the museum are of an adult nature and could be disturbing, with footage of actual deaths shown in our theater, so please proceed through the curtain on your right with caution. Thank you for joining us today."

She sits back down in her seat and returns to her computer. Rebecca looks back at me with a reassuring smile. "Are you ready?"

I take a deep breath, searching for the courage to do this. My mother's death still feels so raw, so painful, so close to where I am now. I don't know if this is what I need. I don't know if this is what I want. But as I told Rebecca, I trust her. If anything, she's been the only person around me lately that I feel I can fully trust. When I don't find the courage, I decide that the courage will come. I stand and follow Rebecca through the black curtain.

I'm not sure what I expected the Museum of Death to look like, but this is hardly it. The Berber carpet continues throughout the rest of the building, which is divided into sections with cheap walls, curtains, and door frames. The walls are filled with photographs and blocks of text—stories about serial killers, grave robbers, murderers, evil surgeons, and any other type of human connected to death that you could imagine. Rebecca meanders on in front of me, looking around casually, as if she's been here many times before, but I take my time. I read about John Wayne Gacy, whose victims were found in his home in the suburb of Des Plaines, just a short drive from Chicago. I read about Aileen Wuornos, who robbed and murdered seven men. I read about Ted Bundy, who was handsome enough to avoid suspicion in luring in, raping, and murdering young women. When I get my fill of serial killers, I move on to the surgeons, some of whom performed unthinkable surgeries on slaves, amputating and reattaching appendages from one person to another. Others used their patients for horrendous experiments, injecting them with God-knows what and observing their reactions.

I've always had a kindred spirit with the macabre. Horror films, true crime, the dark and the dismal. My mother raised me on the classics: *Psycho*, *The Exorcist*, *The Shining* . . . Maybe they weren't the best films to show your ten-year-old, but I never protested. In fact, I begged. The scarier the better. Maybe there is something deeply troubled about me. Maybe I'm not so different from some of these horrible minds surrounding me. Or maybe the way I've been able to cope with the unthinkable atrocities of the world is to acknowledge them. To listen to them. To hear them. To see them. As disturbing as so much of it is, I feel my heart fluttering behind my ribcage. My emotions feel disjointed, disconnected, but as I try to make sense of them, one thing feels anchored within me. And she's standing right in front of me. I'm still not entirely sure of Rebecca's intentions in bringing me here, but for the first time in a long time I feel listened to. I feel heard. I feel seen.

The next room features a wall dedicated to local deaths—some qualifying by dying in the state of Iowa, and others being as local as Fairbury itself. The one photo that instantly catches my eye is of a white-haired reverend with a microphone, preaching to a group of congregants who hold their left hands in the air. Below it is a plaque about Redd Wright and his mysterious death last year. At the bottom of the description is a prophetic quote by the man himself that says, "If I should die among the heavens, lay me to rest below the ground, where I will be closer to my God than I ever was on earth."

When I reach the back of the museum, I'm expecting to find Rebecca, but the room is vacant, save for a display of organs and fetuses in yellowing jars, and yet another black curtain with a sign above it that reads *FILMS OF THE DEAD*. I pull back the curtain and walk into darkness.

Amid the pitch black is a film screen, playing an old film that I can't quite make out. Facing the screen are five rows of pews. They're empty, except for one person. Two rows from the front is Rebecca, watching the screen. I sit a foot away from her on the pew. I know I should be looking at the screen yet I can't help but look at her. At the curve of her jawline. The bridge of her nose. The blue of the movie screen reflected in the whites of her eyes. But she's not looking at me. Her eyes are fixed straight ahead. And it's probably for the best because if she were to look at me, I'm not sure what I would do. The closer I feel to Rebecca, the further I get from Sam. Even now, sitting here with her, it feels as if he and the whole Wailing family are a million miles away. And, to be honest, I like that feeling. I would bottle it if I could. I would kiss her if I could.

It's only then that I hear the voice that's crackling through the speakers. "A leading cause of death in the United States, suicide takes one life every eleven minutes . . ." I turn my head to face the screen. It takes me a moment to understand what I'm looking at. The film may be grainy black and white, but I know instantly that I'm looking at blood pouring out of a woman's wrists. Then the film changes to an older man hanging by a noose. For a moment, I think they must not be real. They must

203

be recreations. But I've forgotten where I am. The girl with the nose ring at the ticket stand warned us that there was footage of actual deaths in the theater, and that footage is playing right before my eyes.

"While heart disease is the number one killer, one of the most feared and devastating is cancer." The footage changes, this time to a middle-aged woman lying in a hospital bed. Most of her hair has fallen out, her eyes are sunken and staring at the ceiling, and parts of her body look slightly disfigured. My breathing stops. My heart drums in my chest. I can feel my throat closing and my eyes begin to burn. Because even though it isn't her, all I can picture is my mother. "Every minute, someone dies from cancer." The film changes to a younger woman in a different hospital room, thin and vomiting. Then an older man on a respirator, his chest heaving up and down. Finally, another middle-aged woman gasps for air, looking like she's inches from death. But in all of those people my mother is all I see. I can hear her voice, crying out in pain. She's screaming from her hospital bed, and the doctors and nurses won't let me near her. "They did this to me!" she cries. "They're trying to kill me! Make them stop. Oh, God, make them stop . . ." Her wails subside as she's tranquilized, and I'm left alone, watching the woman who I once knew to be one of the smartest people I'd ever met succumb to full insanity before slipping into death.

It's happening again. The tears are coming before I even feel the urge to cry, streaming down my cheeks like my pain is surfacing through someone else's body. I can't control them. I can't blink. I can't move. All I can hear are my mother's screams. Even the narration of the film is completely drowned out by the screaming in my head. Today is the day. The day my heart shatters into a million pieces. The day it all becomes real.

"Abby killed herself." Rebecca's words seem to have the power to wake me from my trance. I turn to face her, but her face is still fixated on the screen in front of us. "She left a note for her parents saying that she was sorry she couldn't be who they wanted her to be. That she was sorry she let them down. And that by the time they read it, she would have jumped into the Mississippi River." At long last, she turns and locks my eyes with hers. They're as wet as mine. "I hope it's alright that I brought you here, Margo. I'm deeply sorry if it wasn't. People think grief is about learning to cope with the pain. It's not. It's about learning how to feel it. When I found out Abby died, I came here. I sat in this spot for hours as if something would finally make sense. And eventually, before I even understood how, it did. It helped to see the pain. To *feel* the pain."

My bottom lip is shaking, and I can't get it to stop. "I feel it," I whisper.

I feel her hand on my hand. She squeezes it. "I feel it too."

The air hangs still between us, and for a moment I wonder if time has stopped. Right now, it's just us. The two of us sitting in a dark theater with the worst sights imaginable unreeling on the big silver screen and the only thing illuminated in the darkness is sitting right in front of me.

My body leans into hers, my lips inches from her lips, and with my movement I see her flinch. For a moment, we just look at each other, our eyes begging the question of how far this moment should go. How far this moment *will* go. I shouldn't do this. I shouldn't kiss her. I'm engaged. To Sam. I love Sam. I can't hurt him. I can't betray him. I can't, I can't, I can't . . .

But as loud as the voice of reason echoes in my ears, my heart pounding in my chest drowns it out. I lean in again, and she leans in too. And before I realize what's happening, we're kissing through our tears. Even with my eyes closed, the blue light from the screen burns through them, flickering like a strobe. Rebecca's grasp on my hand tightens as she kisses me back. When we pull away, her eyes are still locked on me, and the sadness is still there, but something about her looks more beautiful than ever. I'm about to attempt to speak when Rebecca's phone chimes loudly, causing me to jump. She shuts her eyes, like she wasn't ready for this moment to end.

"I'm so sorry," she mutters, reaching into her purse and pulling out her phone. I glance at her screen and see that I've been gone for over an hour. Sam knows damn well I can't run for an hour. I'll have to tell him something happened. That I turned my ankle or that I got lost or—

Reality pours down around me as I realize that I'm trying to think of lies to tell Sam because I haven't been out on a run. I've been with someone else. I've kissed someone else. A pang of guilt wrenches my stomach.

Rebecca puts her phone back in her purse and looks at me, but it's not the same look as before. Because that moment, as precious as it was, is over. Even now, it feels so far gone I'm beginning to forget it.

"I should probably go," I say, wiping my tears on the sleeve of my hoodie.

Rebecca shakes her head. "I'm sorry, Margo. I shouldn't have—"

"Let's not ruin this with apologies." I smile as bravely as I can. We stand and make our way toward the black curtain. Rebecca disappears through the curtain, but before I can follow her, my eyes drift back to the flickering room one last time. The movie has started from the beginning again, with the narrator covering a history of human fascination with death. In the back row, a nondescript figure sits facing the screen. I don't know if they've been there the whole time, but I do know that only moments before Rebecca and I kissed, we were alone. Completely and utterly alone.

Chapter Twenty-Two

THE DRIVE BACK to the Wailing house feels twice as quick as the drive to the Museum of Death. I don't want my time with Rebecca to end. I don't want to leave this fantasy that I've created for myself. This fantasy where I'm not a prisoner in a family I don't connect with. A fantasy where I'm not getting married tomorrow. A fantasy where I'm able to feel whatever I need to feel, with a person who understands me on a level I haven't had in a long time.

I've told myself over and over again that there was nothing Sam could do to help alleviate the grief I've felt over my mother. But this experience has made me wonder if that's necessarily true. It's not to say he needed to grieve for her the way I grieved for her. But a lot of the time, I felt like I needed to hide my grief from him. As if letting him see my pain showed me in a weakened state. I don't know if he made me feel that way or if I made me feel that way. If Rebecca taught me anything today, it's that I've needed to grieve for a long, long time. And if there's anyone in my life holding me back from grieving, it's Sam. I used to think it was because he made me happy. That I was so happy around him I didn't need to grieve. That he somehow took the pain away. But the pain was never taken away. It was only pressed down, deep into the darkest parts of my heart. And Sam's fingerprints are all over my chest.

I look over at Rebecca as she parks the car down the street from the Wailings' house. I so badly want to kiss her again. To *feel* with her again. But I won't. Because whatever this is, it's not real. It's a fantasy.

Rebecca turns off the car and looks at me. With all the words between us already said, there's nothing but silence hanging in the air.

Finally, I say the only thing I can think to say. "Thank you."

Rebecca nods her head and looks away, her eyes drifting to the house. "If you need anything at all, or if you don't feel safe or comfortable for any reason, please call me. Okay?"

"I will," I say, hoping I'll be able to find my phone so I can keep my promise.

Even so, I can't bring myself to get out of the car. Maybe it's because Rebecca's story about Abby is at the forefront of my mind, but I have the awful feeling that if I get out of this car, I'll never see Rebecca again. But reality has completely engulfed me now, and I know I can't escape it. I climb out of her car and shut the door behind me. *Don't look back*, I tell myself. If I look back, I know my path will change. And I can't handle any more change right now. Sam is here. Sam is real. Sam is what I know. Sam is who I love.

When I enter the house through the front door, you'd think I walked into a scene from *Home Alone*. Every member of Sam's family, except for Ruth and Selma, is bustling around the house. Alice and Cheryl have white flowers and vines splayed out all over the dining room table and are moving around it, talking to one another and doing something with them that I can't quite see. Mary is talking incessantly, moving from the dining room into the kitchen and back again carrying various random items. Jimmy and Hank come from upstairs, carrying a large, wooden item that looks like it's supposed to be a part of a bigger wooden item.

Hank's face lights up when he sees me. "There she is!"

"Thank God," says Jimmy with a half-grin. "Mary hasn't stopped moving since you left. She was getting worried."

As they walk past me and toward the open door behind me, Hank leans in, his voice low. "She's not the only one."

I hear footsteps coming quickly down the stairs. As Hank and Jimmy push past me with their cumbersome object, Sam appears at the bottom of the stairs. He's looking at me like he's not sure if he should be relieved or angry. If he is angry, he has every right to be. For more reasons than he even knows.

"You're alright," he says, almost like a question.

"Yeah." I let out a long breath and wave my hand in the direction of the road. "I'm really sorry I was gone so long. I got totally turned around." I add an embarrassed laugh for good measure.

Sam nods his head, but I'm not sure he believes me. "I was worried," he says, stepping toward me. "Mary's been worried too."

"I know, I'm really sorry. But at least I'm here now."

He runs his hand through his hair, then reaches into his pocket and pulls out a phone. "I found your phone."

He hands it to me and I take it, powering it on. "Oh, God. Thank you so much. Where was it?"

"It was in your room, on your dresser."

I feel my brow furrow. "I could have sworn it wasn't there when I was looking for it earlier."

"It doesn't matter. At least it's here now, right?" There's an iciness to his voice that makes my throat tighten. Before I can respond, the kitchen door swings open and Mary appears through it.

"I thought I heard your voice!" She walks over to me quicker than I realized she could, placing her hands on my cheeks. I have sudden flashbacks to my childhood as she squeezes them together. "We are so glad you're back!" She removes her hands and gives me a painfully earnest look. "We were getting worried about you."

"I know, I'm so sorry. I got a little lost."

She looks at me with great surprise. "A little lost! How far did you go?"

I shrug. "I'm not sure."

Mary shakes her head and tosses her hands up. "Well, there's plenty to do before tomorrow."

"Right," I say. "How can I help?"

"Oh, no need for you to lift a finger, dear! You can relax and keep the ladies company." She nods to Cheryl and Alice. Cheryl gives me a polite smile and a nod while Alice doesn't even bother to look up from her portion of the flowers.

I force a smile, but if I'm not needed to help, then I don't see why me going for a run this morning was even an issue at all. Besides, all I really need right now is to be alone. To process what happened with Rebecca. "Of course," I say. "Just let me get cleaned up and I'll be right down."

I share a glance with Sam before moving toward the stairs. Mary grabs my arm gently as I reach the bottom step. Through a wide grin she says, "Don't go running off again."

My phone is fully turned on by the time I reach my room. I quickly pull up my messages, looking for my last texts from Rebecca. But when I scroll through my messages, the thread with her is completely gone. I back out of my messages and open up my contacts. She's not there either. She's been erased from my phone entirely. Like she never even existed.

Her business card. I still have her business card. I pick up my jeans from where they're draped on the chair and search the pockets where I know I had it last. But it's not there. It's gone too.

"Are you coming back down?"

I look up to see Sam standing in the doorway, and a thought that's very hard to process hits me. He knows. He knows I've developed feelings for Rebecca. Maybe he even knows she picked me up today. If any of those things are true, then I know it was him. I know he deleted her from my phone.

"Why did you delete Rebecca's contact from my phone?" I ask before I can stop myself.

"What?"

"Her number and messages. They're gone."

"I don't know what you're talking about. I didn't even turn your phone on."

"And Rebecca's business card." I toss my jeans on the floor. "You took that too."

Sam looks at me like he can't believe what I'm accusing him of, and I feel the guilt creeping up my spine. "What is with all this focus on Rebecca?"

I feel my face growing hot. "Nothing. There's no focus on Rebecca. I was going to let her know about our change of plans. She was our wedding planner."

"Sam, I could really use your help down here!" Mary calls from downstairs.

"Be there in a sec!" Sam calls to Mary, then leans in close to me. "She wasn't our wedding planner," he hisses. "She was *your* wedding planner."

Sam turns and leaves the room. I'm so angry at him I could scream. Even if he didn't delete her number from my phone, his words still sting me more than I'm proud of.

I look down at my phone. There are still no bars. Still no service. I feel trapped all over again.

I follow Sam downstairs, practically dragging my feet. When I reach the main floor, Mary is standing there with Sam. She looks from him to me. "You two haven't been fighting, have you?"

Sam looks from me to Mary. "One of Margo's contacts is

211

missing from her phone and she thinks I deleted it."

I gape at him. He feels much more like an annoying brother to me in this moment than my fiancé.

"Who would Sam have deleted from your phone?" Mary asks, aghast.

Sam answers for me. "Her wedding planner."

Mary looks from Sam to me, her expression growing more shocked. "But we have everything planned." They have everything planned? How could they have everything planned? We only decided on the date last night. "Besides, dear, we decided we don't need a wedding planner."

"No, *you* decided we didn't need a wedding planner." In the deafening silence that follows my statement, everyone within earshot turns to look at me. Even Ruth. I watch as Mary's eyes fill with tears, and I suddenly feel like the worst person in the world.

"Didn't you think we'd do a good enough job with planning your wedding?" Mary says, as if she's absolutely heartbroken.

"No, I—" I try to soften, to backtrack. "I do. I just thought it would help to have an outsider's opinion. But now someone has deleted her information from my phone."

"Ha!" Hank lets out a bark of a laugh as he saunters into the room. "Now who would want to do that?"

"I don't know. But it's gone."

I didn't know it was possible, but Mary looks even more wounded. "And you think one of us did it?"

"Maybe you deleted it yourself," Alice offers coolly, not even looking up from the flowers.

I look at her pointedly. "I didn't delete it." But that's when the thought hits me that I've been losing control over what I do in my sleep more and more these days. There's a chance I could have deleted it and not remembered. I push the thought out of my head and attempt to hold what little ground I have.

"Honestly, dear . . ." Mary's tears have dried, and she gives an amused laugh. "I wouldn't know the first thing about how to delete something from a phone. I've never even used one of those contraptions." Mary waves her arms in front of her, like she's waving away the bad energy that Sam and I have brought to the wedding planning ritual. "Look, it doesn't even matter. We have a wedding to prepare for! Margo, has Sam told you the good news?"

I look at her, dread suddenly filling my body. I'm sure whatever news she has can't be good.

Mary holds her pause a few seconds too long, drawing out the suspense for dramatic effect. "We'll be able to have the ceremony at the Evergreen Mansion! Isn't that exciting?"

My heart beats fast. Not out of excitement. Out of anger. The words pour out of me before I can stop them. "I'm not sure if I want to get married at the Evergreen Mansion."

"Don't be silly." Mary laughs and waves my remark off as if she thinks it's a joke. "Everyone who's anyone would kill to be married there. Oh!" She practically cuts herself off. "Before I forget ..." Mary shuffles off to the kitchen. Hank has moved over to the dining table. I'm not sure if he's intentionally giving Sam space or if he's bored with the conversation.

I look up at Sam to find he's already looking at me. His expression is no longer icy or cold. It's sad and hurt. "I promise I didn't delete her from your phone," he says. And whether or not I should, I think I believe him. Maybe I did delete her contact. Maybe it was me. However Rebecca got deleted from my phone, maybe it was meant to be. Maybe this is my chance to have a fresh start with Sam.

"Come here." He holds out his arm, pulling me into a hug. With my ear pressed to his chest, I can hear his heart beating through his shirt, and instantly all my anger towards him vanishes. We're just stressed. We're anxious. We're just nervous about getting married. "I love you," he whispers so that only I can hear.

My eyes fill with tears as I bury my face further into Sam's chest. "I love you too," I say, although my words come out muffled. I pull away and look up at him. He tucks a stray strand of hair behind my ear. "I really want to marry you," he says.

I swim through my guilt to find the words I know he wants to hear. The words I know I need to say to make them real. "I really want to marry you too."

I hear the kitchen door swing and turn to see Mary approaching us with a mason jar in her hands. "Here you go, dear." She hands me the jar. "For the urine sample."

"Urine sample?"

Sam rolls his eyes. "God, Mom. Is that really necessary?"

"Of course!" Mary says with complete certainty. "Jimmy's going to run it through a few tests back at his office. Give it to him when you're done. Need to make sure you're in tip-top shape for the ceremony!"

Tests? To make sure I'm in tip-top shape? I suddenly feel like a show dog. What kind of tests are they running? Before I can ask, Mary bustles off, leaving me holding the jar. Something shrivels up inside of me. Because I know for a fact that, even if Mary hadn't left, I still wouldn't have asked. I would have smiled and nodded and forced a polite, "Thank you," before giving away the last few remaining pieces of myself I've managed to hold onto since we got here.

Chapter Twenty-Three

ONE MORE DAY, I tell myself. One more day and then it's just me and Sam, away from his family. Away from this strangeness. I wish I could shake Rebecca from my mind. I want to see her. I want to talk to her. But I remind myself that whatever happened with Rebecca this morning is not reality. Reality is cold and raw and looming all around me. Reality is tangible. Rebecca is not.

I use the bathroom and fill the mason jar a quarter of the way, with the majority of the urine spraying on my hand, the whole time trying not to think about how ludicrous this is. Then again, it's a relatively normal thing compared to a lot of the other things I've witnessed during this visit. I wash off my hands and the outside of the jar thoroughly and bring it to Jimmy. When I find him, he's polishing crystal in the kitchen. "Here you go." I hand him the jar and try not to think about the awkwardness of this interaction.

He looks at me, confused. "What's this?"

I'm lost for words. He should know what it is. "For the tests?" His brow furrows. "Mary asked me to give you a . . ." I can't bring myself to say *urine*. "A sample."

He suddenly gets it. "Oh! Oh, of course. Forgive me, Margo.

I'm juggling a million things today." He takes the jar. "I will take care of this."

I find Mary next, ready to do whatever I need to do to make this happen. To make this all finally be over. But when I offer to help prepare for the wedding, Mary assures me they have everything they need. Why do they even need me here, then? Why couldn't I have stayed out for the day? As a last-ditch effort, I offer to go into town if there is anything else they need for the ceremony, but Mary insists that there's plenty left over from Jimmy and Cheryl's wedding. While I've never been opposed to hand-me-downs, I can't help but think of Alice. The idea that my groom is going to be a hand-me-down from my future sister-in-law doesn't sit well with me.

Feeling displaced, I wander into the kitchen. I open the fridge, take out the pitcher of lemonade, and pour myself a glass. I've only taken a small sip when Mary walks in, carrying some large, silver trays.

"Don't drink too much now, dear."

I set down my glass. "Why not?"

"Didn't Sam tell you? It's tradition for the bride to hold her bladder until after the ceremony." I laugh uncomfortably and proceed to sip my lemonade. "What's funny?"

I stare at her. "Don't go to the bathroom until tomorrow night?"

"Thirty-six hours," she says cheerfully before leaving the kitchen.

I want to scream. I want to run. But I tell myself that love is about making sacrifices. I remind myself that my small, unusual family may not have always seemed normal to outsiders. That Sam is the one I'm marrying. That for better or worse, this is Sam's family. And I have to stay for him. I take a deep breath and try to be as rational as possible. They can't keep me from going to the bathroom. I'll minimize how much I drink and sneak off to use the bathroom when no one is watching.

I smile and nod and pour the rest of the lemonade down the drain.

I haven't seen Sam since our fight this morning, but I imagine he's busy getting ready. Maybe even working on his vows. I wrote mine the day after he proposed. I thought they were going to be difficult to write, but they weren't. They poured out of me onto a piece of white paper that I've been carrying around with me ever since. I don't know if I want to read them at the ceremony tomorrow, though. Not because they're private, but because I'm not sure if they reflect the true way I feel about Sam at the moment.

With everyone busy, there's nothing for me to do at the house. So I decide to take a walk. And I decide to take my phone with me. Because even if I can't contact Rebecca, my curiosity over the article about the Redd Wright followers that I gleaned the other day is nagging at me. But as soon as I get my shoes on and open the front door to leave, Mary stops me.

"Sweetie, where are you going?"

"Oh, I'm going for a walk."

"No, no. We need you here."

"I didn't think there was anything for me to do, so—"

"Nonsense! I have four dozen xeranthemums that need to be strung together."

She leads me to the back porch and shows me how to string together the xeranthemums.

"Xeranthemums represent everlasting love," Mary says as she ties together the stems of two flowers. "Did you know that, Margo?"

I shake my head. "I didn't."

Once I'm well-versed in the process, Mary leaves me to it. After nearly three hours of stringing together the flowers, my hands have started to cramp up. I raise them in the air and turn my wrists in small circles to keep the blood flowing. When the sleeves on my oversized sweatshirt fall to my elbows, I realize that the red indents that encircled my wrists have now either faded completely or were never there to begin with. I want to ask Ruth, my only witness, if she recalls what happened to me last night, what I might have done to myself, but of course there's no point.

I look out across the cornfield. There's a haze to the sky that I don't care for. It makes me feel trapped. And everything is much too still. I want the earth to give me some movement. Even if it's merely a soft breeze so I can know that I'm in the real world and not trapped in the snow globe I feel like I'm in. As soon as I think it, I get my wish. Way in the distance I see a few stalks of corn swaying back and forth despite the still air. The movement stops, then starts again, moving closer to the house. I get to my feet, but I can't see any better standing. When the stirring is about ten feet into the cornfield, it stops abruptly. I wait for a moment for it to start again, but it doesn't. Whatever it is that's lurking in the cornfield, I wonder if it sees me. I feel like it does, and the feeling makes me uneasy. But it's probably just an animal. There's nothing else it could be.

I sit, pick up the next flower, and tie it to the previous one with tender fingers. I have practically ten feet of flowers by this point, and I'm almost out, so at least that means I'll be done soon.

I'm about to move on to the next flower when my ears catch the faint hum of music in the distance. I listen carefully and my heart beats faster as I recognize the song: "Shine on Harvest Moon."

The corners of my mouth turn into a smile. Sam. He must be around here, somewhere. Maybe he's writing his vows and listening to our song for inspiration. Maybe he's trying to lure me over to him for an apology and a secret, pre-wedding dance.

I follow the music around the side of the house until I come to the cellar. I glance around because I have the feeling I'm not supposed to go inside. But there's no lock on the door, and there's no one in sight, so I don't see the harm. Besides, Sam might be down there. I lift the heavy cellar door and walk the dirt-covered concrete steps into the cool dark of the underground.

The music grows louder, but it's too dark in the cellar to see very much. I feel a thin chain brush against my face and pull it. A dim, hanging light comes on, illuminating what little is within a three-foot radius of me. The music is louder now, and scratchy, like it's crackling through a record player. I wish I had my phone for a flashlight, but I left it outside with the flowers.

"Sam?" I say to the darkness. "Sam, are you here?"

There's no response. Only the music hits my ears.

I look around but I can't make out much of anything. Most of what I can see is old and rusted: a push mower, a carved wooden chest, some farming equipment, some canned and jarred foods . . . Then my eye catches something in the far corner that doesn't quite fit. I take a few steps closer until I see the silhouette of a person and freeze. We stand there for a moment, the figure and I, neither of us moving. He has no eyes, no mouth, and only the subtle bump of a nose. It takes me a single terrifying minute to realize it's only a mannequin. A mannequin with a brown wig and a thick moustache, wearing a suit right out of the 1970s. I recognize him immediately as Redd Wright.

I grab hold of the string on the lightbulb and pull the light in my direction, illuminating the mannequin and the shrine surrounding him. Framed photos hang on the walls. Artifacts, pieces of jewelry, and candles that look as though they've been recently lit are all displayed on the round tables on either side of him, and the whole thing is surrounded by fresh xeranthemums. I back up slightly to get the full picture of what I'm looking at and see bold red writing centered above the shrine: *Quod umquam finis adest.* Below it is an antique podium holding a large, old black book. I take a step forward and run my hand over the leather-bound cover. The very touch of it tingles and warms my skin, and I instantly feel compelled to open it, yet terrified to do so. Before I can so much as lift the heavy cover, I feel a hand on my shoulder and spin around, causing the lightbulb to swing and the beams to bounce off the cellar walls. When I see the faint outline of Sam's profile, my heartbeat slows.

"What are you doing down here?" he asks.

"I heard music." It's only when I say it that I realize the music has stopped. "'Shine on Harvest Moon' was playing."

Sam grins. At least I think it's a grin. It's difficult to tell in the light. "I think you can't help yourself from thinking about me."

Normally I would think Sam was being cute, but right now I want to know who was playing the music. My eyes dart around the room until they land on an old record player. Sure enough, the record on the spinner is "Shine on Harvest Moon" by Ruth Etting, but there's a thin layer of dust atop it. I touch the phonograph; it's as cold as the damp air around me.

"Come on, let's go back upstairs." Sam takes my arm.

I glance over at the shrine, at the book. "Do they pray to him down here or something?"

"I guess? Honestly, I don't really know. I hardly ever go down here. Gives me the creeps."

"Don't you think it's a bit much? The whole Redd Wright thing?"

Sam shrugs and guides me to the cellar entrance. "It makes them happy. It doesn't cause any harm. I don't see anything wrong with it."

"I really don't like the idea of getting married at the Evergreen Mansion. You didn't tell me, but I know why it means so much to your family. I know it was his home."

"I'm sorry I didn't tell you," he says casually. "I didn't think it mattered."

"It's fine. I just don't want to get married there."

He steps closer to me and brushes a strand of hair out of my face. "Look at it as a ceremony for them," he says. "We'll do things however we want when we get back to Chicago. However *you* want. I promise."

I try to believe him, but Sam's promises to me have felt empty for a long time now. Instead of arguing, I decide to believe him, and let him lead me out of the cellar and into the light.

Chapter Twenty-Four

I SNEAK OFF to the bathroom an hour later to pee. I can't imagine Mary was completely serious about that tradition. Then again, she's been bizarrely serious about all the other traditions. When I open the bathroom door after washing up, I'm met with Alice.

"It's bad luck to break a wedding tradition," she says with a smirk. This is it. I've been caught. She's going to go straight to Mary, thrilled to be able to tell her that her true love's fiancé went against her dying wishes. "But don't worry." She leans in and lowers her voice to a whisper. "I won't tell if you don't." She walks off, and I feel both nervous and oddly comforted.

At supper, I eat a veggie burger with roasted potatoes while everyone else has chicken. At the center of the table sits the large pitcher of fresh lemonade, taunting me. I haven't drunk anything else all day. Even though I know I'm not going to be able to uphold their tradition, I might be able to get away with letting Mary think I did if I limit my trips to the bathroom.

"This might be the best lemonade you've ever made, Mom," says Cheryl.

"Agreed," Jimmy adds.

"It's a new recipe I'm trying," Mary gloats. "Drink up!"

After supper, I excuse myself to take a walk. I need the fresh air, but mostly I need cell service. They let me go without a fuss this time, and Sam helps me put my jacket on. "Why are you taking your phone?" he asks when he sees the device in my hand. "I thought you weren't getting service."

"I'm not," I say quickly. "But I use it as a flashlight."

Sam nods. "Ah, got it." He kisses me on the forehead. "Be safe."

I head down the road in the same direction I did last time, keeping my eyes glued to the bars on my screen. After a good twenty minutes, I get one. Then two. I open up Google and search "Redd Wright" again. Instantly, I spot the headline of the article I didn't get to read before and tap on it. It takes a few minutes, but it finally opens, and I see the full title and subtitle of the article in big, black letters: "Group of Redd Wright Followers Accused of 1st Degree Murder: The Deadly Outcome of a Virgin Sacrifice."

I feel my tongue catch in the back of my throat and skim the article quickly.

October 10, 2019—Helena, Montana—
The Helena Gazette

On Friday, October 7, Jeremiah Calhoun was arrested for the murder of nineteen-year-old Brianna Frost. Calhoun, who claimed to be the leader of the cult-like group of seven Redd Wright worshipers who call themselves "The Enders," said in a statement upon his arrest, "I only did what my savior wanted me to do. I only did what was best for my fellow Enders. We are more powerful than the law. We have knowledge no other human beings have. In His eyes, we are forgiven. And that's all that we need."

Frost's body was discovered deep inside the Helena National Forest. The scene in question could only be described as a ritualistic ceremony, with flowers, sticks, and twine. Frost was found, bound and gagged to a stake. Her eyes were gouged out and her torso mutilated. "We have never seen anything like this before in our forest," Park Ranger Deborah Haas said in a statement. "We would like it known that this tragedy in no way represents anything associated with the Helena National Forest."

While all seven of "The Enders" will be tried in court, Calhoun has made it clear to the press that he intends to take full responsibility for what he calls a "virgin sacrifice," claiming that he is the "chosen one" and that "no one else deserves credit" for the act but him. The trial is set to take place on November 2 at the US District Courthouse in Helena, Montana.

I scroll down further until I see a photo of the crime scene. The throne sits in the middle of a forest, with black torches encircling it. The tree trunks, the dead leaves, the brush—everything around it looks like it's just been burned. The only undead thing that remains is a single flower on the ground beside the throne that managed to escape the flames. But it's not just any flower. It's a xeranthemum.

My hands are shaking. Is this article any indication of the intent of Sam's family? Am I the next virgin sacrifice? I open up my dial pad, my finger hovering over the screen, but I don't know who to call. I don't have any friends. The people at my job don't care about me. They can't help me, not really. I can't even call Rebecca without her phone number. The police. My only option is to call the police. But what will I even say? *Hello, my future in-laws may or may not be planning to use me as a virgin sacrifice in a religious ritual?*

Even if I at least let someone know I'm here, I'll be better off than I am now. I dial 9-1-1 and press *Send*. There's no ring. There's only silence. I look at my phone. On the screen, *Dialing . . .* flashes over and over again. I even move forward a few more yards, but it doesn't do any good. *Call Failed* appears and the screen goes blank.

Maybe I'm overreacting. Maybe Sam's family is nothing like "The Enders." I know I may be losing it. I know my thinking may be irrational. But I need to know exactly what's going on. I need to go back to the cellar. I need to look at that book. I need to validate the insane thoughts that are coursing through my mind. I start at a sprint back to the house.

In the dark, with the warm lights from the house's windows contrasting the stark backdrop of the night sky, the home looks normal, almost inviting. I peer into one of the warmly lit windows on my way to the cellar. Mary, Hank, and Ruth are sitting in the living room, watching TV. I can't see what they're watching from my angle, but I can guess. Cheryl and Jimmy must have taken Selma home for the evening. I don't see them in the house, and their car is gone. Watching this scene through the window, I would believe I'm looking at a normal family. That nothing is wrong. Then again, maybe they are normal. Maybe I'm the one who's crazy.

The lyrics of "Shine on Harvest Moon" travel through the cool air and reach my ears like a message meant only for me. I follow it around to the side of the house and open the cellar door.

Once I'm inside, I don't waste time. I take out my phone and turn on my flashlight. At first glance, the shrine looks untouched, but at a closer look, I can see that the candles are lower than they were this afternoon, a thin cloud of fresh smoke hangs in the air, and the book is open. The music continues, swimming through my head. Above me, floorboards creak. I'm right below the living room. I need to turn off the music before someone hears it and comes looking for me. I shine my light on the phonograph. The music is still playing, but the record isn't spinning. It's still coated in the same layer of dust. The song finishes, and I'm left alone in the dark and silence of my mind.

I shine my light over the yellowing pages of the book. Sketches of snakes fill one side, and a description of the healing powers of their venom fills the other. I turn the page. The next one is about beetles. I turn the page again. Ingredients for a hot beverage that supposedly makes the drinker ill over time. I turn to the next page. Peacocks. A man in an elaborate headdress made primarily of peacock feathers. Beside the headdress is a blurb with the heading *Tezcatlipoca*. I glance at the sentence below it: *The divine being should be dressed as the god Tezcatlipoca, and should be not only pure, but selected for his physical beauty and perfect teeth.* I turn the page yet again. Descriptions of different flowers, including xeranthemums. A bathtub filled with blood, with a footnote stating that bathing in virgin blood can heal ailments. My heart beats faster and I keep going. A ceremonial ritual wherein drinking the urine of a virgin can provide longevity. I think of my sample, of the lemonade, the best Mary ever made, and I nearly vomit. Finally, I come to a section that's been bookmarked with a tassel of hair, tied together with a blue ribbon. My heartbeat drums in my ears as I hold the tassel of hair up to my own. Even in the darkness, it's a perfect match. I think of Ruth and her fingers combing through my hair, the hairbrush capturing every fallen strand. I force myself to look down at the book. On the page is an elaborate sketch of a naked woman tied to a stake beneath a full moon. In her hair is another elaborate headdress, and she's surrounded by xeranthemums.

226

Her eyes are black, and her expression excruciatingly pained. Behind her is the ominous, dark shadow of a large beast. With horns and fangs and glowing red eyes, the beast looms over her, feeding off her fear until it can feed on her flesh. I've seen those red eyes before. I've seen that beast before. And I know what he's going to do to her. I can see it. I can hear it. I can feel it. Because I am her.

I tear my eyes away from the drawing to the text below it: *Virgin Sacrifice of Immortality.*

The book slips from my trembling hand and lands with a thud on the floor, a newspaper clipping falling out from the pages on its way down. When I find my strength, I bend down to pick it up and catch a glimpse of the paper's headline: *Televangelist Redd Wright and Wife Die in Tragic Plane Crash on Christmas Day, Their Bodies Still Unrecovered.*

Below the headline is a photo of the crash site, an open field filled with fiery debris. The article fills the page. I skim the words, but the words don't matter. Because what catches my eye in the article is a photo of Redd Wright in a tux, standing beside Ruth. She's wearing a long, white satin gown and on her finger is a ruby ring. My ruby ring. And the caption below the photo reads: *Redd Wright and wife Ruth Wright.*

I almost fall over before I can stand. Because Ruth is Redd Wright's wife. Does that make Mary his daughter? Cheryl and Alice his granddaughters? And what does that make Ruth if she died in the plane crash? I imagine the ring on Ruth's slowly blackening fingers, her inaudible moans, her demented mind, always lost in the waves of the television. Lost in the words of Redd Wright.

No. She couldn't be dead. That's impossible. That's crazy. Maybe she survived the plane crash. Maybe there was a mistake, and she was never on the plane to begin with. I've sat beside her. I've talked to her. I've felt her bony fingers running through my hair. Unless . . . unless that woman in their house isn't Ruth

Wright.

When I finally manage to stand, my head bumps the table. I hear the sound of glass rolling on wood, followed by a garbled shatter. I wave my phone and am nearly blinded by the vast amount of red liquid seeping across the floor towards my sneakers. *Blood.* I stumble backward, away from the mess, clutching the book to my chest. Once I catch my breath, I set it back on the pedestal and open it to the page with the snakes. Then I search the floor until I spot the broken bloody jar. Taped to the glass is a small label. I bend down to take a closer look. It says only one word: *Margo.*

Me.

I remember my dizziness, my pale skin, the hole in my arm—the one that disappeared after Selma's purification. I look back at the blood. My blood. *Virgin blood.* Like my whole relationship with Katerina didn't fucking count. What I wouldn't give to call Rebecca right now. To hear her voice. To talk to her about all of this insanity. She would get it. She would understand.

I cover my mouth and will myself not to vomit. I need to get out of here. We can leave tonight. Or early tomorrow morning, if it avoids suspicion. Tell Sam's family I got sick and we had to go home. Tell them whatever we need to, to get the hell out of here. I take a big step over the pool of blood and make my way out of the cellar and into the crisp night air. But I'm not home free. They'll find the jar. They'll see the blood. I just pray that we'll be long gone by then.

I need to talk to Sam. Unless Sam is part of this. Unless this is why he brought me here. A brand-new wave of nausea rolls through me. My heart pounds so hard I can feel it in my throat, hear the blood pulsing in my ears. I try to imagine Sam being involved in any of this. Try to imagine him sneaking around with his family behind my back. Try to imagine him lying to me.

I shut my eyes. Sam can't possibly know about all of this. He can't possibly be in on it. I tell myself this over and over and over again, partly because I so badly want to believe it, and partly because, right now, he's all I have. I can't leave without him. Or at least without his car.

I expect to find the family still in the living room, watching TV, but when I enter the house, I find the room vacant except for Ruth, the blue light of the television bouncing off the walls. I catch a glimpse of Redd Wright on TV and feel my stomach lurch. Ruth isn't watching her favorite televangelist on that TV. She's watching her husband. Even in the monotone blue light, I can see her arm. It's blacker than I've ever seen it, the ebony creeping up over her wrist—death waiting to consume her, inching across her body. I feel a chill pass through me and think I might faint. But I can't. I need to stay strong. At least strong enough to make it home. I tiptoe up the stairs and am about to knock on Sam's door when Mary approaches me.

"Margo, dear! There you are." She takes me by the arm. "Come with me, I need to show you something—"

"I was actually just about to see Sam—"

"Oh, he's already asleep."

"It's just after nine," I protest. "And I'll only be a minute—"

"He had a headache." She smiles sweetly, and I know there's no sense in arguing with her. I need to keep things as normal as possible if I want to make it out of here. She takes my arm and I let her guide me into my room. Into my cell.

On the bed is a long, white satin gown, the same gown Ruth was wearing in her wedding photo. My stomach churns. Surely if I ran now, someone would stop me. Someone would catch me. They wouldn't even have to try very hard. There's seven of them, and only one of me. They've been able to swap out my pills, to drug me to sleep so they could sneak into my room late at night and draw my blood without me waking. They've made me think I was crazy. That when I thought I saw someone standing in the corner of my room in the early hours of the morning, I was going mad. That when I saw Mary bathing in blood in the bathtub, that my eyes deceived me. They've lied to me, manipulated me, cast a fucking spell on me. Who knows what other tricks they have up their sleeves?

"Isn't it beautiful?" she says, smoothing the ivory gown. "It belonged to Ruth. She wore it on her wedding day."

She isn't lying. Just like she wasn't lying about Ruth's ring, which feels like it's burning off the skin between my fingers.

"Beautiful," I manage.

"You'll wear it tomorrow," Mary says thoughtfully. "And you won't take it off until you've been made an honest woman." She smiles at me, and I feel sick. I want to hurt her. Instead, I keep my fists clenched at my sides. She picks up the gown and hangs it on the back of my door, then sits down on the bed, where she motions for me to sit beside her. Out of necessity, I oblige. "Purity is a sacred thing, Margo. You may call me old-fashioned, but I truly believe it's the greatest gift we can give our Almighty Father."

I bite my tongue. As much as I want to, I will not argue with her. Because even before I found Katerina, not once in my life had I thought of "saving myself" because I believed it was what some higher power had asked of me. Never had I felt that not being intimate with someone would offer me some holy acceptance by a god that may or may not exist.

"I know Sam's told you that we're not his blood family," she goes on, "but he has been more of a son to us than we could have ever imagined. Which is why we've always taken pride in instilling our values in him. He may not speak as openly about his beliefs as we do, but he still believes them all the same. He's saved himself for tomorrow in the same way you have." She smiles at me. "Are you nervous?" She puts her hand on my hand, over the ring. "It's okay to be nervous."

I need to play her game. I need to feed her whatever she wants to hear. "A little," I say sheepishly.

"It's not nearly as scary as it seems. And he'll be gentle."

She squeezes my hand. "What we're most excited about is you joining our family."

I muster a smile and hope Mary doesn't notice the corners of my lips twitching. "Me too."

After Mary leaves, I lie in bed in the dark in my regular clothes, but I'm not going to sleep. As exhausted as I am, as heavy as my eyelids feel, I'm not going to sleep. My restless mind helps keep me awake, my thoughts a jumble of music and words and moments that have tormented me for the past five days. From the second I walked through their door I've been under their spell. Maybe even longer than that. How do I know they didn't have their claws in me before I even knew who they were? I think back to my mother, to the weeks before she died.

"They did this to me! They're trying to kill me! Make them stop. Oh, God, make them stop . . ."

They're trying to kill me. When my mother would say things like that, I always chalked it up to the voices in her head. That incident was no exception. I thought it was a combination of her mental health and the trauma of going through cancer. That maybe she thought the doctors were making her sick since she wasn't getting any better.

But what if "they" weren't the voices? What if "they" weren't the doctors? What if they . . . were them? This family. These people. I try to recall what their spell book said about a poisonous drink, but my mind can't seem to make sense of anything. The one question that seems clear as crystal to me now is, how do I know Sam wasn't sent to lure me into this sticky, tangled web? That's just it. I don't. I can't trust him. But the thing is . . . I don't think I ever did. How could I trust someone who lied to me? Someone who brought me into this hellhole and let me sleep alone every night? And even before this trip, someone who prevented me from grieving someone I loved so dearly? Rebecca was the only person who let me grieve the way I needed to. The only one who truly understood what I was going through. What

I was suffering through. Sam is the one who let me suffer.

I'm unsure if I've drifted off to sleep, but almost instantly the room is completely dark. In the faintest voice, I hear my name being called from outside the window and sit straight up in bed. I put my feet on the floor and walk over to it, cautiously peering through the glass. At first, all I see is the hazy horizon of the cornfields against the night sky. It's only when my eyes fall to the ground that I see a figure staring up at me. Even in the darkness, I recognize the form—it's Rebecca.

As quietly as I possibly can, I creep downstairs, past Ruth, through the kitchen, and out the back door. I run over to Rebecca, and once I'm a few feet away, I realize that she's sopping wet, hyperventilating, and shaking from head to toe. I slow to a stop in front of her. My jaw drops and I'm at a complete loss for words. I realize what she's covered in isn't water. It's blood. Her skin is coated in it, the original color barely visible through the red streaks and smears. A million questions circle my mind, so fast that I'm barely able to process them. Is it Rebecca's blood? Is she hurt? If it's not her blood, whose blood is it?

She takes a few uneven steps towards me. I try to determine if she's injured in any way. Aside from her disjointed steps, I don't see any sign of injury. I don't see any cuts or gashes or scrapes on her skin. Only blood. So much blood. Her eyelids are peeled back as far as they can go, and in the moonlight, the whites of her eyes are blinding and crazed. When she's finally calm enough to breathe, a voice is emitted from her mouth that's broken and barely audible, as if it's taking every last ounce of air from her lungs to speak.

"It's . . . you . . ." she gasps, fumbling for my shirt, my shoulders, my hair. "It's . . . you . . ." She grabs the collar of my shirt and pulls my body against hers, her face inches from mine, her eyes bulging so much I can see the red veins even through the darkness. "Fuck him," she spits. Before I can speak something snaps behind me. I didn't think it was possible, but

Rebecca's eyes grow wider. I spin around and see nothing but grass, corn, and sky behind me. But that doesn't mean that there isn't anything there. I look back at Rebecca; she's no longer looking at me. She's looking past me, to the acres and acres of slowly swaying corn, fear in her eyes unlike anything I've ever seen. She releases me from her grasp as if her hands have gone limp, and slowly backs away. I look to the corn again, trying desperately to see what she's seeing, but I'm blind.

"Rebecca, wait—" I take a few steps forward, hoping she'll look at me, but she keeps her focus on what I can't see. Another snap in the cornfield, and like a deer at a gunshot Rebecca flees, running as fast as her legs can carry her. Another snap behind me, and I whip my head around. There has to be someone there. Or at least something. I take off at a sprint, following Rebecca's trail around the house, but when I reach the front, I find that I'm alone. Only I don't feel alone. I hear my own breathing like it's on speaker in my head. But I hear something else too. Hissing. First, it's distant, like a snake behind glass. Then it gets closer as if it's at my feet. Finally, it slithers up my spine and licks my ear. I wave my hands around my head frantically, spinning around so fast I disorient myself. When I catch my bearings, I run to the end of the driveway and look one way and then the other, hoping to see a glimpse of Rebecca, but she's gone.

I listen for the hissing, but it's gone. I listen for my mother's voice, but it's gone too. I hear nothing, not even the sound of my own breathing, as if my eardrums have burst and I'm listening to the world from within a bubble. My mind reels, stuck on Rebecca. Bloody, frantic, terrified Rebecca.

It's you. It's you. Fuck him.

She's right. *Fuck Sam.* Fuck all of them. I look at the house, at its terrifyingly empty face. God only knows the horrors that are hidden within those walls. The ones I've seen have shaken me to my core, let alone the ones I have yet to see. This monstrosity is not where I'm going to meet my end. I look down the road

233

toward town. I could run. I could keep running until I find someone who will help me. In the middle of the night. In a town where the only other person who knows who I am has disappeared. Or I could drive. But I don't have a car. I don't even have keys.

Sam does.

Chapter Twenty-Five

I GO AROUND TO the back of the house and let myself in through the back door. When I get to the living room, Ruth is still sitting in her chair, watching Redd Wright on TV, but that's not what causes me to freeze in my tracks. It's the outline of a figure standing outside the front window. A figure that's followed me to Fairbury and I'm now convinced hasn't let me out of its sight since. A figure that's only as real as I allow it to be. I walk past it toward the hall, knowing that even if it's still there, I don't see it.

Before I make it to the stairs, I look down the hall and spot the dial phone on the small table by the wall of photos and run over to it. My hand hovers over the receiver, knowing my luck isn't about to change enough for it to give me a dial tone. I lift it up and hold it to my ear, and my fears are confirmed. Silence. Dead silence. I turn the dial anyway in desperation—9-1-1. Still silence. My heart sinks, and I carefully set the receiver back down.

When I reach the top of the stairs, I tiptoe down the hall. If I'm caught, I have no excuse. Because I'm not even supposed to be going to the fucking bathroom.

Sam's door is unlocked, and I open it slowly. When I close it behind me, I lock it. Because even if he's dangerous, his family is worse. Sam's snores are light, but I can tell he's asleep. I turn on my phone's flashlight, covering it with my palm so it's only a glow, and search around his dresser for the keys, careful not to make a sound. With a soft bump, I accidentally wake his phone, the home screen lighting up. I squint my eyes and look at the tiny bars in the upper righthand corner of his screen; each one of them is full. Sam has service. Even though he told me he didn't, he has service. If I can, I'll take it with me when I leave, but right now I need his keys more than I need his phone. I open the drawer to look inside, and the hinges squeak like nails on metal. Sam stirs but his steady breathing continues. I feel around in the drawer until I touch jagged metal. Slowly and carefully, I pick up the keys. But it's not slowly and carefully enough. They jingle slightly and Sam's breathing stops. In a jarring thrash he turns on his nightstand light.

"Margo?" He squints in the light. "What are you doing?" His eyes dart to the keys in my hand before I can pocket them. "Why do you have my keys?"

I have no choice now. Maybe he'll understand. Maybe he'll believe me. Maybe he isn't on their side after all. "We need to leave."

"What? Why? And why aren't you wearing your nightgown?"

I look carefully into his eyes. I need to play this right. I need to let him be on my side. At least for now. "Sam, do you love me?"

"What? Of course."

"Do you trust me?"

"Yes, I trust you. Margo, what is this—"

"Then come with me. I'll explain more in the car, but I'm in danger here."

"In danger?" His eyes dart to the keys, and for a second, I

think he's going to grab them from me. But then, as though a revelation has just come to his mind, his expression softens. "Oh," he says slowly. "I know what's going on here."

"You do?"

He touches a hand to my face. "You're having one of those night terrors like your mother used to. It was probably brought on by all this stress."

I shake my head. "No, that's not it."

"Margo, please." He slips the keys out of my fingers so smoothly I wonder if I actually handed them over to him. He sets them on the nightstand and pulls me close, but my body is stiff in his arms. "You're nervous about tomorrow. This all happened so quickly. I get it. I'm scared too." He offers me a gentle smile. "But I love you. I want to marry you. I want to be with you."

Fuck him, I think. *Fuck him.*

He pulls me in against his bare chest, stroking my hair, then my back. He's wanted me for months. He's wanted me since we got here. Leaning against his hips, I can tell he wants me now. And that's when Rebecca's words hit me.

Fuck. Him.

My heart thuds against my chest, and I pray Sam can't hear it. I need to think. I need to hold on to any shred of rational thought left inside of me. I quickly sift through the emotions flooding through me, my mind on the verge of a breakthrough. Finally, clarity hits me. I know what I need to do. I need to break him. I need to take away every ounce of willpower he has. I need to let him ruin me. It may be my only chance of survival in this house. My virgin blood is worthless if I'm no longer a virgin. Or at least what *they* consider a virgin.

I pull away slightly, but I don't take my hands off of him. "You're right," I whisper. "I've waited so long for this." I trace my fingertips over his chest and down his abdomen. "I think I'm just tense." I keep my eyes locked on his as I pull his hand up to my lips and kiss each of his fingers, letting my tongue touch every tip. He runs his free hand through his hair.

"Margo, we can't," he breathes, his eyes wandering to my thighs. "One more day."

I pull off my sweatshirt, and his eyes fall instantly to my bare breasts. "I can't wait one more day. Besides, it's after midnight. It's already our wedding day." I lean in and kiss him, pressing my chest against his. His lip quivers but he kisses me back, like he can't help himself. He runs his hands over me as I slip out of my leggings and panties and climb on top of him. "Sam, I need you," I breathe against his neck as I kiss him.

He groans into my hair as he runs his hands up the back of my thigh. "Margo, we can't. We need to save ourselves until tomorrow." He squeezes my flesh and lets his hand wander up to my hips and waist. His hips are moving involuntarily under mine. With every small thrust I feel his erection growing harder, more forceful, and I know I'm so close to making him cave. I just need something to push him over the edge.

"You're right," I breathe, but I don't stop kissing his neck. "Our first time together will be so much better than my first with any other man."

He pulls away. "What?"

"What's wrong?"

"I thought . . . you'd only ever been with Katerina."

I look confused. "I said my only serious relationship had been with Katerina. There was also this guy in college. It was casual and didn't mean anything. That's not a problem, is it, my love?" I lean in and kiss his neck again, waiting for some sign that he still wants me.

He puts his hands on my thighs again, mumbles a "Fuck it," and I know that's it. I know I have him.

Before I can think of my next move, he flips me on my back and pulls off his underwear. He has nothing to lose. If I'm no longer pure, there's no point in waiting. Why should another man have taken what he doesn't get to take? His ego wins, and he pulls himself inside me.

The bed creaks under our weight as he thrusts into me. But I'm not here. I'm someplace else. My eyes are glued to the keys on the nightstand and the phone beside it. My two remaining lifelines. Sam groans so deeply I feel the vibrations of his throat against my cheek, and for a moment, I'm hit with the awareness of where I am, of what I'm doing. Of what *we're* doing. This is what it might have been like. Not exactly like this I would hope. Not in his parents' house the night before our wedding, but something like this. With Sam's chiseled body pressed against mine, moving against me. With our bodies intertwined, our breath shallow, our heart rates high, fulfilling our deepest fantasies. But I don't feel fulfilled. I feel hollow. I feel empty. I feel nothing. I shut my eyes. Not to sink into the moment, but to remove myself from it once again. Because this, what's happening between us, isn't the fantasy I've had since we started dating. Whatever that was is long gone. This is nothing. This means nothing.

Sam thrusts harder, the bed creaking even more. I know we must be quiet, and for a moment I fear someone may hear us, but my fear vanishes as soon as it appeared because the act is over within seconds as I feel him come inside of me.

He breathes shallowly into the nape of my neck for a few seconds before whispering in a low voice, "You can't tell anyone."

He rolls off me and I stare up at the ceiling, a newfound feeling of satisfaction washing over me. "I won't."

I pull on my leggings and sweatshirt. Sam dresses and walks me to my door, leaving me no opportunity to grab the keys or the phone. He doesn't kiss me before he goes back to his room like he normally would, but I don't want him to. I go into my room and close the door behind me. I need to find a way to get the keys and get out tomorrow, with or without Sam. It takes me until I'm back in bed before I realize I'm shaking, and my heart is racing. I feel vulnerable, and even though it was my idea and my doing, I feel violated. That's the thing about being a woman. We never feel like we truly have autonomy over our bodies. Maybe because we don't.

I try to wash the memory of Sam from my mind. I remind myself that what we just did was simply a tool, a trick, leverage. It was never like that with Katerina. But if I'm here, I need to play their game. Virginity is a construct. It's only as important as I make it out to be. And just because I let him do that to my body doesn't mean he did it to me. I let myself take comfort in the fact that I'm no longer of use to the people who live on the other side of these walls. I'm no longer chaste. I'm no longer pure. I will not be their sacrifice.

The night will be long without sleep. I set my alarm for two hours from now so I can rest enough to make my escape tomorrow. As I wait for sleep to come, I stare at the painting on the wall at the end of my bed. I've looked at it every night since I got here, trying to solve the puzzle of it in my mind, if there is even anything to solve. But this time, for the first time, it looks different. There's another person on the ground in front of the house with the others, a ninth body—with brown hair and a blue nightgown. I recognize her instantly. She's me.

But that's not the only thing that stands out. I suddenly feel like there's a painting within the painting, trying to reveal itself to me. I squint my eyes and turn my head. And that's when I start to see it. I climb out from under the covers, turn around, and lie upside down on my back, my head hanging off the foot of the bed. Instantly, the piece takes its true form. The farmhouse isn't sitting on the land surrounded by cornfields. It's upside down, beneath the ground, and the cornfields are roots that have burrowed under the surface. In the roots, I see the same three crosses that hang above the Wailing television set and on stage behind Redd Wright, two right-side up and the center one upside down. On the front lawn, the nine figures aren't bowing to the heavens. They're bowing to the shadow in front of the house. And the shadow isn't a shadow at all. It's the beast.

Chapter Twenty-Six

WEDNESDAY

"WAKE UP, SLEEPYHEAD!" Mary's singsong voice wakes me.

I open my heavy eyelids and look at the clock: 12:32 p.m. I set my alarm clock for five forty-five. I know I did. I even set my phone alarm as a backup at six. But neither went off.

Mary bustles over to the white gown hanging on the back of my door and smooths it out. The door is closed, and I'm trapped all over again.

"You're going to be the most beautiful bride," she says, admiring the dress. "I'll let you start getting ready. I don't want you lifting a finger now, you understand?" She waves her finger at me. "This is *your special day*. As soon as you're ready, you come right down to the living room and relax while we finish getting everything ready." She lets out a squeal of excitement and leaves the room before I can say a word. I lie back down on the bed, my eyes drifting to the painting. The figure in it that appears to be me is now wearing a white gown instead of blue.

I stand and walk over to the window. It's only two stories. Selma survived three.

A few hours later I'm sitting on the love seat in the living room with the late afternoon sun streaming through the windows. Someone is constantly watching me. Constantly checking in on me. Offering me food and lemonade, to which I have to respond, "No," politely and without gagging. There has been no chance for me to escape without making a scene. My only hope is that when we make our trek to the Evergreen Mansion, I may have an opportunity. Ruth has been with me the whole time, sitting in her chair, her eyes unwavering from Redd Wright on the TV screen, the hairbrush in her hands, strands of my hair still stuck to it. Her left arm is now completely black, the deadness creeping up onto her neck beneath her collar. I want to go over to her and see if she still has a heartbeat. See if she's truly dead, or just barely alive.

Between us, Selma sits in her playpen, working diligently on a puzzle of some kind. The family's uneasiness over the doll I bought her suddenly makes perfect sense. They were afraid of the angel inhabiting it. If it were possibly inhabited by a demon, I'm certain they would feel differently. For a moment I envy Selma. What I wouldn't give to be unaware of what's going on around me. To not fear that this day might be my last if I can't figure out a plan of escape.

Above the TV hang the three crosses that I can't get out of my mind, two right-side up and the center one upside down. I look down at my hands, folded on the white silk of my lap. After I dressed, I tucked my crinkled wedding vows in the sleeve of my gown, not that the scribbles on the paper mean anything anymore. The paper is now scratching the inside of my wrist and I have half a mind to throw them out. I feel so empty, so hollow. I feel like the opposite of a bride. I haven't done my hair or makeup. I haven't eaten. I haven't drunk. I've been told by almost everyone in the family to take this time to focus on myself, to rest and prepare for tonight's ceremony. They've been in and out of the house all day, driving back and forth to the Evergreen Mansion, preparing for whatever ritual they're going to perform. I look out the window. Sam is carrying several old chairs from the garage over to the pickup truck. It's the first time I've seen him all day. I'm not supposed to. It's tradition.

I feel trapped. Not only in this house, but in my own body. I need to get out, but it has to be timed just right. Every other minute, someone walks past the front door or past Sam's car. I can't even go looking for the keys in his bedroom because Alice is up there, helping Cheryl with her hair.

So far, no one has confronted me about the broken jar of blood, but I'm waiting for Mary to bring it up. Then again, maybe they haven't been down there since last night. Maybe they've been too busy. Maybe if they do find it, I can convince them that it wasn't me. That maybe it was an animal. Maybe it was a beast.

I turn my focus back to the TV. Redd is going on to his hundreds of followers who hang on his every word as if he's God. Then again, maybe he is.

"Time," he says with a knowing grin. "We're always running out of it. Losing track of it. Letting it slip away." There's a murmur of agreement among the audience. "But what if we didn't have to? What if our time here on earth was limitless? *Well,* you'd probably say, *doesn't that mean getting old? So old that our bodies no longer want us to be alive?* I've got news for you." He pauses for dramatic effect. "It doesn't have to mean that at all. It could mean more time to create change. More time to enjoy life. More time with a loved one. But the time I'm talking about doesn't happen overnight. It's something you *earn.* Something that our Almighty Father so graciously bestows upon those of us who are willing to make big sacrifices for Him. He believes, like we all do, that those who succumb to temptation are weak. That sacrificing your impure desires for His reverence is the greatest gift you can give."

He clasps his hands together in front of him and crosses the stage. "We all read fairy tales when we were younger. We all want that happy ending. We all want that happily ever after. But what if there doesn't need to be an ending? What if, when we reach the end, it's not the end, but the Ever End? What if it goes on forever?" He grins. "*Quod umquam finis adest.*" They all repeat the foreign words after him. In my mind flash the words on the walls of the cellar. "The Ever End is here."

The Ever End is here.

Suddenly, I'm back in my childhood bedroom. My mother is sitting on my bed, reading me a story. It was my favorite: an old pop-up book of *Sleeping Beauty* that belonged to my mother when she was little. Every page contained a paper mechanism I could pull or push that moved the scene in front of me. Some of the images were haunting, some beautiful, some borderline grotesque. I wouldn't realize until years later that it was hardly a children's book, but somehow the frightening nature of it enticed me, and I requested that my mother read it to me every night I was feeling courageous enough.

When we got to one of the last pages of the book, where an old woman causes Sleeping Beauty to prick herself with a spinning wheel, sending her into a deep sleep, my mother waited patiently as I reached my small hand up and carefully pulled the paper tab out and in, moving the needle to Sleeping Beauty's finger as her expression remained frozen in time. The next page, when Sleeping Beauty was asleep, was always my least favorite. Not because there were no paper mechanisms and no strings to pull, but because I feared for her vulnerability. My dislike of bedtime as a child felt rooted in the lack of faith I had in my higher power to protect me in my most vulnerable state, and this page encapsulated that.

"Next page," I would say quickly.

My mother probably assumed my only dislike of the page was that there was nothing for impatient six-year-old me to do, and turned to the next page where the prince kissed Sleeping Beauty to wake her. I pulled the paper tab, which moved his lips to hers. My mother turned the page one last time, and the two of them were married in the castle at sunset. I pulled the tab to make the setting sun appear, relishing in the comfort of the familiar ending.

"And they lived happily ever after," my mother concluded, closing the book.

"What happens after the end?" I asked.

"Maybe it doesn't end," she says. "Maybe it goes on forever."

I thought for a moment about her statement. "But if it goes on forever, then why does it say *The End*?"

"I think it's a different kind of end." I expected her to look at me as she spoke, but she looked off, past my right shoulder, in one of the trancelike states she fell into now and then. "The Ever End." Her eyes were suddenly tearful. She let the tears fall for a moment before shaking her head and snapping back, a trance I've found myself falling victim to more and more since her death. She would wipe her face and smile at me, her tone jarringly different from the moment before. "Time for bed."

The Ever End. The Ever End is here.

How did he do it? How did he get into my mother's head over twenty years ago? What kind of power did he have? What kind of power do those who follow him have? I already know at least a fraction of what they're capable of. I already know that I've bitten into a poison apple. That my innocence, my purity, has been used against me. That the only way to wake me up from this nightmare is with the touch of a man. And even then, after last night with Sam, my newfound protection will only keep their sacrifice from working the way they want it to. It can't keep me from whatever other unspeakable things they choose to do to me.

With a wave of hopelessness washing over my body, I look from Redd Wright to Ruth. She turns and looks at me, slowly raising the hairbrush to my head with her blackened arm. She's going to brush it again, but I won't let her. I pull away out of her reach. I look back at Ruth, at her eyes. They widen and she freezes like a statue. She isn't even breathing. Or if she is, it's so shallow no one would ever know. Her periodic blinks and the subtle twitches in her face are the only signs of life she gives. I glance around the room, but I'm pretty sure everyone is outside. I turn back to Ruth and when I speak, I keep my voice low. "What are you?" She doesn't respond, doesn't even look at me. "I know who you are." I look at the TV, at Redd. "You're his wife. That's who you are." I look back at her. "But *what* are you?"

She opens her mouth and lets out a low growling moan. "You ..." she croaks. "Your ... you ..." Her voice gives out before she can say anything else, and she turns back to the TV, back to Redd. But I don't think I can stand to hear his voice another minute. I'd turn off the TV this second if I knew it wouldn't start her screaming again.

Ruth. Screaming.

I get to my feet and flip off the TV. As soon as I do, sure enough, she wails at the top of her lungs. Seconds later, Alice and Cheryl come running down the stairs, hardly acknowledging me as they push past my body to get to hers.

"What happened? What's going on?" says Cheryl, rushing to Ruth's side.

"I don't know, she started screaming ..." In the moment of chaos, I lunge for the stairs, taking them two at a time. In the distance I hear Mary and Hank's concerned voices fill the living room.

"What happened? Is she alright ...?"

I push open Sam's door and go straight for the nightstand, but the keys aren't there. Neither is his phone. They're not in the drawer. They're not on his dresser. They're gone. They're with him.

I come out of the room and walk down the stairs. The TV is back on, Redd Wright is talking again, and Ruth, surrounded by her family, is no longer screaming. The second I leave the last step and head for the front door, Sam enters, nearly running into me.

"What's going on?" He finds his footing and looks at me. "Margo, where are you going?" They all look from Ruth to us. Sam hasn't moved. He's still looking at me.

Before I can come up with an answer, Mary crosses the living room towards me. "Margo, what happened? Why was Ruth screaming?" She looks at me earnestly. "Did you turn off the TV? You know you can't do that, dear."

I take a step back, hiding behind Sam's arm. Not because I trust him, but because he's the closest thing to a shield that I have. I squeeze his arm. "Sam, did you tell them what we did?"

Sam looks back at me, and I catch a glint of fear in his eye. Mary looks between the two of us, her brow furrowed. "What do you mean? What did you do?"

"We didn't do anything," he says quickly, but his face is red and he's beginning to sweat.

Hank lowers his voice to a harsh whisper. "Did you two do something to Ruth?"

"No." I find my courage, the same courage I needed to read that twisted fairy tale, and step forward. "Sam and I had sex last night."

Mary gasps.

"No," Sam interjects. "That's not true."

He's either lying to try to preserve the secret before the sacrifice, or he's lying out of fear of what his family thinks of him. But I need them to know the truth. I need to lean on my only ounce of protection. "Yes, it is. I came into his bedroom last night—"

Mary covers her ears. "I can't listen to this."

Alice walks over to us, her face burning as she looks at Sam. "You had sex with her?"

"No. I swear. That didn't happen."

"Sam, stop this." I'm getting angry. "Tell them the truth. I came into your bedroom last night and I let you fuck me."

Mary starts to cry. Hank pushes forward and grabs Sam by the collar, nearly knocking me onto the steps. "What did you do, boy?" Mary gets on her knees, sobbing and howling. Hank shakes Sam by the shoulders, raising his voice over Mary's wails. "WHAT DID YOU DO?"

In the commotion, I slip behind Sam and out the front door. I practically jump off the front porch, running across to the road as fast as my body will take me. I don't know if anyone is following me yet. I don't have time to stop and look. I push my legs to go as fast as they can, my feet hitting the road harder with every step I take. To my left, the sun is setting. To my right, the sky is nearly black. It will be dark soon. I have no light. I have no phone. I have no idea how long it will be before I see another car. Still, I keep running. Because it's all that I can do.

After ten minutes I'm wheezing, and my legs are close to giving out, but I keep going. The darkness is almost overhead, and I can see in the distance that a full moon is on the horizon. The perfect blend of orange and yellow, rising over the cornfields. I think of the drawing in the book, the woman on the stake. The full harvest moon. The red eyes. The beast. I push my body to run faster, but as soon as I do, I find myself slowing to a stop. Up ahead is the familiar shadow. The figure that haunts me everywhere I go. For a moment, it's only me and him—a Western stand-off between two cowboys on a dirt road. And for a moment, I think I can take him. He's just a man. I'm as strong as him. But then his form shifts into another familiar form. He grows into much more than a man, and within seconds his half-man, half-peacock silhouette is taking up the entire road as it glides toward me. I freeze, but it doesn't stop. It keeps moving closer. I turn on my heels and run back the way I came. But I can feel him gaining on me, like a cold wind threatening to blow.

As fast as I run, it's not fast enough, and the being hits my back with the force of a twelve-foot wave, slamming me to the ground. I hear a crack as my body hits the gravel and seconds later feel a shooting pain radiating through my right ankle and up my leg. I roll onto my side, doubled over in agony. My head whirls around, looking for him, but he's gone. I'm alone on the sunless road surrounded by nothing but cornfields and darkness. Even the moon can't help me see.

I manage to pull myself onto my feet with the help of a sturdy cornstalk, but when I touch my injured foot to the ground, even gingerly, the pain is searing. I can barely stand, let alone walk, and I have no idea how I'm going to make it any farther. If I stay here, it's only a matter of time before they find me. If I don't stay here, if I try to hide in the corn, I hinder any chances of being found by anyone. And risk being found by something else.

In the distance I see headlights approaching fast. I do my best to lean into the dying corn, but my ankle prevents me from hiding properly. The vehicle slows down, its headlights blinding me. As it comes to a stop, I pray the driver is a stranger.

"Margo!" I hear Sam's voice call from the window. He gets out of the car, and it's all I can do not to push through the pain and run, but I know it would hardly be a fair chase. Instead, I fall to my knees, cowering away from him. "Are you okay? Are you hurt?"

I let out a guttural sob. "Get away from me."

He puts up his hands in surrender. I can barely make out the look on his face in the headlights, but I can tell it's soft, pleading. "You were right," he says. "You were right about everything. They're sick. They want you to be some sort of sacrifice." His voice cracks and he covers his face with his hands. "I don't know what's wrong with me," he cries. "All this time, I thought they were a little religious, a little crazy. But it's worse. It's so much worse. Oh, God, Margo . . . I'm so sorry."

Sam falls to his knees, his shoulders forward, his back heaving as he sobs. Seeing him break down has stopped my crying all together. Not because I believe him, but because I've never seen him this upset, this emotional. It's jarring. More than jarring, it's unnerving. I want to know the truth. I want to know what's real and what isn't. Staring at his weak, limp body, I feel my last bit of strength drain from my body. I don't know what to believe and I don't know if I should believe Sam, but my brain is foggy with pain and the headlights are disorienting in the darkness.

He looks at me, his eyes fearful and desperate. "We need to get out of here," he says. "Margo, please. I understand if this is the end of us, but please. We need to leave. Now."

My breathing is shaky, my ankle throbbing. I hear a rustling in the distance and look to the west where the sun has all but set. I pull myself up onto my feet so I can see across the cornfield. Against the stark orange sky, I see a shadow at the source of the noise. It's moving closer, trampling through the dead cornstalks. I look at Sam. His breathing is even faster than mine. He sees it too.

"Help me to the car," I hiss. He rushes to my side and lifts me into his arms. In seconds we're in the car, driving off in a cloud of dust. I can see only what the headlights want me to in the road up ahead, and the uncertainty of what I can't see is agonizing. That's when I feel something in my hand and look down to see Sam's hand. For a moment, I let myself feel safe. We're driving away from the house. Away from whatever is lurking in the cornfields. Away from everything but the moon.

We come to a fork in the road and Sam turns right. "I'm sorry," he says after a few minutes, breaking the silence. "I'm sorry I didn't believe you."

"We need to get home," I say. I won't feel safe until I'm home.

We drive for ten minutes. Another turn. Then another. Even though the darkness is upon us and the headlights don't show me much, I'm oriented enough to feel like I'm on an unfamiliar route.

"This isn't the way we came," I say.

"No, I know. We're taking the back roads. We'll be more likely to lose them this way."

Another ten minutes. I look out the window, trying to find comfort in the touch of Sam's hand, but I can't manage to do so. All I feel is cold.

"Don't worry," he says after a moment. "I was able to convince them."

I keep my eyes out the window, searching for a sign of anyone but us. Up ahead I catch a glimpse of what looks like a store or a house, a small beacon of hope in the enclosing darkness. "Convince them of what?"

"That you're still a virgin."

My hand goes completely numb beneath his touch as his words hit my ears. I don't avert my eyes from the building in the distance because I now know exactly where we are. And what lies ahead is hardly a beacon of hope in the darkness. It's a fire burning in a nightmare.

"I really am sorry," Sam says, his voice cold. He moves his hand to the steering wheel and flips on his turn signal even though there isn't a car in sight for miles. "I did what I had to do."

Before he can say any more, before we can get an inch closer to the Evergreen Mansion, I grab the wheel, lift my good leg over the gear shifter and press as hard as I can on the gas. We veer off the road and into the cornfield, the car bumping and jerking with every stalk we hit. The windshield cracks but doesn't break, and the left side mirror snaps off, but Sam doesn't let go of the wheel. Instead, he elbows me in the face, knocking me off him and causing me to see red. Within seconds, my nose feels swollen to twice its normal size and I taste blood on my tongue. I feel us slowing to a stop, but I can't see clearly enough to know where we are. When my vision finally returns, the first thing I see is the Evergreen Mansion, and I know that if I wasn't in Hell yet, I'm going to be very soon. Before I can so much as scream, something grabs me by the wrist and drags me out of the car from the driver's side.

My bare legs scrape and skid along the dirt road, tearing my dress and causing me to bleed. I try to fight them, even though I know it will do no good. Once I'm away from the car, whoever had been holding my wrist lets go and I see Sam, upside down over my head, pinning me down by my shoulders. I let out a scream, but it doesn't matter. The only people who can hear me are the six surrounding me right now. Sam holds me down tight as Hank approaches me. I feel a pinch in my arm and seconds later I watch Hank's face dissolve into the dark sky behind him.

Chapter Twenty-Seven

I'M DIZZY. SO, so dizzy. My eyes feel like they're closed, but they must be open because I can see colors and blurred shapes moving all around me. The colors are mostly made up of black and green and red, but I can't make sense of any of them. I feel like I'm dreaming, and yet all of my senses are heightened. I can feel, smell, even taste. The taste in my mouth is fruity. It takes me a moment to place it—cherry. The shapes around me slowly begin to take form. They're people. They're not doing much, just standing around, some walking slowly, some talking, some crying. I can't make out any of their faces or what they're saying. The setting begins to form and I find myself outside. Not merely outside, but in a cemetery. I look down at myself. I'm also wearing black—a dress that falls below my knees. In my hand is a red sucker. But it's not my hand. It's different somehow. I catch sight of the hair that falls down to my breasts. It's not my hair. It's stick-straight and golden yellow.

I sense movement to my left and turn to see a girl beside me. I can't tell if she's really young or really old. She's shorter than an adult but taller than a child. She has very thin, blonde hair, and her skin looks thin and blue and delicate. Her mouth hangs open and her eyelids droop, tears falling out of them.

"Cherry," she says, and I assume she's talking about the sucker. But when I hand it to her she waves it away and taps my arm with her tiny hand. "Cherry, I miss Mama."

With a pull from behind my navel, I'm suddenly somewhere else entirely. I'm in a church filled with people. They're dressed like they're from a different time—the 1960s or 1970s. They're all standing, singing, chanting, their arms in the air. It's only then that I realize I'm standing too, my arms raised up over my head. I hear a familiar booming voice echoing in my ears and, through a parting in the crowd, see the man who's speaking at the front of the church. He holds a microphone in his hand. Beads of sweat roll down his face, past his sideburns, past his thick moustache. He thrusts his fist into the air, his Adam's apple bobbing up and down as he chants at the top of his lungs. I manage to look to my right and see that I'm not here alone. Mary and Hank are standing beside me, their eyes closed, their hands in the air. Aside from less gray in their hair, they don't look much younger than how I remember them.

There's another pull from deep within my stomach and suddenly I'm surrounded by sterile white walls enclosing a small room. Hank is there and Mary too. They still look the same age, and for a moment I think I'm in the same time period as in the church. But the computer on the desk of the doctor's office gives it away. It reminds me of the one my mother had when I was a child. Hank and Mary are talking to Jimmy, who's wearing a white medical coat. He's smiling and nodding as he talks to them. Hank turns to face me, holding out his hand to me. I move forward, catching Jimmy's attention. He holds out his hand to me, grinning. I take his hand, feeling the warmth of his touch beneath my fingers. For a moment I feel safe. Then my world melts again.

The scene around me morphs into a car. I'm staring straight ahead from behind the wheel. My hands grip it tightly, only they're not my hands. The skin on them is dark, the knuckles thick. I glance in the rearview mirror and see Jimmy's face looking back at me. I hear a soft wheezing and glance to my right. There's a young man, maybe in his late teens, sitting in the passenger's seat. He wears a cap, and underneath it I can see he's bald. His frame is thin and bony, his clothes hanging on him like he's not even there. He covers his mouth to cough and on his arm I see thick veins and puncture marks. When I look up ahead, I see the Evergreen Mansion in the distance. A few clouds part, and the sun shines through the windows of the car from high above us. It's bold and blinding and bright, so bright that I have no choice but to shut my eyes.

When I open them, I'm in front of the Wailings' house, and I feel wind hitting my face, strong and cool. My lungs hurt. I'm breathing fast. I'm running. At first, I don't know if I'm chasing or being chased. Then, up ahead, I see a boy, maybe a teenager, with a mop of brown hair and a tall, skinny frame. He's running fast, away from me. He looks over his shoulder and smiles. I would know that smile anywhere. It's Sam.

He yells something to me and keeps running. I can't make out what he said, but I do hear one word: Alice. I keep chasing him. He stops abruptly, and I crash into him. We fall to the ground. I'm lying on my back and he's leaning over me. His smile dissolves as he reaches a hand to my cheek. I feel his fingertips against my skin, and for a moment I think he's going to kiss me.

I let my eyes close as he leans in, but when I open them, Sam is no longer in front of me. Someone else is—a young woman with white-blonde hair and brilliantly blue eyes. And we're no longer in front of the Wailing house. We're in a car. The girl is smiling at me, but there's a sadness in her smile. Something catches my eye—a glint. I follow it to the rearview mirror. Hanging from it is a chain with two pendants on it. One is a cross, and the other is a small metal rectangle with the word *Abby* etched on the front of it in cursive. Above the keychain I glimpse my reflection in the mirror, but it's not my reflection. It's Alice's.

The familiar pull rises up inside of me once more, and with a jolt I'm standing in front of the Wailing house again, but something feels different. The sky is cloudy, and it looks like it might rain. I look down at my arms and see that they're covered in lace sleeves. In my right hand is someone else's hand. I look up and see a very young version of who I can only assume is Hank, grinning at me. I turn my head and am staring down the lens of a very old camera, complete with an accordion-style body. It's positioned on a tripod, and there's a man standing behind it.

With a bright flash of light, I'm back in a church. Only this one is different. It's small and dark, lit solely by candles. The windows are made up of stained-glass images of animals. It feels familiar. I've been here before. For Selma's purification ceremony. The church isn't crowded. There are about fifteen of us, twenty tops. I'm in the front row, my arms outstretched to Redd Wright. He wears a suit, but it's different than the one I've seen him wear on TV. It's older. Much older. I look around and see that the other men in the church are wearing similar suits. The women are all wearing dresses, long ones that hang past their knees, some even grazing the floor. Many of them have hair that's short and curly, tucked under small hats with lace trim and netted veils.

Redd Wright is looking at me, a grin spreading across his face. He reaches a large hand in my direction. It comes at me slowly, deliberately, getting bigger the closer it comes to my eyeline. Finally, his hand covers my face, and everything goes black.

Chapter Twenty-Eight

I'M AWAKENED BY the sound of squawking. When I open my eyes, the first thing I see is a path leading either directly away from me or directly to me, illuminated by torches. I can't see much past them except for the dark sky and various shadowed figures brushing against the stark backdrop of the cornfield. My eyes focus enough to make out a large white wall up ahead with movement dancing across it. A movie screen? A large television? My eyes follow a series of thick wires and cords running from the screen down the side of the aisle, past my feet to someplace behind me that I can't see. I look back down the aisle. At the end of it, a few feet away from the screen, is a row of three dark silhouettes kneeling toward the cornfield. The squawking continues, with bouts of cooing. It sounds almost like chatter, a conversation in a foreign language. I follow the noise with my eyes until I come to the blurry outline of a woman talking to a large, birdlike shadow. As I regain my consciousness, I realize the woman is Mary and the birdlike shadow is the same figure from the road: the menacing half-man, half-peacock demon of my nightmares.

When I make a pathetic attempt to move, it takes me only

seconds to realize my body is bound to the large wooden chair I'm seated in. My wrists are strapped to the arms with twine, and although I can't see them, I can tell my legs are in the same state. I'm still wearing the pure white gown. Although it's no longer white and no longer pure. It's covered in dirt and a spattering of blood that I can taste in my mouth and feel, dried and crusted, on my lip. My blood. Only it's no longer virgin blood. They'll be angry when they use it and it doesn't work. But it doesn't matter because I won't be here. I'll be dead.

I shake my heavy head in an attempt to wake myself up faster and feel something scratching my scalp. With a drunken clumsiness, I shake my head more until something falls off and into my lap. It's a floral crown of sorts, made out of the same flowers I was stringing together yesterday. Xeranthemums.

"Thank you, Savior," I hear Mary whisper to the shadowy peacock creature. Suddenly, a gust of wind hits me with a loud *woosh*, knocking the crown onto the ground. I look up and see the creature flying through the air, past the moon, over the dying cornfields, and into the darkness. A moment later, one of the dark figures approaches me and in the dim glow of the fire I see that it's Cheryl, wearing a long black dress.

The taste of cherry fills my mouth, and suddenly I remember—the black dress, the cherry sucker, the girl beside me. *Cherry. Cherry.* The girl wasn't saying *Cherry.* She was saying something else. *Sherry.* Cheryl. Was that a memory? And more importantly, was it *Cheryl's* memory? The thought clouds my vision as I try to see the Cheryl in front of me through the darkness and orange glow surrounding us.

Cheryl smiles at me affectionately, picks up the crown, and places it gently back on my head.

"Help me," I manage to croak.

She doesn't respond, but keeps smiling as she turns and walks back off to another figure who I presume is Jimmy, holding what appears to be Selma.

I look to my left and see a figure sitting on a chair, facing forward, her body stiff and still, her eyes wide. It's Ruth. I follow her eyeline to the movie screen. This time my eyes are focused enough to recognize Redd Wright's face, larger than life against the dark sky. I can hear his voice even from a distance, but the only words I catch are "power" and "redemption." My eyes drift from the screen back to the three figures at the end of the aisle. I stare at them, my mind filling with fresh, raw memories. I've seen these figures before, in my dreams. But there should be four. One is missing. Sam is missing.

"Oh, my dear, you're awake!" Mary walks up to me, dressed in a long black gown like Cheryl's. I flinch when she gets close and she looks instantly hurt. "Do you think I'm going to hurt you?" I try to speak but choke on my own blood and spit instead. "Oh, my dear . . ." She reaches out a hand and caresses my cheek, causing me to wince. "We would never, ever hurt you. I'll admit," she says with a laugh, "I was very disappointed to discover you'd been snooping around the cellar. Oh, what you must have thought when you found the blood! I hope you know we only took what we needed, never more." She offers me a reassuring smile that makes me want to vomit.

"You can't do this," I hiss.

"Oh, Margo. You're going to have to trust us. We would never hurt you." I squirm pathetically beneath the ties that bind me, but it's no use. She leans in and looks at me with deep concern. "Are you uncomfortable?"

"Let me go," I manage. "Please. I won't tell anyone. I'll leave and you'll never hear from me again."

Mary laughs. "Well, we can't have that, can we?" She smiles at me fondly as she reaches out her hand and strokes my cheek. Her finger feels like a hot iron against my skin.

Hank approaches her. "Darling, it's almost time."

"Oh! We must get ready." She bustles off and Hank gives me a polite nod before following her.

Even in my disorientation, I'm finally able to make out all the faces of the family members. Sam still hasn't shown his, but I imagine his entrance will be a grand one. Isn't he their prince? Their very own Tezcatlipoca? I feel tears falling from my eyes. There is no good. There is no God. At least none that will look out for me. The god that they pray to, that Redd Wright prays to, is not a god at all. He's the ruler of Hell, and they are his worshipers. I just want them to do it already. Just kill me and get it over with. But I know that's not going to happen. There will be no mercy on my soul. Not if they can help it.

"Attention!" Hank's booming voice echoes across the yard. "The time is now. Please proceed to your places." Jimmy finishes stabilizing a long, wooden contraption at the end of the aisle that looks like a combination of a catapult and an upside-down cross, then takes his place one torch away from Cheryl. Alice helps Ruth turn in the seat of her chair to face the aisle, and everyone lines up on either side, one person between each fire-lit torch. The three kneeling figures on the other side of the wooden contraption still haven't moved. I wonder if they even can, or if they're prisoners of this ceremony just like I am. If they're sacrifices too. Or if they're dead like Ruth.

Hank doesn't stand with the others symmetrically on either end of the aisle. He takes his place at the end of it, in front of the wooden contraption opposite me, and addresses everyone.

"We have been blessed, for most of our lives, with a beautiful gift. We've been given the gift of time. Of course, this is not a gift that has come easy. It is something we have earned. That we have sacrificed for." He looks right at me. "Tonight, we are going to ask Margo to do the same. But not without an understanding of what her sacrifice means. As we all know, this sacrifice must be willing. While everything in our lives has been *His* choice, this must be *hers*." He smiles at me. "Your choice, Margo."

I shake my head and open my mouth, but no words come out. Hank laughs. "No, no. You don't get to decide yet." He turns

261

to Cheryl. "Cheryl, my dear, would you care to start?"

Cheryl hands Selma to Jimmy and takes Hank's place at the end of the aisle. When she speaks, she speaks directly to me. "I know this must all seem very overwhelming to you, Margo. It was to me too, after my sister and I lost our mother back in '71. But much like you, finding the Wailings changed my life for the better. My saviors." She gives Hank and Mary a watery smile, which they both return. "They offered me the opportunity of a lifetime. But at a cost." She turns to the three figures on display and gestures towards the small one at the end. "My sister was born premature. She spent her life struggling with health problems, ailments, pain. She never went to school, never took a lover. My sister was exactly what *She* would have wanted."

Cheryl smiles widely, wider than I've seen her do before. My eyes flicker to the small figure she had motioned to, and suddenly it hits me that Sam isn't going to be the fourth body at the end of the row. I am. I am the body that they lured into their trap, the pure sacrifice they need to sustain their way of life. I feel the blood pumping through my veins, what's left of it anyway. My mind is racing to keep up, to put the pieces together. But the more I understand, the less I wish I knew.

"It isn't killing," Cheryl continues, a defensiveness in her tone. "It's a sacrifice. By making that sacrifice, in return we receive the greatest gift of all: time. Mary, Hank, and I, were blessed by Her. We'd proven ourselves worthy. And one day Selma will join us. Once she's of age, she'll have the opportunity to receive the same gift we have." She smiles and steps back into her place. She then takes Selma from Jimmy, who steps into Cheryl's place at the end of the aisle and speaks to me.

"I didn't believe Cheryl when she first told me the truth about her family. I'm a man of science, not religion. Why would I believe something like this was possible?" He lets out a grim laugh. "But the more she showed me, the more I saw, the more I began to believe. When they offered me the same opportunity that they'd had and said that it would not only prolong their lives, but mine too, I agreed to do my part." Jimmy's voice breaks and he looks away, his gaze falling on the tallest figure in the center. I remember driving the car as Jimmy. The young man beside me was nothing but skin and bone. Who was he? A friend? A patient? Whoever he was, how could Jimmy do this to him? Don't doctors take an oath? An oath to take care of people, to help people. Everything that's happening here goes entirely against that.

When Jimmy meets my eyes again, I see tears streaming down his cheeks. "I wasn't happy with my decision, not at first. Not as I saw the sacrifice take place. But within minutes— seconds—I changed my mind. Because the gift had already begun to take effect. I saw the Wailings transform from sick and dying to healthy and alive. I, myself, felt more alive than I had in years. I knew it had worked. And I knew I hadn't truly lived until that moment." Before stepping back, he pauses and looks at me again, a glimmer in his eye. "I trust you to make the right decision, Margo."

He smiles and takes his place beside Cheryl, allowing Alice to take the spotlight. Her petite figure looks even smaller following Jimmy's large silhouette, but I know her size doesn't mean anything. I know what she's capable of. "The Wailings taught me everything I know. They gave me a life I could only have dreamed of. And when I was old enough, they gave me something else." Her voice turns cold. "They gave me a choice: either bring them a sacrifice . . . or become one." There's a resentful glint in her eye that I think might break her, but she presses on. "They showed me what I needed to do to join them. I befriended a naïve young woman with a religious upbringing. She was struggling with her identity—feeling that her family would never accept her for who she truly was." My eyes land on the charcoal gray figure with straw hair on the far right and my stomach churns, but I know it shouldn't. I've known all along what these people were capable of. I just didn't want to see it. I stifle the urge to scream. I remember the girl in the car when I was Alice, with white-blonde hair and endless blue eyes. The girl with the sad smile. The girl whose rotting corpse is kneeling on the ground in front of me. But she's not just a corpse; she's not just a body. She's Abby. Rebecca's Abby. My Katerina. "So, I guess in some ways, I'm a pretty decent actress after all."

As Alice grins and steps back into her place, Mary steps in, smiling at me. "Hank and I met at church in the summer of 1932," she begins proudly. I remember the feeling of lace against my skin, of the bright light from the camera as our picture was taken. I remember the old wedding photographs in the attic, the couple that looked so similar to Hank and Mary they could have been twins. I think of Sam and wonder how many lies he's told me, how many I may never even know about. "We fell hopelessly in love and married the following spring. We wanted to start a family, but soon realized that wasn't in the cards for us."

She looks over at Cheryl and Alice and smiles. "Well, not yet anyway." She turns back to me. "When we found Redd Wright, we knew right away that he could offer us so much more than any church ever had." I can see Redd Wright standing at the front of that small, dark church. The same one from the purification ceremony. The same one from my memories. I can feel his hand closing in on my face, suffocating me. "We followed him from the beginning. He took a liking to us and shared his secrets, his powers. It was all exactly as it was meant to be." She gives a watery smile that suddenly turns into a frown. "When that tragic accident took our beloved Redd Wright, we thought it might be the end of our way of life forever. But we should have known that he wasn't truly gone, not really. He's simply taken a new form. He's still here with us."

In my mind flash visions of the peacock man, their savior in his new form.

"He still wanted to help us. All he asked for in return was

that we care for someone who was so dear to him." Mary smiles at Ruth, whose eyes are still glued to the screen, to her husband. "They were married for almost ninety years when Redd passed. Recovering her body was easy. Keeping her alive has been a challenge, but we've had help." Her eyes meet mine. "But she's growing weak, Margo. She needs you. We need you." A few tears fall from her eyes, but she doesn't wipe them. She keeps looking right at me. "The Almighty Father that Redd and Ruth prayed to was unlike the God we knew growing up. He was so much more. He could offer us things that our God never could. Most people know him as Satan, but to us he will always be our Almighty Father."

In the distance, an ungodly sound shakes the cornstalks. Everyone looks off across the cornfields for a long moment, and all I can hear in the abrupt silence that follows the roar is my own breathing. When Mary turns back to me, her smile is even wider. "She's hungry."

"Who?" My voice shakes when I speak. "Who is She?"

"Amrita Diabolus, daughter of our Almighty Father." Even in the dim light of the torches and the moonlight, I can see the corners of Mary's mouth twitching. "And what better way to show our love of His daughter than by presenting him with the granddaughter of Redd Wright?"

Chapter Twenty-Nine

I HAVE CARRIED every encounter I've had with the figure around in my memories. Every memory of him is etched on my mind and will stay with me forever. Not what I saw, but what I felt. The fear of being alone. Sitting outside the first-grade classroom, two years after I first saw him, I was overcome with that feeling in its strongest form. I was waiting for my mother to pick me up, and the mere sight of him was enough to turn me pale as a ghost.

He stood across the shaded, quiet street, a dark, twisted anomaly amid the normalcy of the suburbs. "Do you want to be alone, Margo?" he asked. In fear, I shook my head. "You don't need to be. You have been given a gift, but your mother has been keeping it from you. She's been lying to you."

A car drove by, and as it passed, he vanished. I looked around, but he was nowhere within my sight. Then I heard his voice again, closer than before. He was no longer speaking into my ear. He was speaking in my head. "You could have everything, Margo." It was then that I saw him again, standing to my left, a few feet away from me, a grim reaper in the midday sun. When he spoke, his cold breath beat against the side of my face, sending a chill down my spine. "You could have time. You could have power. You'll never have to be alone again. Would you like that?"

I didn't move. I didn't even look at him. Instead, I covered my ears as tight as I could. But as it didn't work when I was four, it didn't work then. His voice wasn't next to me. It was inside me. Deep inside me. "Your mother wants to keep you from us. She's not protecting you. She's preventing you from being everything you could be."

He reached out his sickly gray hand, a long, bony finger lingering over my cheek. I shut my eyes and prayed for him to go away, but he didn't. The tip of his icy finger grazed my skin, and even with my eyes squeezed shut, I could suddenly see more clearly than if they'd been open. I saw a blaze of red and orange, an inferno of heat. In the center of it was a woman, her hands raised high over her head, screaming. But she wasn't screaming in pain. She was screaming in power, as though she herself were part of the flames that surrounded her. As though she made them, built them, controlled them. The flames burned higher, and as they grew she stopped screaming and met my eyes. For a moment, she did nothing. Then a wide grin spread across her face, like she was thrilled to see me, an old friend she had been waiting for, after years and years. It's not until this moment, over twenty years later, that I finally recognize her. She was me.

Before I could see any more, I was jolted back to earth by the honking of my mother's car. I looked around, but the man was gone. I picked up my knapsack and on shaky legs walked to the car. I never told my mother about the man. She had assured me before that the man's appearance on that stormy night outside our house had all been a dream, so this time I assured myself of the same thing. Because even if it was real, even if I hadn't been dreaming, I didn't understand what any of it meant, and I didn't want to. I still don't want to. But now I don't have a choice. And all that does is confirm what I've known all along. That history repeats itself. I should have been able to see it coming.

I should have done the math. I shouldn't have let the traumas of my childhood be locked away in the darkest corners of my mind. If I hadn't, I wouldn't be here right now. I would have seen what Sam was capable of. I would have calculated the risks, the danger. But I didn't. Because when history repeats itself, it always does so in the most sneaky, conniving way. I couldn't predict the future. I could only have listened to the past, to the right voice inside my head.

Mary looks past me, towards the mansion. "Samuel! It's almost time."

For a moment, everyone is silent. In that moment, something catches my eye in the corn. I look, but there's nothing there. Before I have time to dwell on it, Sam appears to my left, wearing a headdress and face makeup. He doesn't meet my eye, just walks directly to Mary. They exchange a kiss on each cheek before Mary turns back to me. "When we found out where you were, that you were alive and well, we knew we needed to bring you into our family. To continue the legacy of your grandfather. Redd agreed. He wanted to do whatever He could to help bring you to us. Of course, we couldn't just kidnap you!"

She laughs and I catch a crazed gleam in her eye. "We needed to earn your trust, your love. Redd knew that there was no way your mother would ever approve of you joining us. She disowned her father and mother years ago." She gives a sad, knowing glance at Ruth, then turns back to me. "The gift she was born with was a complete waste on her. But it won't be on you. We've already seen just the beginning of what you're capable of. And after tonight your powers will reach their full potential."

Mary turns to Sam. "Sam, is there anything you'd like to say to Margo before we begin?"

Sam gives a small nod and turns to me. In his makeup and costumery, he's barely recognizable. But he would be unrecognizable to me anyway, even without the disguise. Because with the lies he's told me these past six months, everything about

268

him is completely distorted.

"I'm truly sorry, Margo," Sam says. I can see his lip quivering but I feel no pity toward him. If anything, it only makes my rage stronger. "A year ago, my family had all but given up on trying to bring you in. Redd had tried so many times, but your mother was always there, always in the way." I involuntarily thrash my arms at his mention of my mother, but the restraints only allow them to barely move. Sam either doesn't notice or doesn't care, because he continues without missing a beat. "When Redd passed on, they knew they had to act quickly if they wanted to sustain the life they'd built. I was their last hope. We knew we couldn't do anything with your mother in the picture, and I am sorry for that—"

I feel fire burning inside of me. "What did you do?"

"We had no choice."

"What did you do to my mother?" I say through gritted teeth.

"She was only holding you back, my dear," Mary interjects.

I think of Sam in the coffee shop with his million-dollar smile, watching me as I read my book—usually the latest James Patterson novel. I think of our first conversation on the train, where he told me they were his favorite books. I think of the peppermint tea I brought my mother from that coffee shop, and I think of the note in the book in the cellar about a hot drink that can keep someone ill. I think of the guest who knocked on our door, day after day, until my mother finally let him in. How that was the start of her disease. *They* were the start of her disease. I squirm and writhe beneath the ties. I want to hurt them. I want to hurt all of them so badly they finally know what real pain is like. So badly that they'd put an end to their own immortality to stop the agony.

"We did what we had to do," Sam says firmly. "She was the only thing standing between us and the power we needed to sustain this way of life. And by bringing you here, I too would be part of that way of life."

"Fuck you," I spit.

Mary walks back over to Sam. "Amrita has not turned her back on us these past fifty years, and as long as we continue to provide her with the pure sacrifice she so desires, she will continue to give us what we want." Even in the dark light of the flames, I can see Sam's eyes shift and his makeup begin to run at his temples. Because he knows I'm not the pure sacrifice their God desires. Because even once I'm dead everything they've built could end.

"So, Margo, that leaves you with your choice." Mary nods to Hank, who carries a large spool of rope over to Sam. He grabs Sam by the wrists and pulls him up against the upside-down cross.

Sam looks around, startled, his eyes stark white orbs in the black circles of paint. "What are you doing?" Jimmy steps in, holding Sam's body against the wooden contraption as Hank rapidly ties the rope. "What the fuck are you doing?" Sam starts to fight it, but Hank and Jimmy fight harder. In the distance, the familiar ungodly roar echoes through the cornfields, only it feels much closer now. In the moonlight, I see a monstrous shadow moving through the crops.

Mary calmly ignores Sam's yells as Jimmy and Hank tie him even tighter to the upside-down wooden cross. She moves forward and kneels at my feet. Cheryl and Alice do the same. Selma, who has been placed in her wooden, hand-carved bed, begins to cry. "Margo Sterling Moore Wright, granddaughter of our savior Redd Wright," Mary says, tears streaming down her cheeks. "Will you do us the honor of sacrificing Samuel Peters Lowe to our dear Amrita Diabolus, daughter of our Almighty Father?"

While Alice and Cheryl keep their heads bowed, Mary looks at me with hope in her eyes. I hear another one of Sam's yells as he's hoisted up against the cross, his feet dangling over a yard off the ground. One by one, cornstalks break, and Amrita's distant roars move closer, echoing off the walls of the house behind me. With a particularly loud roar, I catch a glimpse of something moving in the forefront of the cornfields again on the far west side of the yard. A female figure darts from the field as silently as a shadow, slinking behind the house. I am not certain who it is, because I know I can't be certain about anything, but I pray that it's who I want it to be.

With Sam fully suspended on the cross, Jimmy and Hank step back, watching him struggle and scream. But as much as he struggles, he can barely move. Finally, he stops yelling and writhing and looks into my eyes, pleading for mercy.

"Margo, you don't have to do this." He's crying. I can see the tears in the white face paint giving way to his pink skin, but his pathetic sobs only fill me with disdain. "Please. I know what I did was wrong. I'm so sorry. We don't have to do this. Just say the word and they'll let me down. There doesn't need to be a sacrifice. Margo, please . . ." He trails off in a pained sob as Amrita roars louder than ever. His teeth are clenched, his jaw locked as he looks at me with fear in his eyes. Even against the white makeup around his mouth, his million-dollar smile glistens. I think instantly of Tezcatlipoca, of the pure specimen with a beautiful physique and perfect teeth. It was never me they wanted to sacrifice. It was always him. He who needed to be kept pure, he who was tricked into tricking me. I am not the fool. I was played by the fool.

Behind Sam, the harvest moon appears from behind the clouds, and Amrita's thirty-foot-tall monstrous shadow finally comes into full view. The sketch from the book in the cellar falls into place right before my eyes, and I know what I need to do.

"Margo, please don't," Sam begs in one last pathetic attempt to save himself. But it doesn't work. Because he doesn't deserve to be saved. None of them do.

I look right at Sam, right into his soulless black eyes.

"Sacrifice him."

Mary breaks down into tears of joy as Jimmy and Hank turn Sam's body around on the wooden cross to face the cornfield. "No, please don't do this! God, please, no—" But Sam's cries are drowned out by Amrita's ominous howl as she reveals herself fully to us, fully to me, for the first time. Her eyes are redder than the flames around us. Her body looks like it's made up of fur and earth and skin and lava, as though she truly were born a beast in Hell. Beneath her tight skin embers burn. Her mouth protrudes, filled to the brim with hundreds of fangs. As she steps forward out of the cornfield I see, for the first time, the disturbing length of her limbs. Like an ape, she uses her abnormally long arms to move her body forward. Only at the end of each of her arms is not a foot or a hand, but one long, sharp claw. She lets out her loudest roar yet, her head turning in a mangled fashion against the backdrop of the yellow moon.

It's only then that I realize the family has all turned to face her, bowing before their God as they chant, "*Quod umquam finis adest. Quod umquam finis adest. Quod umquam finis adest. Quod umquam finis adest…*"

Amrita reaches her single claw slowly, carefully, up to Sam's face. I hear him whimper, but his body seems to have gone limp. Then, with her beastly cry, she rips her claw down the center of his body, splitting him like a scrap of fabric. She puts the bloody claw to her mouth and eats what I can only imagine is his heart, swallowing it whole. In that moment, the chanting stops. Everyone's eyes watch as Amrita goes completely still, Sam's body hanging lifeless on the upside-down cross before her. After a long moment, she lets out what sounds like a distressed grunt. Seconds later, it turns into a roar that breaks my eardrums. Mary shakes her head, her eyes wide and afraid. Without hesitation, Amrita turns and runs on all four limbs back into the cornfield, leaving nothing behind but the broken crops and Sam's mangled body.

Mary's voice shakes when she speaks. "What happened?"

Cheryl lets out a cry and runs over to Jimmy, who puts his arms around her.

Hank staggers backwards as he searches for his footing.

Mary spins around wildly, touching her hands all over her body as if checking to make sure it's still there. "Oh, no. Oh, please, no . . ."

Alice appears out of nowhere, grabbing both sides of my chair and screaming in my face, "WHAT DID YOU DO?"

Before I can speak, Mary begins to wail. Hank grabs her, holding onto her as if she'll crumble into a million pieces if he lets go. But then, as if by force, he lets go of her, flying backwards and hitting the ground. He lets out a guttural, pained cry. Mary starts to step toward him, but freezes, falling to her knees and howling. And it's not only the two of them. Within seconds, they all begin wailing in pain. I look at Alice, who's still inches from my face. Her eyes have gone black and the skin around them is melting off, as if she's a plastic doll being engulfed by flames. She staggers backward as if no longer able to hold herself up. I look around at all of them. Every one of their faces is melting, deteriorating right in front of my eyes.

Cheryl reaches for Selma, who's crying uncontrollably, but her arm melts before she can grab her from her bed. Jimmy's skin has all but fallen off, revealing his skull and teeth only briefly before they begin to melt too. Hank manages to grab Mary, holding her as the two of them morph into a pool of black and red and charcoal. The only bodies that remain untouched are Sam's, which is gutted and dangling from the sacrificial stake, and the three lost souls facing the cornfield, forced to kneel indefinitely to a God they never chose to believe in.

And then there's Ruth, who continues to sit, motionless, staring at the large screen with wide, unblinking eyes. The screen is glowing brighter than ever. On it, Redd Wright is still speaking, calling to his followers. He's calling for power. He's calling for redemption. He's calling for more time. Then he stops. Because the screen bursts, shredding, as though something that I can't see has broken out of it and entered this world. Out of the dark sky swoops the peacock creature, Redd Wright. He lands a few feet in front of me, his haunting, birdlike frame a silhouette against the flames burning behind him.

Even though I can't see his eyes, I can feel him staring at me. For a moment, it's just the two of us. I feel every ounce of joy, every shred of happiness left inside of me, seeping from my body. As I'm about to come to terms with the fact that this might be the last moment I'm alive, a new, orange glow catches my eye as something intervenes between me and this ungodly creature. Rebecca waves a torch at Redd Wright, a guttural yell emitting from her throat. He stares at her, and the three of us know what he could do if he wanted to. We know all too well what he's capable of. But instead of destroying both of us in a single swoop, Redd spreads his gigantic wingspan and lifts himself off the ground in one swift motion. Then, with his three-foot-long talons, he grabs Ruth by her shoulders and takes off, the force from his wings causing the torch flames to burn higher. As quickly as he appeared, he's gone, and within minutes it's all over. There are no more wails, no more howls. All I hear are Selma's cries, a sound that feels both insignificant and like crucial proof that I'm still alive.

The torch falls from Rebecca's hand and she turns to me, a curtain of matted brown hair masking half her face. I don't care. Because it's the most beautiful half a face I've ever seen. She lands on her knees in front of me, quickly untying my ankles from the chair. Once my ankles are free, Rebecca moves on to my wrists, her eyes locking with mine. I let out a sob as she sets my hands free. As if my bones have been removed, I fall limply against her. She helps me stand, and I realize the crown still rests upon my head. Even though I can barely feel the pain of my injured ankle, I let myself put my weight on Rebecca as I stare at the wreckage around me. The wreckage that's nothing but a symbol of Sam's one mistake that could not be undone. Because God is not forgiving. *Their* God is not forgiving.

In the distance I see the crest of sunlight peering over the cornfield. I turn and look at the house behind me. The house with nobody, nothing inside. The house that should have burned to the ground years ago. My eyes fall on the torch Rebecca had been holding, its flames slowly eating away at the dead grass around it. I look to Rebecca, who seems to read my mind. I hobble over to the torch and lift it from the ground as Rebecca grabs another. With my free hand, I take the crown off my head and toss it in my chair. It's only then that I realize my chair wasn't only a chair surrounded by xeranthemums. It was a throne, and I was the one they wanted to worship. As I touch the flame of the torch to the crown and watch it spread across the flowers, slowly devouring the dying petals, I wonder how close I came to the power I could have held. However close it was, it was too close for me. The only thing I am grateful for is that now I know the truth. His blood runs in my blood. His thoughts are in my thoughts. His powers are my powers. But none of that means anything. Because it's just blood. They are only thoughts. And power is only power if I let it be. The voices inside my head were only His when He possessed them. He had no control over the voice that kept me safe, and He had no control over my mother's. We didn't always have the strength to know the difference between the two. But I do now. And I will never listen to His voice again.

We make our way around the house, torching every dried bush, every piece of wood we see. As I limp around the back of the house, I pause, the same familiar music of "Shine on Harvest Moon" hitting my ears like an ocean wave.

"*The end is here* . . ." a small, familiar voice inside my head whispers. "*Let the end be here* . . ."

Through the torch's pole, I feel my hands growing hot. I drop

275

the torch, and the flame goes out, but my hands are burning. I look at my palms. They're red, like coals, so hot that the tips of my fingers may very well ignite at any moment. I press my hands to the house and feel the heat coursing through my body. The siding ignites, the flames spreading like they've seen years of drought. I move on to every window, every door, pressing my hands against them and watching as they melt and catch fire through my fingertips. Then I step back and watch it all burn, the music growing louder in my ears, drowned out only by the roar of the fire building in front of me.

Something suddenly feels like it's scratching at my wrist. I reach up my sleeve and pull out a folded piece of paper: my vows to Sam. The vows he'll never hear. The vows he never fucking deserved. I don't even bother to unfold the paper before I let it ignite between my fingertips, bursting into flames and ash.

By the time I meet Rebecca in front of the house, I expect more work to be done, but there isn't. The house is burning as though it's the home of Satan himself, which it might as well be.

The two of us watch the flames stretch high above the house, licking the dawning sky. Watch as the front porch collapses into itself. Watch as the windows shatter into a million pieces. Watch as the home that will bind me for the rest of my life burns to the ground in front of me. And as I watch, the thought crosses my mind—that even if their God is not forgiving, perhaps there is a god that's just, a god that throws lightning bolts from the heavens on Christmas Day to smite those who deserve it.

In the fire's roar and crackle, I listen for the familiar music, for the voice in my head, but I hear neither. Among the roar of the flames, another sound travels back to my ears. Selma's faint cries in the distance stop my beating heart. I look over at Rebecca.

"Do you hear that?"

Rebecca's face falls. "She'll die."

We run around to the back of the house where the once

ceremonial setup of torches and chairs is now consumed by fire. Whatever remained of the family members has now burned like oil across the ground. Flames engulf the makeshift stage, illuminating the dark, kneeling figures that I can only hope will now be laid to rest. The wooden cross and Sam's body are completely ablaze in a vision that can only be described as biblical. I hear a loud crack and watch as the wood gives out and Sam's partially burned body hits the ground, the sound of the landing drowned out in the fire.

I spin around, disoriented by the blaze of crimson and gold, until I spot the bed with Selma's name engraved so preciously into the wood. I hobble over and grab her up into my arms as the bed's legs begin to burn. She coughs and cries as I hold her against my chest. Rebecca takes my arm, and with her help I limp as fast as possible away from the fire and smoke.

The front door of Sam's car is still open when we reach it, my blood still spattered on the window. But then I see another car, a much more comforting sight down the driveway: Rebecca's yellow Volkswagen Beetle parked on the other side of the iron gate. Once we manage to get to the gate, we pull it open and hobble over to the car. Rebecca helps Selma and me into the backseat. I hold her tiny body as close to me as I can without suffocating her. Rebecca shuts the door and runs around to the driver's side. Finally, my heart begins to slow. I look down at Selma. She has fallen silent, but her eyes are still red from tears and smoke. I want to reassure her that everything will be okay. But I don't know if it will. I don't know anything anymore.

Rebecca climbs in and starts the engine, then looks back at me over her shoulder. "Are you okay?"

I nod my head. "I will be."

Rebecca faces forward again and drives the car off the property. As we pull onto the road, I half expect Redd Wright's birdlike form to swoop down on me and refuse to let me leave. But he doesn't. Because he has no reason to help the Wailings anymore, and no reason to stop me. In the rearview mirror, the Evergreen Mansion continues to burn against the sunrise. As I stare, hypnotized by the flames that I created with my bare hands, I can't help but think of my mother. Of the woman who vowed to always keep me safe. The sacrifices she made to always protect me from the monsters under my bed. The monsters that I now know to be real. Very, very real. She raised me to be strong, to never look back. I refocus my eyes on the road ahead of us. I won't look back again. Because whatever this was, this is where it ends.

It ends here.

Acknowledgments

I would like to take a moment to thank the many people who made *The Ever End* possible.

From the moment I pitched *The Ever End* to Bywater Books, I knew my story had found the right home. They fell in love with *The Ever End* for all the reasons I'd hoped for in a publisher—its characters, its story, and all of its weirdness. Thank you to Salem and Christel for taking a chance on this unsettling read. Thank you to Ann for the beautiful cover design that truly captures the essence and eeriness of the book. And thank you to Kit, my editor, who truly understood my intentions with this story, and helped me shape it to be the best it could be.

As an only child, my friends have always been my siblings. For Will, my brother and favorite game night companion. For Rachel, who I will always love belting "Summer Paradise" with at the top of our lungs on our annual beach trip. For Shaina, with whom I share not only a love of books, but also our wonderfully endless conversations. For Brittany, a kind, generous person who I am so lucky to have as a friend. For Alyson, my very first sister, who I have grown up with, shared sleepovers with, and who I cherish as if she were my family. For Hannah, my first writing partner, who allowed me to continue playing pretend well into my teen years with all the wonderfully ridiculous movies we made together that will never see the light of day. For Maggie, my Learning Community sister, whose friendship and creativity helped me through college in so many ways. And for Becca, my inspiration and my dear friend. From Brunswick hugs and mini-Cadbury eggs to countless emails and late-night conversations, my life would not be the same without her.

Much like Margo, my family has always been incredibly important to me. I have been very fortunate to have so many people in my life who love me, support me, and always encourage me to be the very best version of myself.

As someone who is fortunate enough to get to share their love of writing with their partner, I have always been inspired by my cousin Kara and her husband Scott. Not only has Kara shared her love of literature with me throughout my whole life, supplying me with many of the children's books I grew up reading, but Kara and Scott's working relationship as coauthors has been a huge inspiration for me as well. I would also like to thank my cousin Kent and his wife Marie-Claude for showing me the importance of art and creativity, my Aunt Carol and her partner Joe, for sharing their stories with me and inspiring me in my TV and radio career, and my Aunt Margie and Uncle Keith, whose love, generosity, and family stories have shaped my way of seeing the world, and inspired me time and time again.

My grandparents, Bryant and Sharon, have always shown me support, love, and encouragement. Their knowledge and wisdom have taught me so much about life, people, and the world. My grandma Shirley taught me generosity, love, and warmth, with every visit I had with her. My grandma Joanne taught me kindness, understanding, and a love of all creatures big and small. I'm very grateful that her words and stories live on through my mother and have reached me through her.

I would not be where I am today without the love and support of my amazing parents. They make me happy. They make me proud. They have been there for me every step of my life, from their patience with me as an energetic and creative child, through my teen years, where I turned our home into a movie set on more than one occasion, and finally through my adulthood, as they have continued to show their love and support of me in everything I do.

My in-laws are, thankfully, nothing like the Wailings—they have been welcoming, generous, and have raised three wonderful children, including the man I love, which leads me to thank my husband, Danny. He has been nothing but kind, loving, and supportive, not only throughout our relationship, but through my entire writing journey. In him, I not only have a partner in life, but a partner in writing, a love that we both share and will enjoy together for years to come.

About the Author

Audrey Wilson is the award-winning author of *Wrong Girl Gone*, *Only Human*, and *Landing Like Rain*. With a BA from Columbia College Chicago, she is also the award-winning screenwriter of over a dozen short and feature screenplays, with her career in film, radio, and television earning her a regional Emmy nomination. Audrey has spoken professionally at numerous writing events, both nationally and internationally, and loves supporting writers at every stage of their careers. When she's not glued to her laptop screen, you'll find her going to the movies or reading a good book.

Audrey lives in the suburbs of Chicago with her husband, rescued dog, and two cats, where she continues getting swept away in her writing on a nightly basis.

Visit her website at www.AudreyWilsonAuthor.com, and follow her on social media at @AudreyWilsonAuthor.

Bywater Books believes that all people have the right to read or not read what they want—and that we are all entitled to make those choices ourselves. But to ensure these freedoms, books and information must remain accessible. Any effort to eliminate or restrict these rights stands in opposition to freedom of choice.

Please join with us by opposing book bans and censorship of the LGBTQ+ and BIPOC communities.

At Bywater Books, we are all stories.

For more information about Bywater Books, our publishing mission, authors, and our titles, please visit our website.

https://bywaterbooks.com

www.ingramcontent.com/pod-product-compliance
Lightning Source LLC
Chambersburg PA
CBHW020401110726

47899CB00006B/1813